Jo Silva is the author of the co[r]

the World Detective Agenc[y]

Cornwall, and also writes hist[o]

under the name, Melanie Huds[o]

bookbub.com/authors/jo-silva
facebook.com/melhudson
twitter.com/Melanie_Hudson_
instagram.com/melly.hudson71

Also by Jo Silva

The Edge of The World Detective Agency

The Wrecker's Curse

MURDER ON A CORNISH ISLE

The Edge of the World Detective Agency

JO SILVA

One More Chapter
a division of HarperCollins*Publishers* Ltd
1 London Bridge Street
London SE1 9GF
www.harpercollins.co.uk
HarperCollins*Publishers*
Macken House, 39/40 Mayor Street Upper,
Dublin 1, D01 C9W8, Ireland

This paperback edition 2023
3
First published in Great Britain in ebook format
by HarperCollins*Publishers* 2023

A catalogue record of this book is available from the British Library
ISBN: 978-0-00-862283-1

This novel is entirely a work of fiction. The names, characters and incidents portrayed in it are the work of the author's imagination. Any resemblance to actual persons, living or dead, events or localities is entirely coincidental.

Printed and bound in the UK using 100% Renewable Electricity
by CPI Group (UK) Ltd

This book contains FSC™ certified paper and other controlled sources to ensure responsible forest management.

For more information visit: www.harpercollins.co.uk/green

For Becky. Thank you.

'Old sins cast long shadows...'

Agatha Christie

Prologue

Oxford, 1982

Seventeen St George's Terrace was a very pretty house to begin with. Not beautiful – that would be too much – but it was certainly pretty, at least that's what Sylvie thought as she admired it from the front gate, standing behind her little sister, hands resting on her shoulders while Mother searched in her handbag for the key. They moved in (Sylvie's mother called it 'taking possession') on Sylvie's ninth birthday, and from the moment her buckled shoes crossed the threshold, she felt at home. The Victorian tiled mosaic on the hall floor told the story of dancing fairies, and although the tiles were cracked and a little jaded, those fairies were just as precious to Sylvie as if they had been skipping across a relic from a Roman Villa. On Sundays, when Mother was still in bed, Sylvie would park her bony backside on the fifth stair, between sharp tacks that once secured a carpet to the staircase, and watch the sunlight filter through the stained glass window of the front door. She tried to capture the dancing fairies on paper, which wasn't easy with only a pencil case of broken crayons and a Christmas colouring book to work with, but she managed it.

Sylvie managed everything.

The stained glass depicted a sunrise – gold and red and warm – and when they stepped into the house on that first day, Sylvie's mother said the sunrise was a symbol of a bright new beginning for the three of them – their new start as a family. And she had laughed then, Sylvie's mother, a big, bold laugh, which led Sylvie to take her sibling Sam's cold hand in hers, glance up and ask, 'Will you be OK this time, Mummy?' At which her mother thought for a moment, promptly took off her coat, and headed straight through to the kitchen.

'Of course I will, darling,' she said, opening the oven door. 'Look! The cooker is electric!'

But by the time Sylvie's tenth birthday came around, number seventeen looked and smelt like all the other houses looked and smelt before it, and by the time her crayons had worn to the point where little fingertips became sore with colouring, the sun in the panel above the door, like the light in her mother's eyes, had disappeared. Sylvie's beloved fairies were hidden, too – buried and gasping for breath – their little hands clawing upwards through the dirt on the mosaic, trapped underneath an abandoned archaeological dig, caught under the grime of a nasty winter and a tsunami of unopened mail. Layers of dirt marked the ages of the children now, you could have sawn into them, like tree rings.

But Sylvie always knew that the real problem with Seventeen St George's Terrace – the reason she felt a constant sense of unease – was not the empty vodka bottles hidden under the sink, but the absence of a back door. Mrs Chang, the next-door neighbour, who played Old Maid with Teddy as often as she could, said that in all her years living in St George's Terrace, happiness never came to number seventeen, because the flow of energy was wrong: 'Bad feng shui!' she said.

She was right.

With no back door, there was no escape; no Narnia to step into.

And no back door meant no back garden, either. No tree to climb, no ball to throw, no dog to play with. With the sash windows painted shut, the genetic memory of old meals – the DNA of Captain Birdseye – clung to every curtain, every wall and every blocked-up fireplace. There was a slither of a front garden and, like the house, it looked quite pretty from the road. But closer inspection revealed that the roses – ruby-red to match the front door – were imprisoned by an iron fence and were being strangled into submission by a sticky, suppressing weed. Eight steep steps led up to the door, where hobnailed boots of past generations had worn the slate into a lethal downward-sloping camber. Sylvie always made sure that Sam went down the steps behind her, just in case, and grew to hate those steps, the last mountain to climb while carrying string bags full of tinned food – mixed fruit, spaghetti hoops, and sausages with beans – hauled from the corner shop, lugged up those eight treacherous steps and deposited with a final hurl at the feet of the fairies.

At eight o'clock in the morning on the 20th March 1987, Sylvie and Sam stood staring at Mother who was sprawled at the foot of the stairs. Her eyes were open, but so were her wrists, allowing her pooled blood to drown out the last gasp of breath those poor fairies could muster.

There were no hysterics. Sylvie and Sam stepped over their mother, followed the trail of blood into the kitchen, and closed the door. Sylvie poured out Sugar Puffs and milk into two bowls before wiping the blood from the floor with the dishcloth. It was important, she explained to Sam, to have breakfast on a day like this, and anyway, Mother's dead body was not a shock to either of them. It was a sight they had both played out in their minds many times before – had even discussed at length before.

Mrs Chang said, 'She probably tried to stick her head in the oven first, and then remembered it was electric.' Mrs Chang was full of advice. She once told Sylvie to be careful of the direction she allowed her thoughts to wander. One night, as Sam dealt the cards and Sylvie did indeed allow her thoughts to wander, Mrs Chang had shaken her shoulder gently and warned that dark thoughts could soon turn into dark reality, leading Sylvie to wonder, as she ate her Sugar Puffs, if she had somehow brought this moment about herself, just by imagining it. She also wondered how on earth she was going to get the blood stain off the fairies because surely the cracks and the grouting would be soaked through with her mother's blood for an eternity.

After breakfast, Sylvie shepherded Sam into the lounge, having wiped the blood off their feet on a tea towel first, shut the lounge door behind them, and they sat, Sam and Sylvie, side by side on the back of the settee with their bony legs hanging down the back panel. The net curtain was draped over the top of them like a drab, bridal shroud, and on account of being unable to open the front door because of the dead weight of their dead mother, and unable to open the windows because of the paint, they waited for someone to walk past. Sam glanced up at Sylvie and said, 'A body must be heavier when it's dead. You would have thought she would have been easier to move.' And Sylvie said, 'I have no idea but you're ever so clever, I'm sure you'll know the answer one day.'

Two days later, the police forced their way through the door and Mrs Chang, who had been away visiting her sister, took the children into her home and made apple tea. Mrs Chang cried for a while and told Sylvie that it would be OK for her to cry, too, at which point Sylvie did have the good grace to break down, but really, she was crying for the fairies. Mrs Chang told Sylvie she was certain that Mother mustn't have meant to die, not really, or else why would she have gone from the kitchen to the door? The smeared blood across the rising sun was surely a sign that she'd tried to open it, to cry out for help, and they would always have that thought to comfort them. But it didn't comfort Sylvie. Sylvie wished that Mother had kept to the kitchen, where the floor was covered with lino at least.

Sylvie, you see, knew the truth.

A lady policewoman rang the doorbell and filled out a form in red ink because neither she nor Mrs Chang had a blue or black pen. It bothered Sylvie for some time afterwards that she had come so unprepared. Sam and Sylvie were led from the house towards two cars parked in the street. Sylvie was led to one car, Sam to another. When Sylvie realised what was happening, she flailed around and even bit the woman who had no pen, but her body – the angular body of neither a child nor a woman – was dragged backwards by what seemed to be an octopus of hands, towards the open car door.

'I'll find you, Sam!' screamed Sylvie. And little Sam, a portrait of blank confusion, was bundled into the car.

It would be ten long years before Sylvie saw Sam again.

Chapter One

DONNA

My name is Belladonna Nightshade. I'm a private detective and flower farmer based at the edge of the world in Cornwall, where the tip of the toe is on the map. I'm alone in the kitchen at my ancestral home, Penberth Manor, which is a rambling old pile that sits very comfortably just above a pretty fishing cove close to Penzance. It's mid-morning on a grey January day and I'm sitting at the table with a notebook in front of me. The end of a well-chewed pencil is in my mouth. On the top line of a fresh page, I have written, *New ways to make money*. But the rest of the page, like my mind, is blank. The flower farm is ticking over, not so much now because it's the middle of winter, but I was hoping that the deficit would be made up by taking on a little detective work – missing cats, missing husbands, maybe a murder or two. Five months into my new venture as a private detective, however, and The Edge of the World Detective Agency is yet to pay its way, which is why we're skint, and by 'we' I mean me and my family, the Nightshades, an infamous

Penzance family with a history of piracy and derring-do. We're also the custodians of *The Book of Ye Deadliest Curses*, but we don't tend to stray to the wrong side of the law these days, at least, not too much.

So no, The Edge of the World Detective Agency hasn't been the successful enterprise I hoped it would be, which is odd because my business plan was foolproof, incorporating such strategies as asking my mate the vicar to pray for us, handing out swish business cards with a fab logo in the local pubs, a mood/visualisation board (A1 size) and *loads* of visualisation work ('I'm sorry Mrs Jones but I simply can't investigate the suspicious death of your uncle this week because I'm absolutely snowed under with dead bodies', etc.). And yet, the phone does not ring, the emails do not spout forth and the bodies – those ten-a-penny corpses that litter the streets in the likes of Shetland and Midsomer – are notably absent. Cornwall has gone quiet all of a sudden, which is weird because it's a county whose landscape and history surely cries out for copious amounts of wickedness (or a missing cat, at least).

I got off to a decent start last year by nabbing a drug cartel *and* an actual killer, and one would think that such proficiency with my first case would have spawned lots of fresh cases; but the truth is, my montage of enterprises (including an Ella Fitzgerald tribute act) does not bring in sufficient income to run the house, which is vast, and ancestral, and expensive. And the bad news is that a winter storm blew off a portion of the roof last month, which we can't afford to mend. We do own several houses in the Penzance area, but we rent them out to low-income families for under-value rents and donate a percentage of the income to a homeless charity, so the cost to maintain and administer them is often greater than the income they generate. What's a girl to do?

(Not complain about it, that's what a girl has to do.)

There are five of us in the family: my younger and musically talented sister, Lamorna, Uncle Jago (eccentric, also musical, academic), and my spirit-junkie auntie, Kerensa. That adds up to four. The fifth is Aunt Kerensa's identical twin sister who shares my name, Belladonna Nightshade (Donna for short) and is spending the next couple of years in prison having already spent many years there for the attempted murder of her husband (and also for being certified a danger to public health due to psychotic tendencies). The good news is that Uncle Jack is now finally dead thanks to a few dodgy shenanigans last year, but really, Auntie Donna didn't deserve to be 'sent down' in the first place because honestly the man was an absolute arsehole.

The prison is in Cornwall on Bodmin Moor, so not too far away, and luckily, it's a fairly casual kind of prison designed to incarcerate the type of woman who hasn't coped well with the menopause and has resultingly lost her way by wielding knives at husbands, that kind of thing. I discovered last year that, being identical twins who have always shared everything, Kerensa and Auntie Donna have been trading places now and again without any of the prison wardens noticing (well, either that or Auntie Donna has been paying them off). All of which means that Kerensa is very generously sharing the burden of 'doing time' with Auntie Donna. She says she doesn't mind doing this because it gives her time to work on her Kundalini meditation, but Lamorna says that Kerensa's got the hots for the prison governor, so who knows what's afoot where those two are concerned. All of this means that sometimes we have Auntie Donna at the manor (medieval with battlements) and sometimes we have Auntie Kerensa. The two of them carried out this little deception for a number of years before I cottoned on that our pet macaw, Ruby, was sometimes nice but sometimes nasty to Auntie Kerensa – Ruby absolutely *hates* Auntie Donna. If I'm ever in doubt which witch is which, I just pop Ruby onto her shoulder and if Ruby adopts 'attack mode', then, hey presto, I know that we have Auntie Donna at the manor.

But back to my blank piece of paper ...

What I really need is a juicy murder to get stuck into, where some wealthy woman (or man, but let's face it, it's most likely to be a woman and almost certainly posh) rocks up at my door and says, 'Donna! There you are. Excellent. I'm in a terrible fix and I wonder if you could help me out. Only, someone has been murdered and I could really do with your help.'

Nah, that's never going to happen, is it?

Time to drop my forehead onto the table and pray to the angels.

'Ah, Donna, you're here, good.' It's Uncle Jago. He's just walked in and is taking off his coat while ushering a stylish woman of middle years into the kitchen. I lift my head from the table. The lady in question is called 'Lady Helen' and she's the owner of St Michaels Mount, a tidal island situated not far from us near Penzance. The Mount is one of the most impressive (if not *the* most impressive) landmarks in Cornwall and is linked to the mainland by a tidal causeway. It has a castle and chapel stuck on top of it.

Lady Helen is looking a little ruffled.

'Sit down here, Helen, dear,' says Jago, pulling out a chair. 'And do tell Donna all about it while I pop the kettle on. Are you still off dairy?'

'I am,' she says. 'But only because of my bowels. If you can cope with the farts, I'd love an Irish coffee ... Pile on the cream and have a heavy hand with the brandy.'

'Oh, don't worry about a little morning breeze,' he says, putting on a pinny and heading to the Aga. 'Farts are compulsory in this house.'

'Super!' says Lady Helen, who pulls out a chair and turns to face me. 'To be honest with you, Donna,' she says. 'I'm in a terrible fix.'

This looks promising …

'Go on.'

'The thing is, I've got a high-profile guest coming to stay next weekend who is in a spot of ... let's call it 'bother'. Murder threats and so on, and I could really do with your help … I'll pay you appropriately, of course.'

I pat her hand and glance up to the heavens. 'Thank you, sweet angels,' I whisper under my breath. 'Thank you.'

Chapter Two

DONNA

While Uncle Jago dollops a spoonful of cream on the top of three boozed-up coffees, Lady Helen opens her Harris Tweed handbag and takes out a piece of good quality card.

'This is what I'm worried about,' she says, handing me the card.

On the occasion of …
The twenty-year anniversary of the Pimpernel Club
You are invited to attend a weekend reunion at
St Michael's Mount, Cornwall
Dinner Dress: black tie
Goodie bags of local produce provided
Date: 27–29 February
Boat leaves Marazion at 15.30
(Sensible shoes for the climb to the Mount)
Lest we forget…

'Seems benign enough,' I say, running an eye over the card while Jago takes a seat at the table.

Lady Helen takes a deep breath and sighs. This is not a great sign as she is from a breed of stoic women who do not easily succumb to throwaway sighs.

'The guests are all friends of Arthur's godson, Rupert Pendleton,' she says. 'There are seven of them coming in total, that's including Rupert.'

'The Godson?'

'Yes. You may have seen him on television. He's one of those weather-forecaster chaps on the BBC ... Ex-Royal Navy.' She dips a finger in the cream and licks it. 'He did *Strictly* last year.'

'Never heard of him,' says Jago. 'Does he do the shipping forecast?'

'No.'

'There you are, then,' concludes Jago, dismissively.

Lady Helen turns to me. 'It all started when Rupert emailed to ask if he could bring a few friends along for the weekend, but we didn't realise he was going to make such a big event of it, so we said yes. Arthur felt that we couldn't really say no because they're all war veterans ... He thought it would be a bit poor-spirited of us.'

'Right. Tell me more about Rupert.'

Lady Helen looks away to have a think.

'Where to start? Both parents died in an avalanche in the Alps when he was a teenager. Dreadful business. Arthur took him under his wing, what with being his godfather, you know. Then he joined the Royal Navy after Oxford ... I suppose rudderless vessels often turn to the forces for a safe harbour, and that's where he studied for all his meteorological bits and bobs, in the Royal Navy as a met officer. The guests are all ex-forces, actually. Well, more or less. That's how they all met, in Iraq. They worked together on the general's deployed staff. It's the twenty-year anniversary of the war this year, of course.'

'*Tempest fugit*,' offers Jago, with a shake of the head.

I look at the card again. 'And why do they call themselves the "Pimpernel Club"?' I ask.

Lady Helen shrugs. 'Rupert said it was an 'in joke' and offered no more. They were all living in tents in the desert, hiding from the Iraqis behind the front line, until eventually HQ was established permanently in Basra at the airport. He said they used to meet up for a cigarette several times a day throughout the war, and then, once they were settled at the airport, they would arrange a time in the evening when they would go onto the airport roof – hidden beneath the parapet, so to speak – for some downtime, like a little social club, I suppose. I believe they even managed to get hold of a few bottles of gin, but don't ask me how.'

'Sent by friends and smuggled in through care packages, would be my guess,' says Jago.

'Quite possibly,' agrees Lady Helen. 'Arthur made an effort to keep Rupert stocked up with Haribo and baby wipes, but I don't think he sent booze, at least, none that he told me about. Anyhow, none of them stayed in the forces for very long after the war, except for one, and he's done jolly well out of it. He's a brigadier now, I believe.'

I'm beginning to think Lady Helen could chatter along similar lines all day. I need to focus her thoughts.

'And you're worried about the reunion because of one

particular high-profile guest who's attending, you say?' I pick up my pencil. 'You mentioned something about death threats? Who is this guest, exactly?'

She fixes me with a stare, as does Jago.

'Here's the rub,' begins Lady Helen, who glances towards the door before leaning in with a whisper. 'It's the Home Secretary!'

'The actual Home Secretary,' I say. 'That Nadine woman ...What's her name again?'

'The Right Honourable Nadine Pinkerton-Smyth,' says Uncle Jago.

'She's been getting death threats, according to Scotland Yard,' adds Lady Helen. 'One of the chaps there phoned Arthur for a bit of a chat.'

'Arthur is Helen's husband,' explains Jago.

'Yes, thank you, Uncle. I *have* met Lord St Clement on quite a few occasions ...' I say.

Jago sniffs. 'Only trying to help.'

I glance down at the sheet of paper in my notebook. It's still blank. I'm struggling to see in which direction Helen is going with this. 'And, as far as the weekend goes ...You're worried because?'

'Isn't it obvious?!' says Jago. 'Poor Helen is worried out of her wits that this Nadine woman will be bumped off while she's staying at the Mount!'

'Is that likely?' I ask, thinking that surely someone as high profile as the Home Secretary will bring a security detail with her. She's staying in a fortress castle, a castle that is very easy to defend but not so easy to infiltrate, which is kind of the point with castles, so ...

Lady Helen and Jago exchange frustrated glances. She leans in closer to explain.

'Think about it, Donna. What if someone has found out that she's going to be staying at the Mount?'

'A mount that has a display room full of every possible antique murder weapon you can think of ...' adds Jago, who I fear isn't helping in terms of calming Lady Helen's nerves. Quite the contrary: he's bloody loving it. 'It's all very sinister!' says Jago. (As I said, loving it.)

'Or, very safe,' I offer. 'After all, once Nadine is inside, all you have to do is lock and bolt the main door and she's as safe as houses. I'd have thought an impenetrable tidal island was the perfect place to put a high-profile guest for her to enjoy a perfectly safe weekend with old friends ...'

Lady Helen and Jago exchange glances once again, only this time they both shrug and look almost ... disappointed.

'That's not to say that someone on the *inside* couldn't pop her off,' I say, hoping to buoy them up a bit on the potential-murder front, and also remembering that Lady Helen mentioned paying me actual money.

'Well, quite,' says Jago, perking up.

'That's rather unlikely,' says Lady Helen, with a bit of a bristle. 'I'm sure Arthur's godson keeps only the best company.'

Jago and I take a turn to exchange glances, and here's why: the Home Secretary is a fifty-year-old woman who has a reputation for being a piece of work i.e. a hardnosed player who would have made Maggie Thatcher look like a pussy cat. She was banned from Twitter last year for being too outspoken – on Twitter!

Our impasse is broken by our pet macaw, Ruby, who flies in through a thin slit of opportunity afforded by the open, kitchen window. She flies with the skill, speed, and grace of a fighter jet on manoeuvres and lands on Lady Helen's shoulder, causing not one inch of a reaction, but then I did say she was stoic (the lady, not the macaw. Drama-queen Ruby is the very opposite of stoic).

Lady Helen commits to a full swig of her coffee, opens her handbag, removes a neatly folded and initialled handkerchief and wipes a line of cream from her top lip.

Noblesse oblige.

'Have you spoken to Rupert about your concerns?' I ask.

'Yes. But Rupert says not to be a ninny ... and so does Arthur. But there *was* that additional phone call from Scotland Yard ...'

This sounds more promising.

'Go on.'

'Apparently, Pinky is ...'

'Pinky?' I say, interrupting.

'Oh, that's what Rupert calls her – Nadine *Pinkerton*-Smyth. AKA, 'Pinky'. The thing is, she's refusing to bring a protection officer with her, or have any police presence on the island at all, which is bonkers because I've googled the organisation that's been sending her death threats (she extradited one of them to South America a couple of months ago; it was all over the news) and they aren't the kind of people that you want to be leaving yourself open to. It wouldn't be so bad, but Arthur and I will be away for the weekend, so we won't be on hand with the old blunderbuss et cetera.'

'Ooh, going anywhere nice?' I ask, hoping to lighten the mood.

'Antarctica,' she says, offering an additional, 'Penguins', by way of explanation.

'And this last line ...' I say, glancing again at the invitation card. '*Lest we forget*. Forget what? The war, presumably.'

'That's my guess,' says Lady Helen.

Jago's eyes narrow. 'Although ... it could be some kind of secret code between them, referring to something *truly* sinister,' he offers. 'It could refer to some nefarious shenanigans they all got up to in Iraq ... or afterwards. They could be an international crime ring all by themselves. What about that, eh?'

Somewhere in the distance a crow caws.

'Can't you simply call the whole thing off, Helen dear?' asks Jago, offering what is clearly the only sensible solution.

Lady Helen says not. 'Arthur says I'm being silly. He was very close to Rupert's father at school, and he thinks it would be pretty rum of us to go back on our word, especially as all of the invitations have gone out already.'

'And who wrote the invitations?' I ask. 'Rupert, I suppose?'

'I think it was Nadine's PA,' says Lady Helen. 'But I'm not one-hundred per cent certain on that. Rupert can be a little woolly sometimes.'

I make a few notes, just to look professional, but really all I'm writing is a shopping list for later.

'Just to confirm, Lady Helen,' I say. 'You've come to see me because there's going to be a reunion party at the Mount, and you think that one of the party has a chance of being murdered over the course of the weekend.'

'Exactly that,' says Helen.

'Right. And how do I fit in?'

'Isn't it obvious?' asks Jago.

I ignore him and wait for Lady Helen to answer.

'Well, dear. I'd be very grateful if you could come along for the weekend and basically run the show – look after the place. To be honest, you simply *have* to come as I've told Scotland Yard, who are understandably nervous, that I'm putting Cornwall's best man, who happens to be a woman, on the job – the job of protecting Pinky. Godson or not, I think there's something very definitely *épineux* about this reunion ...'

'Dodgy,' says Jago. 'She means dodgy.'

'Quite,' says Lady Helen.

How to word my next sentence ...

'Don't you think you might be overthinking it ... just a little bit?' I resist the urge to pat Lady Helen's hand. 'I doubt a cabinet minister would be willing to put herself in perilous danger. She must be fairly sensible, what with being a politician ...'

Jago and Helen burst into spontaneous laughter and proceed to laugh out loud for a good minute, which I ignore and wait for an answer from Lady Helen. Once she's stopped dabbing her eyes with that handkerchief, she says,

'You're right, of course. But then there's the return of the samurai to consider ...'

'Isn't that a film?' I say.

'Don't be facetious, Donna,' says Jago. 'You know perfectly well that Helen is referring to her resident ghost.'

I do. But, really ... ghosts now? This is turning into a *Scooby-Doo* mystery.

'He's been a bit busy lately – our samurai friend. On the prowl type of thing,' explains Lady Helen. 'He keeps swishing the library curtains whenever I sit down to watch *Countdown*, and I know there isn't a draught in that room because Arthur only recently put the secondary glazing in.'

'I think he's trying to tell you something, Helen,' says Jago, glancing over his shoulder to double-check that the samurai hasn't followed her to Penberth.

Lady Helen takes another swig of her brandy coffee.

'Right then,' I say brightly, positioning my pencil above the page for the umpteenth time. 'Let's start with the basics. Who exactly is coming to this shindig? Names, ages, backgrounds… Tell me everything you know.'

Helen grabs her handbag and takes out a Filofax.

'I'm glad you asked that,' she says, her eyes more animated now. 'Because I've made a few notes…'

Chapter Three

DONNA

'Start with the juicy MP!' shouts Jago from across the kitchen. He's returned to the Aga and is wearing his best pinny to prepare brunch. It says, *Prick With A Fork* on the front. 'I bet she's got a secret or two tucked up her sleeve,' he adds. 'Or my name's not … well, Jago Nightshade.'

I turn in my chair to face him. 'Since when did you, my dearest uncle, refer to anyone as, "juicy"?'

Jago points a fish slice in my direction. 'I wasn't always middle-aged, you know.' (He was. I bet he appeared from the womb wearing a tweed suit and carrying the minutes of a village council meeting.) He returns his attention – and the fish slice – to the pan of potato and chorizo hash he's knocking up (Jamie Oliver. Delicious) while I turn to the back page of my notebook and write *The Guest List* across the top.

'Right then, Lady Helen. The Pimpernel Club… What have you got?'

Guest One.

The *Right Honourable Nadine Pinkerton-Smyth (AKA 'Pinky')* graduated from Oxford with a degree in international politics and law in 1994. There are pages and pages of guff about her on the internet, so much so that you really can't see the wood for the trees, but the bottom line is that most of Twitter hates her while the Prime Minister loves her; at least, he does at the moment, but twenty-four hours is a long time in politics. Pinky is one of two of the seven guests who never served as a member of the armed forces. As a young, thrusting, civil servant at the time of the war in 2003, Pinky was deployed to Iraq to act as the political advisor to the major general. According to Helen (and therefore, according to her godson, Rupert), Pinky has always pedalled the story that she spent the war as the general's right-hand woman, operating as a key link between the government at home and the military at the front. After being promoted quickly through the ranks of the civil service, Pinky reached the dizzying heights of assistant private secretary to a cabinet minister. After which time Pinky came to the, quite correct, conclusion that she could most likely do the job better herself. She quit the civil service and used her influence and contacts within the party to nab herself a Home Counties' safe seat and found herself gracing the back benches of the House of Commons quicker than she could say, *get me the Prime Minister on the phone*, or, *why wasn't I told about this immediately*. It was her 'front line' credentials that helped her to win the support of her constituents, but in reality (again, according to Rupert), she swanned about the Iraqi desert for the duration of the war wearing designer combat trousers and silk blouses, with a pistol and gas mask hanging from her belt, while basking in her own self-importance. (I'm beginning to think that Rupert might be a tad jealous of Pinky.) Pinky's journey from the back to the front benches was stratospheric and Helen's final summation describes Pinky as being very attractive 'for her age'. (I *would* pull Helen up for ageism, but I'll let it slide as she's older than Pinky and so entitled to say such things.) In summation, Pinky is 'made for politics', which says absolutely everything I need to know about the Right Honourable Nadine Pinkerton-Smyth (or plain old Nadine Smith as she was known before becoming an MP). Anyhow, according to Scotland Yard, who've been on the blower, there's a killer on the loose with a bullet with Pinky's name on it and (even better) some kind of blow-your-mind-scandal is about to blow about her. All in all, it's perhaps not the best of times for Pinky Smyth. No wonder she wants to escape for the weekend.

Guest Two.

Atticus Black. Mr Black was Special Forces Liaison Officer on the general's staff. Helen knows nothing about him except that when she googled the army website, he didn't look at all as she expected. When asked to elaborate, she says, 'Well, what can I say? He looks like just an ordinary man and not the least bit like Daniel Craig!' Atticus is the only one of the Pimpernel Club to have remained in the armed forces for a full career. He was the 2004 Olympic champion at rifle shooting. (Was he now?)

Guest Three.

Miles Johnson was the United States Marine Corps liaison officer on the general's staff and the only officer who was allowed to access US intelligence services via his laptop. According to Rupert, Miles was a bit full of himself during the war, and having seen a picture of him on the internet taken at a swanky business dinner a few years ago, Helen feels that his teeth are a little too white, his hair a little too well-groomed, and his biceps a little too buffed for him to fit in well at the Mount. He's now an entrepreneur of some description, but Rupert has no idea what commodity he's dealing in these days. Miles was living in the Middle East, last he heard, Abu Dhabi or maybe Doha; Helen can't quite remember.

Guest Four.

Sienna Blackville was one of several officers from the Intelligence Corps working at Headquarters. Her particular strength on the team was her in-depth knowledge of the oil industry, having done a doctorate focusing on the socio-economics of the Middle Eastern oil industry only a year before (timing is everything). She was also the go-to person for any tricky photographic interpretation during the invasion. Sienna Blackville is now a famous TV journalist. I have never heard of her but that means absolutely nothing as I rarely watch TV and never watch the news – who wants to be depressed *that* badly on a regular basis? She is divorced and has a grown-up daughter who is in her late teens and has a life-limiting genetic condition that manifested in adolescence. Sienna is understandably bereft and has taken a break from journalism to spend more time with her.

Guest Five.

Matt Lewis is a handsome (Lady Helen's words) ex-RAF pilot who was deployed (begrudgingly, in Rupert's opinion) to work with the army as a liaison link between the general and the RAF, who were safely tucked away with their aircraft in the likes of Kuwait and Qatar. Rupert said that (being RAF) Matt was automatically despised by his colleagues because the army tend to view the RAF with an unhealthy dose of jealousy and suspicion that is often, but not always, warranted. Nevertheless, he's a 'decent kind of a chap' according to Rupert, and Helen quite fancied him after looking at a photo online. (The internet really is a blessing for this type of caper.) Apparently, he has an uncanny resemblance to that actor who played Captain Townsend (Princess Margaret's love interest) in the first series of *The Crown*. Matt now flies the Boeing 777 long haul for British Airways. On hearing this, Jago said, 'What a dull job! No wonder he accepted the invitation to come to Cornwall. There are only so many times one can fly to Bora Bora without becoming bored to death of the damn place…'

Guest Six.

Dr Jane MacAvoy. Dr Jane was the chief medical officer in Iraq. She spent her days at Headquarters on the radio advising which assets should go to which casualties on the battlefield – deploying helicopters and manpower to recover the wounded and so on. She returned to Iraq a year later for a tour as a battlefield surgeon, then left the army after a second Iraq tour, and is now a doctor at a medical institution near Oxford. She gives lectures around the world advising on medical facilities and operational requirements for military deployments. The summation of Dr Jane is that she's seen some terrible things, has a brilliant mind and is impervious to shock. (She won't mind coming across the samurai ghost then.)

Guest Seven.

Rupert Pendleton is Helen's godson and was the meteorological officer who gave weather briefings to the army several times per day. He was injured in Basra after getting caught up in a roadside, bomb attack and had to have his right knee rebuilt, which left him with a limp. It was Dr Jane who applied battlefield first aid and thereby saved his life. He's now a weatherman for the BBC and lives on the outskirts of Marlow. His ambition is to take over from Carol Kirkwood on *BBC Breakfast*, but he doubts she'll ever leave, so he'll have to make do with the six o'clock slot instead. He's a solid, all-round good egg, according to Helen, although I have the feeling that Helen is keeping something back.

'And that's it. That's your lot,' concludes Lady Helen.

I look down at the guest list and whistle.

'A TV met man? Famous journalist? MP? It's quite a list.'

Lady Helen mops up the egg from her brunch plate with a piece of sourdough toast while Jago pours her another cup of tea, the brandy coffee having long since been polished off.

'So, you see,' she says. 'There is absolutely no way I can leave Rupert and his friends in the castle without proper supervision – who knows what these types of characters might get up to when they've had a few snifters! Donna, you and your sister are to provide the entertainment for Friday evening – a little singing, a bit of soul – you know, the Ella Fitzgerald numbers you do at the pub. Lamorna can play her little harp during dinner; and if Jago does the cooking, well, together you will all provide a lovely night while keeping an eye on things.' She narrows her eyes and leans in. 'After all, St Michael's Mount is a very lonely – one might say, dangerous – place to leave a group of ... let's call them "interesting" people for the weekend.'

'Especially when one of them has a price on her head,' says Jago.

Hmm. As much as I have prayed for the detective agency to bag a job like this (thank you, angels, by the way) this all seems so unlikely, so melodramatic. And if *I* were the honourable Pinky Smyth, I'd definitely want to escape for the weekend without any hangers-on like us.

'But a potential murder in a castle on a tidal island,' I say. 'Isn't that just a bit ... 1920s?'

'I'll pay well above the going rate, obviously,' says Lady Helen, patting my hand. 'And you can all stay in one of the holiday cottages down at the harbour. They're all empty until Easter – it'll be like a little holiday for the family!'

Ruby, who has transitioned to Jago's shoulder, squawks and fluffs her feathers a bit.

'And of course, you can come too, Ruby,' says Lady Helen. 'Just don't shit on the Persian rugs ... or the samurai soldier, will you?'

Ruby throws me a side eye just as my sister Lamorna walks through the door with a guitar in her hand, playing *Hopelessly Devoted to You* in the style of Cornish singer, Daisy Clark, who also does a cracking cover of the timeless classic. She's barefoot and wearing an old, twill suit of Jago's that's pulled together at the waist by a broad belt. The ensemble somehow looks amazing, but poor Lamorna hasn't had any new clothes in years...

'In that case ... we'd be happy to help you.' I hold out a hand to shake Lady Helen's already outstretched one.

'Help with what?' asks Lamorna, resting her guitar on a spare chair.

'Murder!' screeches Ruby.

'Ooh, our speciality!' says Lamorna, opening the biscuit tin and taking out a Jammie Dodger. 'Are we committing the murder this time or solving it, because things got a bit unnecessarily complicated last year, didn't they, Jago?'

'Murder! Murder!' screeches Ruby.

Jago looks away and I jump up to shoo my sister out of the kitchen while throwing some reassuring words over my shoulder in Lady Helen's direction.

'My sister!' I say, my accompanying laugh far too high-pitched. 'She's such a joker!'

Chapter Four

Detective Sergeant Joe Enys of Devon and Cornwall Police (Penzance station) is standing in a small kitchen in a newly refurbished townhouse in a lovely part of Penzance. He's in Chapel Street, to be precise, where the Brontë sisters' mother was born (there's a blue plaque). Joe is admiring a copper sink with such delight that you would think modern plumbing is a revelation to him, especially as he doesn't usually care about sinks – the stainless steel one in his flat of ten years has always been perfectly adequate – but this particular kitchen, with its quartz worktop (non-porous and scratch-resistant), Neff appliances and wine fridge, is the dog's whatsits. And so is the rest of the house; a three-storey, newly renovated townhouse to be sold fully furnished (IKEA, but nice) with no onward chain. Joe wouldn't normally be able to afford a townhouse on Chapel Street, this is Cornwall, after all, and the locals aren't used to being able to afford the really nice places, but Joe's grandad – who owned the type of farm up Zennor way that sits well with the type of bored housewife belonging to a London banker who is looking for a Cornish smallholding from which she can keep alpacas and distil gin – died last year (the grandad did) leaving Joe a tidy stash of cash. The house on Chapel Street has no parking and it's only a couple of doors down from a popular pub, which is not ideal for a copper, but number fifty-one screams out 'home' to him.

'Can you get me a few quid off?' asks Joe, addressing Chris, the estate agent.

Chris pulls an, 'I don't know, mate,' expression just as Joe's phone rings. It's Chief Inspector Penworthy, his boss lady from Truro.

'Better get this,' says Joe, wandering through to the lounge and taking a seat on what's likely to become his new sofa, a green velvet two-seater from Loaf.

'Yes, ma'am?'

Penworthy isn't known for pleasantries. 'Where the hell are you?' she asks.

Why lie?

'I'm viewing a house that I'm thinking of buying, if I can get the price right,' says Joe, throwing a knowing glance in Chris's direction. Chris shrugs and starts turning off lights.

'Where?'

'Chapel Street.'

'On *your* wage? Did someone die?'

'Grandad.'

'Ah. Nice one. You on speaker phone?'

Joe hates speaker phone, seeing it as just one of many indicators of the end of decent behaviour on *so* many fronts. 'No.'

'Good, because I've got a job for you and it's a bit hush-

hush. Well, it's completely *hush* actually, not just hush-hush, if you know what I mean.'

Joe does. He steps out onto the street. If he concentrates hard enough, he can hear the sea as it breaks across Battery Rocks. He's only a stone's throw from the promenade, too, *and* the lido, and the Yacht Inn, and the fish and chip shop... Yep, he's definitely buying this gaff.

'All clear,' he says.

'Right. How do you like the sound of having a cabinet minister pay a visit down your way?' asks Penworthy.

'I don't like it at all. Which one?'

'Nadine Pinkerton-Smyth. And before you say, "Who?" that's the Home Secretary – or ma'am to you. She's the one that's always in the news for saying the wrong thing.'

Joe examines the paint colour on the exterior walls. The developer has chosen a very stylish dark olive colour. Farrow and Ball, Joe reckons, or something pricey like that. The windows are proper quality, too. There's no garden, but who needs the hassle of mowing grass when you've got the sand and the sea literally on your doorstep? Shame about there not being a shed, though. A man should have a shed. Where will he keep his fishing gear?

'Oh, yeah. Blonde woman.' Joe stops himself from saying, *Great legs, looks like a right goer*, because he's done the 'Inappropriate Behaviour and Unconscious Bias Awareness Course' and knows that you can't say that kind of thing anymore.

'That's the one,' confirms Penworthy. 'Massive tits. Bit of a tart, I reckon.'

Joe allows himself a smile.

'Why all the hush-hush?' he asks, 'Sorry,' he corrects himself. 'Why all the complete hush?'

Penworthy lets out a long (can't be arsed with this) sigh. It sounds to Joe like she's loading the dishwasher while talking, which is understandable as Penworthy is a single mum with a teenage kid, a dog, *and* she's a detective chief inspector. 'Because the Yard have been onto me with their "concerns",' she says giving enough stress for Joe to imagine the air quotations. Joe hears her kettle click on. 'Anyhow, good old Nadine is determined to ditch her protection officer and wants to arrive in Penzance incognito, which isn't at all like the Right Honourable Pinkerton-Smyth, not according to the Yard. She never usually goes anywhere without leaking it to the press and then banging on about it on Twitter, apparently.'

'Shouldn't be too big of a deal, should it?' says Joe, glancing upwards to inspect the guttering. 'We coped with G7, and no one died. Where's she staying?'

'St Michael's Mount. Some kind of reunion for the weekend. Ex-forces lot. She's staying there for two nights. There's a driver bringing her down.'

Joe heads back into the house. He isn't really paying much attention to DCI Penworthy because, frankly, he doesn't really give a crap about a cabinet minister who's going to a party. Nor does he see why it's a big enough deal to involve the police, at all, let alone Scotland Yard *and* a busy detective chief inspector like Penworthy, who hasn't even had the time to make herself a cup of tea without being on the phone sorting out yet more nonsense. He's also supposed to be going on a fishing trip this weekend and nothing short of murder usually stops Joe from heading out on his little boat. He says as much to Penworthy (missing out the fishing trip detail, clearly).

'And I agree with you,' says Penworthy. He hears her slam the dishwasher door closed. 'But the Yard have told us to keep an eye out because she's had these death threats.'

'Haven't they all?' says Joe.

'Not like this,' says Penworthy. 'There's a price on her head – an actual price, like it's the bloody Wild West. She extradited this South American bloke last year who was the head of a London crime ring and they're out to get her – are happy if anyone gets her, hence the price on the head.'

'When's she coming?' Joe is starting to realise that he might have to take this thing a little more seriously.

'This weekend,' says Penworthy. 'I've spoken to Lady Helen already – you know her, right?'

Know her? He went to school with her nephew.

'Yep, nice woman. Is it a big do?'

'Not especially. I think there are seven of them coming down. But I think the Yard is right, and my copper's instinct is telling me that there's something fishy going on with this weekend of theirs, especially now that Donna Nightshade is involved.'

Like a March hare listening out for a predatory fox, Joe's ears prick up to full height. Donna Nightshade, with her long, dark wavy hair, lithe limbs and beautiful complexion, who wears sexy shorts and a T-shirt or vest top from April to October, was his childhood sweetheart, but he had to arrest her when she was eighteen because she got involved in a tiny smidge of drug dealing (not technically her fault). Because of this minor issue of her arrest leading her to serve time, she didn't speak to him again for many years, probably because she came out of prison wearing an ankle-tag monitor, which didn't go down well in the Nightshade household, or in Penzance generally – Donna is a bit of a local hero. But having brushed herself off and started down a squeaky clean path of righteousness as a flower farmer at the Nightshade baronial manor, last year Donna decided to open her very own detective agency, which happened to be at exactly the same time her uncle – Jack – got himself murdered, and Donna found herself playing not only the part of prime suspect for the murder, but also the self-appointed private investigator to crack the case. (At the time Penworthy told Joe to lock her up and throw away the key). Joe and Donna struck up a bargain of sorts to work together to uncover the true murderer (Joe called it an act of friendship, Donna wasn't so sure) and after a high-speed boat chase involving some *really* dodgy crooks, Donna and Joe solved the murder together (well, kind of … Joe genuinely solved it, whereas Donna just thought she did). With Donna off the hook, Joe thought – hoped – that she would forgive him for past misdemeanours and subsequently fall in love with him again. Furthermore, Joe (who, let's face it, has loved Donna for all of his life) ended the shenanigans by buying Donna a dog for her birthday– an actual woof-woof – as a sweetener. He crashed her birthday party with the express intention of telling her, once and for all, that he loved her. But wouldn't you know it, this damn ripped Interpol officer – Jase Clarkson – who had been working undercover on the case (total arsehole, as far as Joe was concerned) pitched up wearing a head brace and immediately declared his undying love for Donna. She couldn't turn him away because he'd saved her life and nearly got killed in the process, hence the head brace. Joe rebounded from this disappointment by taking his desk sergeant, Demelza, out on a date (to be fair, he'd promised to take her to dinner if she hushed something up about the Nightshade family) but this decision, as with all rash decisions made on the rebound, proved to be a course of action he regretted later, and continues to regret to this day: there's just no shaking Demelza.

'Donna Nightshade?' repeats Joe, trying to sound nonchalant but there's a definite sudden sweatiness to his brow.

'Yes. And get this!' Penworthy's disdain cuts through the airwaves like rapidly thrown knives. 'Lady Helen has hired the whole of the Nightshade clan to do the food and the entertainment for the weekend, having fallen for the guff that Donna is a private detective now. Apparently, Lady and Lord St Clement are going to be away in the Antarctic that weekend. What a bloody shit show. The Yard wants me to put a man on the ground and I've spoken with Lady Helen, and it's all sorted. You'll stay in one of the holiday cottages on the harbourfront.'

That's Joe's fishing trip well and truly flushed down the toilet, and he *would* usually be cross, but he's just been handed a weekend with Donna Nightshade in a spooky castle that's perched on top of a rocky island and cut off from all humanity when the tide is in… Joe could think of worse things to do with his time.

'Won't the guests think that it's a bit odd that the local detective sergeant has pitched up on the island for no justifiable reason whatsoever?'

'I don't give two shits if they do,' says Penworthy, her voice is raised now because she's moved on to another domestic chore – hoovering. 'But just in case the Right Honourable Pain In My Arse kicks off, I've decided to pass you off as a waiter.'

Words fail Joe. Act as Donna's waiter for the weekend? She'll love that.

'Anyway, must be off.' Penworthy turns off the hoover. 'I've got the kid to pick up at four and a dance class in Redruth at six.'

'Ballet?' asks Joe, returning his attention to viewing the house.

'Nah. I'm doing tap now. Ballet was too rough on the toes. Keep me updated, yeah?'

'Yes, ma'am.'

'And, Joe?'

Joe has started playing with the tap again. 'Yes, ma'am?'

'Listen. I know you're desperate to get into those Nightshade knickers, always have been. But honestly, kiddo, take it from me … it's *never* going to happen!'

The phone goes dead, leaving Joe standing in front of the kitchen sink staring at his phone.

Chris meanders in from the lounge. 'Well? You interested?'

Joe takes a deep breath and scrunches his face. 'Knock off twenty grand and I'll take it off your hands.'

Chris laughs out loud, which is not the response Joe was expecting.

'You're dreaming, aren't you? It's a fixed price, mate. This developer's minted, so he'll just sit on it until it goes. I'll tell you this, though; you won't get a copper sink and genuine mosaic tiles anywhere else in Penzance for this price. No worries if it's not for you, though. A second homer will have it as a holiday home.'

Joe's nostrils flare.

Over his dead body.

'OK. I'll have it!'

(*Oh, Joe. He was bluffing!*)

Hands are shaken just as Joe's phone pings. It's a message from Donna. At least three heartbeats are skipped.

A little bird just told me that you've volunteered to be my manservant for the weekend.

How? How had she heard so quickly?

Be cool, Joe. Don't fire a message back straight away … leave it an hour.

Sod it. He starts to type, his mouth edging into a lovely little smile.

It's your gig, clearly. I'll just be there to observe – and to serve wine, apparently.

Donna replies,

The dog says 'hi' by the way. Oh, and you owe me fifty quid for a new rug – genuine Afghan. He chewed it. And Ruby needs counselling because she can't cope with the dog barking. I do love the little shitbag, though, so thank you. See you at the Mount on Friday for a bit of fun.

Joe (smiling) steps out onto Chapel Street while Chris (also smiling) locks the door and puts in a call to the developer. Thirty seconds later there's an even wider smile and a thumbs up from Chris.

Woo-hoo! A new house *and* a rendezvous with Donna Nightshade!

He'd better not mention any of it to Demelza, though, except that he's going to have to, what with her being his desk sergeant and all. Joe types out a reply message to Donna, but immediately deletes it. He's not a game player or anything, but perhaps it's best to leave her waiting for a response for an hour or two…

Oh, Joe. Who are you kidding?

Chapter Five

Matt Lewis has woken up with his face pressed against the cold glass of a train window; saliva is dripping down his chin. He has no idea where he is or why he's there, but taking a moment to recalibrate, he vaguely remembers landing at Heathrow airport very early this morning. Yes, of course. He captained the red eye Boeing 777 from Chicago last night. Not for the first time he reminds himself that life as a long-haul pilot really is rubbish – so much for spending his off days basking in rays of endless sunshine in the likes of Bora Bora… Matt was lucky if he got a Dubai trip in the bag. He *would* throw the towel in – the Pimpernel Club has certainly seen him right for cash over the years – but what would he do with his time if he did? A person needs something – an occupation – to get up for every day, and the BA pension will come in handy too, especially now that he's got this unexpected responsibility hanging off him. He wipes his chin with the back of his hand and decides that another couple of years of setting the 777 to autopilot while he has hairdresser-chat with the stranger sitting next to him (BA has a ridiculous number of pilots) won't kill him.

After straightening out his face he notices that the train has just departed Truro, which means that there's about half an hour to go before he reaches his destination – Penzance. Not for the first time he wonders why on earth this reunion was called for. The war was over years ago, let it remain so. Reunions only ever dragged up bad blood. Wasn't it time to let it all go and just carry on as they had been happily carrying on for years – as silent partners?

Well, yes and no.

Matt knows full well that while the Pimpernel Club will almost certainly raise a glass to the fallen – damn awful business it was – and while there will be hardly a dry eye in the room when they toast absent friends, the real reason they are meeting in person is less to do with a reunion and more to do with money – lots and lots of money. He sighs. Oh, well, in for a penny, in for a pound. He reaches into the front pocket of his rucksack, grabs a can of Red Bull and a breakfast cereal bar and stares out of the train window at the rolling film of the soggy detritus of a wet and dreary winter's day in Cornwall. Taking a swig from the can, he returns his thoughts to the 'letting it all go' and remembers that there are certain things – certain consequences of past events – that simply cannot be let go of. So really, the previous stream of thought was pointless because he had absolutely no choice but to come here today. And couldn't it all work out in his favour, anyway? Being trapped on an island in the company of the Pimpernel Club (ridiculous name thought up by that Rupert idiot) might just provide the perfect opportunity to get his own particular issues sorted out once and for all…

His mind wanders to the last time he saw Pinky. He recalled accosting her on the street as she'd left a House of Commons Select Committee meeting last year.

'What do you want, Matt,' she'd said, carrying on walking down the road. 'Because if it's about what I think it's about, then my answer is still no.'

He'd grabbed her arm. 'What we did in Iraq had consequences beyond your career, Nadine!' he'd shouted. 'I had no damn choice but to be caught up in this, and you should be involved, too.'

Pinky had stopped walking, shook free her arm, and with eyes narrowed said, 'That whole thing was your particular idea at the time, I seem to remember.'

Matt shook his head. 'Rubbish! There's a build-up to that kind of thing and you were more than happy for me to go through with it at the time. For God's sake, woman, don't you want to do the right thing as a basic human being?'

Eventually, she looked him in the eye and said, 'No. I'm not going to get trashed in the papers for this. If you leak it, I'll deny it. I know the boss of British Airways by the way. He's having dinner at mine next week.'

There had been a cavernous pause then before she had simply turned away and carried on walking.

'You're a heartless cow, Nadine Bloody Smith!' he had shouted down the road.

And Nadine, for her part, had simply turned around, smirked and said, 'Moo!'

Meanwhile, on a National Express bus heading down the only arterial road in Cornwall, the infamous A30, fifty-two-year-old Miles Johnson is considering how it has come to be that he is utterly devoid of cash and travelling by bus. He's being bored to death by an elderly woman sitting next to him (something about her genius grandson), and if that wasn't bad enough, the pilot of his flight into London last night was that freakin' RAF guy from Iraq.

Ex-US Marine Corps, Miles Johnson – once known as the hero of Basra by the people of his hometown, thanks to a fabricated story told by Miles to his mother – was once a millionaire businessman. He smiles remembering how Tatler named him 'Top Man to Watch in 2007'. But nobody did watch him, mainly because Miles is the kind of guy who has done lots of things 'once'. He was once the man who gave Elon Musk a significant leg up in his early years in Silicon Valley (utter crap, but Miles has told this story so many times he's started to believe it) and he was once the go-to contact who could get investors a foot in the door of the oil industry in the Middle East. That story, at least, is true. But that was all a very long time ago. Having sold up his apartment in Dubai last year, Miles is now the kind of man who doesn't have his return fare home. His stomach growls as he runs a dry tongue over perfect, pearly white teeth. (Dang it! Why the hell had he paid ten-thousand bucks to get the damn things straightened and whitened in the first place?).

But then, a smile crosses his smooth, tanned face. He'll soon have plenty of money – squillions of the stuff. Miss High and

Mighty and the rest of those British assholes could bail him out – they've got enough money floating about, probably swimming in it, and all thanks to Miles's idea in the first place. And if they don't cough up? Well, he's got his book to fall back on... His lovely, lovely book. Yep, when he thought of the fallout, it was worth the trip into this quaint old English shithole.

'But listen to me,' says the old lady. 'Here I am going on and on about myself, and I haven't asked one single thing about you yet and we're nearly there...'

'What about me?' asks Miles, dipping a hand into the lady's packet of Werther's Originals.

'Well, for a start, where are you from?'

'The Midwest originally. I live in Chicago now.'

'And what do you do for a living, Mr...?'

'I make money.'

'Very nice. And how do you do that, my grandson will want to know.'

He nudges her playfully, sucking on his sweet. 'By swindling the shit out of people, usually.'

She rolls her eyes. 'Oh, you are a joker, Mr... But seriously, come on now, what brings you to Cornwall on a rainy afternoon? It's not exactly tourist season, is it? And there's a storm coming in tomorrow...' She glances up at him, her watery eyes full of excited expectation.

Miles glances out of the window. 'I told you, lady. I'm here for money. And ... just a *tiny* bit of revenge, maybe?'

The lady shakes her head. 'Get away with you. A nice man like you can't possibly mean something like that?'

He turns his head to look at her. 'I'm not a nice man,' he

says, popping the wrapper of the Werther's Original back in the packet. 'And I do mean it.'

Earlier in the day, investigative journalist and war correspondent, Sienna Morris, was sitting in a tearoom in Marazion looking across the causeway towards the stunning and iconic St Michael's Mount. Her mind, however, was racing too much to enjoy the view. She looked at her watch: 10am. It was time to head across to the mount if she was to get there before the causeway closed at eleven. She had two books in front of her. The first was the latest Coleen Hoover (she pretended when last interviewed on *This Morning* to read only Booker Prize type fiction, which was absolute bullshit as she'd grown up with Jackie Collins and wasn't going to change her reading habits for anyone). The second book was the proof copy of her memoir, *The Diary of an Ordinary Woman – Confessions of a War Correspondent*. She smiled. Nadine wasn't going to like it – none of them were, but that was nothing compared to the diatribe of whistleblowing crap that she'd heard Miles was writing. What. A. Cock. Putting her two beloved books away, Sienna pulled the rain cover over her rucksack, grabbed her suit carrier and took the first steps of a short walk across the causeway towards a very long weekend.

Later, while Sienna is settling nicely into the Mount and Miles is nearing the end of his bus ride, a black Range Rover is working its way around the narrow streets of the picturesque village of Marazion. The driver, Brigadier Atticus Black, is looking for somewhere to park. He found the main car park half an hour ago but, noting the price of a ticket, began to cruise the streets for a free spot – because hell would freeze over before he'd line the pockets of the *Just Park* brigade. After a final cruise of Marazion's quaint, narrow streets, he turns off the engine outside a cottage that has a sign saying, *please don't park here as I'm an old lady and you'll block the light to my windows.*

He pulls on his polar-proof padded jacket, grabs a large holdall and a suit carrier from the back seat, and with long determined strides, crosses the road outside the Godolphin Hotel and ventures into a quiet cafe. He's an hour early but he needs to gather his thoughts … look through the accounts … formulate a plan … consider what to say to Nadine. God, she'd got some balls that woman.

He orders a coffee – black, like his name – and with the first sparks of excitement building into a fairly decent burn-up as the buzz of a new deal begins to tingle its way from the ends of his gnarled fingers to the tips of his hairy toes, he takes out his laptop and opens a document titled, *The Poldark Project*. And then his laptop dies. He looks at the wall by the table. No plug socket. He walks around the room while being stared at by a middle-aged couple who are feeding scraps of bacon to their dog. Still no plug. The waiter appears with his coffee.

'Where can I plug in my laptop,' asks Atticus, not offering even a glimpse of a smile.

'You can't,' says the waiter. 'This is Cornwall, mate. Not Costa.'

To which Atticus has no answer.

While Atticus is scowling at the waiter, BBC weather presenter, Rupert Pendleton, is sitting opposite a radiant-looking woman at the bar in the Godolphin Hotel, Marazion. The lady is Dr Jane MacAvoy, eminent battlefield surgeon, decorated in Iraq, Afghanistan, and various other war zones less known about around the globe. They're trying to look easy and relaxed in each other's company – just old mates catching up over a glass of vino. But the truth is that they spent the whole of last night shagging while on the sleeper train from Paddington, the joke between them being that there was no sleep involved whatsoever. They've spent the day walking the beaches, despite Rupert's limp, admiring local artwork, sitting down to a Cornish cream tea, and all the while trying desperately not to be recognised by all the other out-of-season tourists wandering around doing exactly the same thing. Although Dr Jane is divorced and as free as a bird (a big blue one is what she usually imagines), Rupert is not free. He's married, has a teenage daughter and lives near Marlow. ('I just don't know where my marriage is going, Jane, to be honest. Sally and I … well, we live two completely different lives now. I'm only staying at home for my daughter' etc. etc.).

Dr Jane puts her hand on the table next to her glass and considers how pleased she is that she had taken the time to get her nails daubed with Gelac. It will be a bugger to get off, but she's probably got some decent chemical back at the lab that can manage it. Rupert glances at her hand before quickly brushing his own over hers as he picks up his drink. There is a spark. A frisson. Their eyes lock. Dr Jane glances down, blushing. A woman on the table next to them throws her friend a knowing glance.

'The question is,' begins Rupert, edging forwards in his seat to speak in a whisper. 'How am I supposed to behave myself for the next few days with you around?'

'You aren't...' says Dr Jane, her eyes emitting the kind of sparkle that only emanates from a middle-aged woman who has rediscovered sex for the first time in years and has just had a full night in the sack.

He leans in even closer and after taking a sip of wine, leaving his lips nice and moist, he says, 'Last night ... it was...'

'Incredible,' says Dr Jane, and she actually means it for once, because if Dr Jane MacAvoy had a pound for how many times she'd told a man that their night together had been incredible when really it had been an absolute snore-fest (at best) then she'd be a very wealthy woman (if ten pounds makes you wealthy).

Rupert leans back in his seat, content to have had his feathers fluffed.

'I suppose we'll have to pretend to be the old us for a few days,' she says. 'Especially in front of Pinky. She's like a ferret, that one. Doesn't miss a trick.'

Rupert adopts a wry smile and says, 'Pinky will have enough to worry about this weekend without concerning herself with us, don't worry about that.'

'Really?' Dr Jane takes a rather large gulp of wine. 'Tell me...'

He shakes his head.

'Come on, Rupe. What do you know?'

'Only that one of the group *might* be about to get one over on The Honourable Nadine Pinkerton-Smyth…'

Dr Jane looks doubtful. 'They'd never manage it,' she says, glancing down at her glass. 'I watched a clip of her in the Commons the other day. No one gets the better of Pinky, but then, no one ever did.'

'Miles might be about to,' he says.

'How so?'

'Something about a scandal. This weekend was all his idea, really. Which I'm supposed to keep quiet so don't tell anyone, will you?'

Dr Jane removes her hand. 'You agreed to arrange all of this just so Miles could get one over on Pinky? I thought the whole idea was so that we could spend the weekend together in private?'

Rupert shrugs. 'It was, babe. Honestly, it was. Miles just sparked the seed of the idea, that's all. And we did always say that we'd have a reunion at the Mount, didn't we? Hey, did you see Pinky on *Question Time*? Talk about hot! Maybe Miles is just after her in another way, if you know what I mean. Cracking legs.'

He downs his drink.

And so ends a wonderful day, thinks Jane.

'You don't fancy her too, do you?' she asks.

He takes a moment to think about his answer, which is, as far as Jane's concerned, a moment too long. His phone pings meaning that he misses the flash of … is it despondency or anger, that crosses Dr Jane's face? He selects a text while saying. 'What straight man wouldn't fancy her?'

Jane takes a moment to digest those last three lines of

conversation, in the way that all women digest conversations with men they have fallen in love with when realising that the man concerned is a player, having previously convinced herself that he has changed his spots, only to find out that he still fantasises over other women, which, 'come on', Jane says to herself, of course he does, all men do. But wouldn't a true gentleman – a gentlemen who wanted a long-term relationship with a woman – keep such observations to himself and at least maintain the act of the game of romance? Yes, he would. Somewhere in the restaurant, a bubble bursts. Dr Jane glances from his glass to his wedding ring, then to his right leg, which is sticking out from under the table at an angle.

'Has today been difficult for you?' she asks, resting a hand on his knee.

'Difficult?' repeats Rupert, his tone suddenly dismissive, flicking off her hand and putting his phone away. Dr Jane has no idea what was in that text, but it wasn't good – his face has taken on a kind of clenched menace. 'Don't be ridiculous,' he snaps, before standing and grabbing his coat from the back of the chair. 'We'd better go,' he says, walking away from the table. 'Get the bill, will you?'

Chapter Six

DONNA

It's the day of the race and with a high tide this afternoon we're crossing to the Mount on our little motorboat, *Nightshade*. According to Uncle Jago there is a storm of unprecedented ferocity approaching and will have arrived with full ferocity by tomorrow. As we bounce across the choppy waters of Mount's Bay I have a feeling of unease – trepidation, one might say – growing in my belly. My sister is on board, as is Uncle Jago, who is at the helm. As master mariners, neither Jago nor Lamorna give a stuff about the choppiness of the sea, or the oncoming storm. Nor does my dog, Patch, and a finer dog to be bestowed upon a family with pirate blood pulsing through their veins there never was. He's in my arms as we look out towards St Michael's Mount which is growing in stature as we gain closer. Every now and again a wave hits us smack on the chops and he glances up at me as if to say, 'We're living our best life, Mum. And I'm bloody loving it!'

We have left Aunt Kerensa at home looking after Ruby, the

macaw, who hates to be left alone but gets seasick. It's perhaps best as I don't think I could have coped with Ruby's dry wit and constant jibes this weekend. Late January is a surprisingly busy time for my flower farm business and Kerensa has instructions to wash the seed trays out before sowing a variety of annual flower seeds and popping them on hot beds in the polytunnel. Kerensa is also the lollipop lady for the local school, so she couldn't take Friday afternoon off, really.

The boat is running low in the water as we have everything we need on board to create a banging weekend, such as food for the banquet, musical instruments and a microphone and amplifier for the evening entertainment. I've even brought several buckets of early daffodils, camellias and foliage to arrange in the reception rooms. Lady Helen has provided the booze, having been sent a cash advance from Rupert. As we enter the Mount's sheltered harbour and the boat begins to settle, I see Helen's trusty butler, Perkin, standing on the far harbour wall. Perkin is one of Jago's best pals; they are rarely sober in each other's company and Perkin doesn't suffer nonsense, so this should be fun. I glance upwards towards the rocky mass of the Mount and that sense of unease in my belly turns to definite queasiness. St Michael's Mount is a big slab of granite that rises up and up out of the sea, with a castle plonked on top and complete with towering turrets and blooded battlements. It's basically a goth's dream. Let's just hope it remains as a dream and doesn't venture into nightmare territory. (Lamorna is secretly hoping that it does.)

My sister grabs Patch while I throw the mooring line ashore to Perkin. Jago, having cut the engine, works his way around the boat dropping fenders over the side.

'Fantastic, isn't it?' says Lamorna, looking up at the castle, her face full of fun and sea spray, her hair a bright red mass of medusa curls. 'Do you think there really might be a murder this weekend?' she asks. 'Because if there is, I'll *definitely* need to see the body.'

'Why?' is the obvious question.

'Because the last time I visited Auntie Donna in prison, she said that TikTok can be a right little earner so long as you post interesting content, and – come on – the dead body of the Home Secretary could get us ... ooh, sixty-five million or so views at least? And Auntie Donna reckons that when you start generating *that* amount of interest, TikTokers can earn as much as fifty dollars a day! I've no idea how much that is in our money, but hey, every little helps!'

Madness. We have already descended into madness. Although ... an earner's an earner...

'And how does Auntie Donna know all this?' I dare to ask.

'Oh, she's been posting clips of what she calls "Prison life". Her username is @cornishbird. The governor made her change her name to that from the previous one, which is a shame...'

It's got to be asked...

'Which was?'

'@pirateslasher. Cool, eh? If a bit gruesome. I don't think Auntie Kerensa approves of Auntie Donna's antics. That's why the TikTok account goes quiet sometimes.'

Dear God, help me.

'Tell me... Why am I always the last to know about my family's ridiculous antics?'

Lamorna shrugs before jumping off the boat and popping Patch down.

'Maybe because over the past few years you've turned into the steady one?'

Me?

Steady?

I begin to unload the boat while chuntering about being the wild and indefatigable Belladonna Nightshade while Lamorna dances up and down the harbour like a fairy. Meanwhile, Jago is shaking hands with Perkin and they've both started singing a sea shanty – 'Yo ho ho and ten bottles of rum', et cetera – and I can't help but wonder if my family aren't too Cornish for their own good. But me … steady? Nah. I'm the dodgy one – the girl who just got rid of her ankle tag. The woman with the wild eyes, the scar on the leg and the sexy tattoo. There's no way I'm steady, now.

No way.

Chapter Seven

By 5pm DS Joe Enys has arrived at Marazion, the gateway village to the Mount and where the causeway runs from (or the boat if the tide is in). Joe is trying to hide his growing frustration because he's pretending to be 'staff'. Nadine Pinkerton-Smyth was an hour late arriving in Penzance (via a chauffeured Range Rover), which meant that he also had to pretend to be late too, in order to chaperone her, and all because she missed the transfer boat, literally this time, rather than figuratively, because if there's one thing Pinkerton-Smyth never does, Joe has deduced, it's miss any kind of boat without a reason.

And that is why poor Perkin, who ferried the other guests across the bay an hour ago and is exactly as long in the tooth as all good butlers should be, has had to don his oilskins once more and despite a flurry of sleet that has started to edge its way across the bay, and the strengthening wind, has had to chug the little boat back across Mounts Bay to pick up Pinky and Joe. For his part, Joe has been standing on the beach talking to an old Marazion mate freezing his tits off, while Nadine sat in the back of the Range Rover, engine running, warm as toast. It's not a good start; Joe already despises her. All of which means that it's the dark of night by the time the boat begins its last crossing of the bay, its green and red navigational lights bouncing up and down as it skips across the waves. Perkin's little boat isn't covered, either, and while Joe takes the full blast of the icy sea, Nadine, who is dressed sensibly in jeans, an Argyle sweater, a Barbour Mileset and Le Chameau's neoprene-lined Vierzonord boots (channelling Kate Middleton, Joe reckons) is huddled inside the cockpit with Perkin, whose failing eyesight, he informs them, is not altogether suited to driving at night.

'There's a storm coming,' he shouts, nodding towards the west. He looks pointedly at Pinky, his face illuminated by the cockpit light. 'There will be no getting off the island once it's in…'

Pinky, who is somehow managing to stay upright without holding on, shrugs the shrug of the unconcerned. 'That sounds just about perfect to me,' she says.

Perkin nods curtly which leaves Joe – who is half-in, half-out of the cockpit – an opening to flash up easier conversation by shouting, 'Hi, I'm Joe,' in Pinky's ear. 'I'm your waiter for the weekend.'

To which Nadine replies, 'Really? And here was I thinking that you're an undercover policeman.'

Joe has no answer to that.

It's a short crossing (long enough with *this* ice maiden, thinks Joe) and when he offers a hand as she steps off the boat, Pinky bats him away in such a manner that he decides not to bother offering to help carry her luggage up the *many* steep steps to the castle. Perkin, dressed in yellow oilskins over the top of his usual tweed suit, seems in no mood to offer assistance either, but it doesn't matter because Pinky has come prepared. She throws her large rucksack over her back easily and, having been given a head torch by Perkin, begins to trip trap up the long path of slippery steps that, centuries ago, were carved out of the steep granite bedrock that forms the base of the castle, steps that culminate at a set of imposing doors.

Once inside a small foyer and with the doors shut very firmly (and somewhat overdramatically) behind them, the three of them remove and shake off their various over-garments, and now that Joe can have a good look at her in the candlelight (there *is* an electric light but Perkin has clearly decided to go full-on gothic this weekend), the Right Honourable Pinky seems younger to Joe than her fifty years would suggest. The blonde highlights add a subtle shine, the menopause-defying trim waste allows for well-fitting jeans to sit smoothly without the first hint of a muffin top, and the face … well, it's not so much pretty, as striking and wrinkle-free. *Botox and fillers,* surmises Joe, although he very much doubts this woman is ever likely to smile broadly enough for him to know for sure.

Pinky turns to Perkin, who is still removing his oil skins.

'I won't dine with the others tonight,' she says, offering the hint of a smile. 'I'll have a tray brought to my room. I don't do gluten, any dairy must be lactose free, no red meat and absolutely *no* nuts. The last point is most important, so I'll repeat it – NO NUTS!'

Perkin pauses a moment before hanging his oilskins on an

obliging hat stand. Eventually, he says, 'This is Lady Helen's home, Madam, not a hotel.' (His diction is an absolute delight.) 'If you are hungry, you must dine with the rest of the party in the Chevy Chase, which is our beautiful grand dining room, at 8pm. If not, then please find yourself the makings of a tray in the kitchen, but if you do venture into the kitchen then I advise you to keep well out of the way of Mr Nightshade, the chef, who is an absolute devil when he's preparing a meal.'

Pinky reacts in no way whatsoever (that'll be the politician in her) but quickly glances at Joe. 'What about you?' she says. '*You're* a waiter, apparently. Can't you bring me something?'

Joe is tempted to reply with, *'I'm a policeman, so sod off.'* But he's too sensible for that, and wants the opportunity to check out her room, seeing as how his sole purpose for being on the Mount is to protect her. He nods his acquiescence and goes with, 'I'll see what I can do.' (Perkin's harrumph can probably be heard in Timbuktu, or at least Hull.)

'I'll show you to your room,' says Perkin, who picks up a posh-looking paper bag – the kind with bamboo handles – from a side table and hands it to Pinky. 'And here is your complimentary goodie bag. I understand that it contains a wonderful selection of Cornish-made goods.'

Pinky has a quick look inside. 'Who's it from?' she asks, looking from Perkin to Joe.

'I have no idea,' says Perkin. 'But all the guests have been given one, so perhaps they're from Lady Helen. Would you like me to check it for nuts?' (Sarcasm drips from every word.)

Pinky stares at him for a moment before taking the bag.

'The policeman can check it out when he pops up later,' she

says. She looks directly at Joe. 'Come to my room in half an hour. I want to talk to you.'

And so, the weekend begins, thinks Joe, who grabs his holdall and heads for the kitchen, which is, without a shadow of a doubt, where the Nightshade clan will be hanging out.

Butterflies gather.

A pulse begins to race.

Palms begin to sweat.

Yep. Donna Nightshade must be close by.

Oh, Joe.

Chapter Eight

DONNA

When I began this private-detective malarkey last year, I did not expect to find myself standing at the kitchen table at St Michael's Mount peeling sweet potatoes while wondering how to prevent the murder of the Home Secretary – ridiculous notion. I'm not going to focus on Pinky-Smyth right now, however, because I'm simply enjoying being at the Mount. This kitchen is incredible; not because it's kitted out with the latest Neff appliances, but because it is the original kitchen of the original monks who kicked off the whole 'let's live on an island' vibe. It is a cold, foreboding room of stone and marble work surfaces with an open fireplace housing a spit – an actual spit! Having spent the late afternoon exploring the castle with Perkin, and then having had a truly awesome game of hide and seek, we're now playing catch up and working hard at preparing the evening meal – that's Lamorna, Jago and me. Perkin has tootled off to his quarters to finish the bottle of rum Jago brought with us because Perkin does not cook, and he certainly does not act the butler for any old Tom, Dick or Pinky. Patch is curled up on Jago's jacket, which I positioned on the floor by the Aga. I'm not sure where Joe's got to but he'd better pitch up soon if he's to prove at all useful. (An image of his girlfriend, Demelza, flashes into my mind, and in that image, she has a knife in her neck and is sinking to the bottom of the deep dark sea. *Get a grip, Donna.*)

Tonight's dinner is a veggie curry affair, which sounds pretty bland as a first-night dish, but under Jago's expert tutorage, it will be anything but bland. In fact, I'd go as far as to say that it will be explosive! Dessert is sherry trifle – you can take the man out of the eighties, etc. but I'm yet to meet anyone who doesn't love a bit of trifle. Lamorna has found a local history book in the spirits cupboard and is trying to peel carrots while reading.

'It says here,' begins Lamorna, 'that Lady Helen's husband's great-great-great-grandfather – or was it great-great-grandfather? Doesn't matter – the tenth Lord of the Mount, who was a bit of a cad by all accounts, spent a bit of time in the Royal Navy (they all did in those days – character building and all that) and he got himself caught up in the Anglo-Satsuma War during the Bombardment of Kagoshima.'

'Busy chap,' I say.

'Less chat, more work,' says Jago.

'He was on the gun-boat *Havoc,*' continues Lamorna, 'and he personally set *five* Satsuma junks on fire.' Lamorna glances up. 'Poor Junks! Are they a samurai tribe or something?'

'Who?' I ask.

'The Junks,' says Lamorna.

Jago puts down a knife and sighs. 'A junk is a type of boat, you silly girl!' His shirt is beginning to show signs of damp in the underarm area.

Lamorna throws me a, 'who rattled *his* cage' glance, before continuing with, 'Anyhoo, there was a bit of a scrap between the Brits and the samurai, and no one came out on top, so to speak, but Charles – that was his Christian name, the Lord of the Mount – wound up with a spot of shrapnel in his shoulder. As with all these things they eventually put down their muskets, or whatever they were fighting with, and Charles ended up going ashore to negotiate a settlement on behalf of the Royal Navy. That's when the local people gave him the samurai costume – the one they have on display here, the one that's displayed in the Garrison room…' She reads on. 'Oh, and ten bottles of whisky.'

'They make a good whisky, the Japanese do,' says Jago.

'Charles thought he'd done rather well out of the deal,' explains Lamorna, 'but then it turned out that the costume was haunted by the last warrior who wore it – a complete psychopath, by all accounts. The last laugh was on poor Charles for bringing a ghost home.' Lamorna flicks through a couple of pages before adding, 'And what do you think of this? There's an afterword here by Lady Helen – our Lady Helen – saying that Arthur – that's her husband – recently went through Charles' diary entries for the return sea voyage and discovered that the poor man's journey home was plagued with misadventure. He died shortly after arriving back at the Mount when – Jesus Christ, listen to this – an old, lodged cannonball landed on his head when he was clearing the guttering out on the lower battlements! All of this bad luck was blamed on the curse of the samurai. Do you think that's why all the walls are dripping with medieval weapons – the swords and spears and crossbows and everything – so that Lady Helen is ready for action against the ghost, whichever room she finds herself in when he comes for her?'

I say that it probably is.

Jago would normally be engrossed in such a story, but he's gone full Gordon Ramsay on us and is throwing trays of vegetables to roast into the oven with alarming vigour. I trade potato peeler for wooden spoon and stand over the Aga making custard for the trifle while Lamorna adds spice to her history lesson. I'm only half-listening though because Jago will throttle me if this custard doesn't come out at the absolute correct consistency, which he described as stodgier than gloss paint but not as thick a Swarfega.

'Did Lady Helen happen to mention when it was that the samurai started showing up again?' asks Lamorna, who is resting her elbows on the table and is now contributing diddly squat to the preparation of the meal. I throw a tea towel in her direction, which in my family is our way of saying, 'Wash up, lazy bones!'

'Oh, I can answer that,' I say, turning momentarily from the custard. 'It was on the night she received the first email asking if they might hold the reunion here – make of *that* what you will!'

'Which was when?' asks a male voice coming from the direction of the kitchen door.

We all look up.

It's Joe Enys. Actually standing at the door. He has come.

I would tidy my hair but that's what 1940s starlets used to do when the hero walked in and I'm a feminist and I don't want to fall into the trap of displaying obvious attraction for any man, especially a copper. We are a family with a history of derring-do, after all, even if we do run a flower farm now. Also, I made sure my hair looked good earlier with an extra bit of beach spritz.

I'm stirring the custard with a wooden spoon in my right hand while holding my phone with the other, having googled, 'How to know when custard is ready?'

'No idea,' says Lamorna, who gallops across the kitchen to hug Joe. (That's the last work we'll see out of her, then.) As does Patch, my dog, who, once Lamorna has let go of all the hugging, jumps into his arms like a long-lost love. 'Thank you so much for coming, Inspector,' she says, 'I'm sure we all feel much safer with you here.'

'For the last time, Lamorna, he's not an inspector,' I say, throwing Joe the sort of smile that thirteen-year-old Donna would have given thirteen-year-old Joe across the playground.

'Not *yet*, he's not,' says Lamorna, hooking her arm around Joe's and leading him to the table. 'But it's only a matter of time if we keep throwing murders in his direction. Cup of tea?'

'Something stronger for me,' says Jago, looking up from a Nigella Lawson cookbook. He's searching for tonight's canapé recipe which is honey-coated cocktail sausages with devilled eggs and peanut-butter hummus. He's also making Nigella's 'Roquamole' which is an avocado dip mixed with Roquefort cheese, sour cream and jalapeno peppers. Delicious.

'But has anyone ever seen this ghost?' asks Lamorna, who has handed Joe a bowl of carrots and a peeler and taken the hint by filling the sink with soapy water before clicking on the electric kettle.

'The samurai? Not *seen*, exactly,' says Jago. 'But Helen has certainly heard him mooching about the corridors late at night. She says that it's the only explanation for all the odd noises and these weird hot and cold spots she keeps finding around the place.'

I'm more inclined to believe that the return of the samurai is merely a cause-and-effect issue of Helen putting the central heating back on for the winter, but why spoil a good story when Lamorna is enjoying it so much.

Joe, who is still holding Patch and nuzzling his nose into his fur, crosses the kitchen to stand next to me at the Aga. He offers me an awkward but endearing 'Hello'. The last time I saw Joe properly to talk to was last September when he pitched up at my birthday party and gave me a present of a dog (my beloved Patch) to mend the many years of hurt and pain between us. (Like I said, it's a long story). Then Joe got the impression that I was shagging this Interpol guy called Jase Clarkson (I wasn't at the time but, all right, I did later, but only when I knew that Joe was hooked up with his desk sergeant). The fling with the Interpol guy was only ever going to be the occasional brief encounter because he's rarely in Cornwall. He's deep undercover somewhere in China at the moment, although thinking about it, why would he tell me where he was operating if he was truly undercover? Wouldn't that be against protocol? He's probably living in Hull while infiltrating a drug ring. Joe, on the other hand, is still stepping out (as Jago would put it) with Demelza, and I know this for certain because Aunt Kerensa saw them walking along the prom hand in hand last week (I bet that was Demelza's idea). All of which means that Joe, my childhood-sweetheart-cum arch-nemesis (although I've more or less got over that now) is no longer on my radar, except that I seem unable to keep my heart to under one-hundred beats per minute when he walks into a room. Maybe I'm just coming down with a cold.

I offer Jago a spoonful of custard and he commits to a 'not bad' face. Meanwhile, Joe returns Patch to Jago's coat and mouths, 'I'm hungry,' at me, like it's 2005 and he's standing in the kitchen at Penberth all over again. I delve into a bag for life and throw a packet of crisps in his direction.

'Did you know that half of them are orphans?' says Jago, who's thoughts have clearly wandered down a new and fairly random path.

'Who are?' asks Lamorna.

'The guests – the so-called Pimpernel Club. They found a commonality in Iraq because they discovered that three of their number were orphans. Helen told me. And four of them – not necessarily the same ones – studied classics at Oxford.'

'Of course, they did,' says Joe, tearing into the crisp packet.

'Classics, tragic childhoods, fags, booze and war…' says Lamorna. 'No wonder they're all wonderfully mixed up!'

'Who says they're mixed up?' I ask.

Lamorna shrugs. 'I do.'

'Well, it's no wonder Helen is expecting trouble,' offers Jago, who removes a tray of prepared vol-au-vent cases out of the fridge. 'Orphans who like a drink, who are versed in the classics, are celebrating their collective survival in a war while mourning the passing of those who didn't make it home… Let's just say you've got yourself one hell of a party brewing.' He allows himself an indulgent shake of the head. 'Yes, one hell of a party brewing.'

'Have you brought a gun, Joe?' asks Lamorna, turning away from the washing up for a moment. 'Because don't worry if you haven't. I was having a nosy around the place earlier and Lady Helen has got a whole load of ancient weapons in this fancy armoury room down below – guns, swords, jousting poles, various implements of torture, crossbows ... it's all there. Ooh, and let's not forget that we could harness the spirit of the samurai chap to help us out if things kick off. His costume is in the same room in a display case. I've got it! Maybe we ought to throw a quick seance? I mean, we'll need to have the samurai on side if things go belly up. Shall I have a hunt round for a Ouija board? Perkin will know...'

Joe starts to rub his temples.

I need to grab control of this.

'Let's not get carried away just yet,' I say. 'I bet they're all lovely people and it'll be a wonderful weekend... Spooky, what with it being held at an ex-monastery turned castle with a storm brewing and a ghost floating around and everything, but it will all be wonderful and there is absolutely nothing untoward to concern ourselves with whatsoever.'

'Exactly,' agrees Joe, crunching on crisps. 'The biggest concern we have regarding the Home Secretary's welfare is having a stray nut find its way onto the island.'

'Stray nut? What do you mean, stray nut?' asks Jago, whose expression has taken on even more of a wild-eyed, frazzled look.

Joe looks at me. I look at Jago. And Lamorna, sensing tension, leaves the washing up, picks up her lap harp and pulls out a chair. Her fingers start to dance out the opening bars to

Libertango which is her go-to music to add a little spice to a tense atmosphere.

'Tell me, boy!' says Jago. 'What do you mean by "stray nut"?'

Joe pauses before saying, 'I mean that Nadine Pinkerton has a severe nut allergy. Surely you knew?'

Jago starts to turn red from the neck up.

'It's why she, er…' Joe pauses. 'Why she doesn't want to eat dinner with the rest of the party tonight. She's asked for a tray in her room.'

Jago doesn't answer but simply crosses to the bin and empties the contents of a large bowl into it. He then turns to Lamorna and rests a hand on the harp strings to silence them. Eventually, he finds some words.

'As an ex-member of the House of Lords, I will not be led into a dick-dance' – Lamorna gasps at this but Jago has more – 'by Little Miss Prim. Nut allergy or no nut allergy, she can eat with the rest of the party tonight, or not eat at all! She has absolutely nothing to fear from *my* cooking!' – we all glance at the bin – 'And no, I will not make up a tray and you will not take anything up to her. I shall now wash my hands and we will remove all traces of nuts. Lamorna and Donna, you will disinfect the kitchen where the peanuts may have lingered, and we shall never speak of nuts again.' He wanders towards the fridge shaking his head. 'Mark my words,' he chunters. 'It's like the gluten-free brigade all over again, and I bet this abomination of a woman has no more got a nut allergy than I have. It's attention seeking, that's all it is.'

Jago puts a clean bowl, two cartons of cream and a whisk on the table in front of Joe.

'Whisk that. And remember, more work, less chat, people,' he says. 'Let's go, go, go.'

Truly. I have never seen this side of my uncle before. And the sooner I get him safely back in front of his fire in his study at Penberth, the better.

Chapter Nine

After the cream is whisked and feathers are unruffled, Joe finds himself standing outside Pinky's bedroom door holding a consolatory gin and tonic and waiting to give her the news.

'Well, if it isn't the local police officer. Popped up to see if I'm still alive?' says Pinky, opening her bedroom door. She has changed out of her day clothes and is now wearing a long, silk dressing gown. Joe has to hand it to her; she has the look of Amanda Holden about her. That is, a different kind of Amanda Holden who has developed the icy stare of a psychopath. She waves her arm theatrically to beckon Joe into the room.

Joe laughs and shakes his head in denial at her comment, but he's never been a good actor. The best acting part he was ever given was in the nativity play at primary school. He had the part of 'Wise Man holding frankincense'– the frankincense being an egg box painted a gold colour by his mum and she'd said that he'd been 'marvellous' in his performance, while his teacher had agreed that he'd been 'certainly unique'. There was this one time in Year 9 when Joe failed to be cast as 'lead feather duster' in *Beauty and the Beast* because the drama teacher felt that he just wasn't quite convincing enough, even though his mum had made him a fabulous feather-duster hat. Joe never got over that particular rejection, especially as he was asked to donate his feather hat to the guy who got the gig. Life really can be cruel sometimes.

Joe steps inside Pinky's bedroom and glances around at what can only be described as a baronial heaven … four-poster bed, oak panelling and tapestry wall hangings – the lot.

'No, I'm afraid that I'm just plain old Joe,' he says. 'Joe the waiter, that's what they call me.'

Pinky closes the door and tips her head to one side.

'Is that right?' She opens her handbag and takes out a packet of Benson and Hedges and a lighter. 'Because I did a Google search when we arrived, and I found a photo of a person that looked just like you in the online version of the local rag. You're standing on a harbour wall holding a massive fish with a daft grin on your face. The caption underneath reads something like, "Local detective bags his bass" and in the comments section someone – I'm guessing a local – wrote "Shame he spends more time catching cod than crooks…" Any further comment, Detective Sergeant?'

'Not really, no,' says Joe. He holds out a silver tray and offers Pinky a glass of gin and tonic. 'Don't worry, not a nut in sight,' he says.

She gestures that he place the glass on the bedside table, lights up the cigarette, takes the long, satisfying drag of a professional smoker and crosses the room to the bed. Joe considers telling Pinky that St Michael's Mount is a strictly no-smoking kind of castle, but when he sees the look on her face as she turns to him holding a folded piece of paper in her hand that was conveniently sitting on the bed, he thinks better of it.

'As you're here, you might as well have a look at this,' she says.

Joe reads aloud from the paper.

Going away, Pinky? Haven't you heard? Cornwall is MURDER at this time of year…

'Where did you find it?' he asks.

'It was delivered in the post to my home in London this morning – the postcode is Penzance. And before you ask, I have no acquaintances here.'

'Who have you told about this?" he asks.

She crosses to the window. The room faces west. The heavy drapes are open and the streetlights of Penzance are glinting in the distance across the water. It's a pretty sight, but then Joe would think so. He loves his town.

'Told? No one,' she says, taking in the view in the kind of dramatic way that befits the moment.

He wants to say, 'Are you a complete idiot all of the time, or just at the weekend.' But goes with a simple, 'Why?'

She sighs (dramatically) and turns around to face him, still drawing on that cigarette. If she doesn't find an ashtray soon, Lady Helen will be furious.

'I've had enough of it all,' she says. 'Had enough of the whole ridiculous game of politics and all that comes with it. Does that surprise you?'

Joe shrugs. 'I'm more surprised that you chose not to bring your protection officer,' he says.

Pinky knocks back the gin and uses the empty glass as an ashtray, which Joe finds both annoying and an immense relief.

'They're all dull as dishwater,' she says. 'And anyway, I knew the yard wouldn't let me have my way and I was right because hey presto! I now have you to look after me, Detective Sergeant Enys.'

Joe glances at his watch. Half an hour until dinner is served. 'You do indeed, ma'am,' he says. 'And bearing that in mind, I'll start with a sweep of your room.'

An eye roll from Pinky later, Joe gets down to business and opens a wardrobe looking for … to be honest, he has no idea; but creating the image that he's a super-cool super-sleuth, rather than a blundering village copper, is everything.

There's a knock at the door.

'Come in!' shouts Pinky much to Joe's annoyance; it could be the potential murderer, after all. 'Jane!' exclaims Pinky, surprising Joe by looking positively joyful as another woman in her middle years walks in. This one does not look like Amanda Holden.

Dr Jane, to be fair, also looks surprised by the greeting, that's until she notices Joe, who is prostrate on the floor looking underneath the wardrobe, at which point she throws out her own exclamation of greeting and even goes so far as to throw her arms in the air and rushes over to greet Pinky with a hug. It is the oddest melding of socially awkward people Joe's ever seen. Now, the Nightshades are people who know how to hug, thinks Joe, that is until they take a dislike to you, then they put you in their book of ye deadliest curses and then you die or are badly maimed at the very least.

The two women abandon the hug and peck cheeks.

'It's so wonderful to see you,' says Dr Jane, stepping back to take in Pinky. 'You look amazing! How *do* you do it?'

Pinky laughs the kind of laugh that only Bette Davis usually pulls off in one of those black-and-white films Joe used to watch with his mum.

'*I* don't manage it,' says Pinky. 'My plastic surgeon does!'

They laugh. Pinky turns to Joe. 'If there's nothing else, Detective Sergeant? I think you can rest easy leaving me with Jane. I can't imagine she has her mind set on murder this evening. Have you, Jane?'

Dr Jane, after looking somewhat bemused, eventually strings a sentence together.

'Murder? What do you mean? Is it one of those mystery weekends or have I missed an in-joke or something?'

Pinky shows Dr Jane the letter. Her face is blank, unreadable.

'It's nothing but a load of crank nonsense,' says Pinky, patting Dr Jane on the arm. 'Let's forget all about it and have a good time!' She nods towards the door. 'So, if you don't mind, officer?'

Joe takes his cue to exit. He considers listening at the door but doesn't bother, but only because the doors are too thick to hear anything through.

Sienna Blackville's room is two doors further along the hallway and is furnished with a lighter touch than Pinky's room – less heavy on the oak panelling and swag curtains. It, too, overlooks Penzance, but with whitewashed walls and light blue furnishings, it has a neutral beachy feel … that is, if any baronial castle can ever feel truly 'beachy'.

It's a shame that Joe has decided to dash back down to the kitchen to resume waiter duties, because if he'd walked back along the corridor and put an ear trumpet to Sienna's door, he would have heard the beginnings of a bit of a row.

'You shouldn't be in my room, Matt,' says Sienna, despite having smiled at him when she answered the door and subsequently left it open for him to walk right in. He closes the door, unbuttons his dinner jacket and pulls at his collar. Sienna, dressed in a stunning black, strappy evening dress, no shoes on yet, offers Matt the occasional flash of a toned leg when the split in her dress swishes open.

'Why shouldn't I?' asks Matt. 'Because people might talk?' His expression is one of bored indifference. 'I think we're about twenty years too late to worry about that.' He picks up an ornament of a dog from a side table, looks it over and puts it down again.

Sienna turns away to take earrings out of a box – princess-cut diamonds.

'You needn't remind me of any past mistakes,' she says. 'With the storm coming I thought you might not have bothered going through with it, that's all.'

'Not bothered? Not a chance!' he scoffs. 'I'll never get another chance like this.'

Sienna shakes her head dismissively before popping in an earring.

'Everything is in position, so to speak,' he says, flopping onto her bed. 'And our wonderful, unflappable Nadine won't know what the hell has hit her when I pull out my little surprise. I still can't believe she's come.'

Sienna pops in the other earring then dabs her lipstick with a tissue. She checks herself out one final time in the mirror and turns around, holding out her hands towards him and smiling. 'Come on,' she says. 'Let's see how they've all turned out. Fifty pounds says Atticus is as up his own arse as ever, Jane is a drab old maid, Rupert is still playing on his limp but hasn't aged a bit and Pinky is glammed up to the nines.'

Matt takes her hands and quickly pulls her onto him on the bed. She doesn't repel him so he kisses her nose.

'What about Miles?' he says, tucking hair that had fallen forwards behind her ear.

'What about him?'

'You didn't guess how *he* might have turned out. Should I be jealous?'

Sienna pushes herself up. She crosses to a suitcase sitting on a luggage rack.

'If I didn't mention him, it's because I don't need to guess. I already know *all* about Miles Johnson.'

Matt sits up on the bed. 'Oh?'

'He's broke and on the brink of alcoholism. He contacted me a couple of months ago and asked me to submit his tell-all book to *my* publisher. As if!'

'Tell-all? Tell-all about what exactly?' asks Matt, looking decidedly less excited, suddenly.

Sienna takes a pair of sparkly six-inch heels out of her suitcase, drops them on the floor and slips them on.

'He's going to blow the whistle about the time when he was in Iraq and was part of a secret club – a secret club that included a very prominent politician, a senior army officer and a famous war correspondent – that's me, by the way.'

'Shit,' says Matt.

'People like Miles will do anything for money,' she says. 'Worry not. It'll blow over. He'll never finish it. He never finishes anything.'

'You're being a tad naïve there, dear one,' says Matt. 'But you're right not to worry. When Atticus hears about it, he'll kill him. Either that or Pinky will run him through with a sword. And what do you mean, he's broke? How is that possible? He had a bigger cut of the money than any of us.'

Sienna ends her preparations by standing in front of the mirror and putting a brush to her chestnut, glossy, bobbed hair.

'Because he's an idiot,' she says, turning around with a flourish. 'He spent it all.'

'How do you know all this?'

'Let's just say that I have contacts that can look into this kind of thing.'

'Do any of the others know?'

Sienna steps towards the bed. Her eyes are dancing. 'I thought I'd drop that particular bombshell after dinner.' She flicks a small white feather from Matt's shoulder. 'Just about when the port comes out will be about right, I think. But let's all at least try to pretend to be best friends first, before all the crappy, pent-up history and angst comes out.' Sienna turns her back to Matt, her long silk dress – black, stylish, figure-hugging, but she can pull it off due to all the wall yoga she's been doing – is gaping open. 'Zip me up?' she says.

Matt takes hold of the zip and the back of his fingers brush Sienna's skin tenderly as the zip goes up.

'Forget it, Matt,' she says, stepping away and turning the door handle. 'That ship has long since sailed.'

Two floors down, Miles Johnson is playing snooker in the billiard room having knocked on Atticus' door and invited him to shoot a few holes. His first reaction on seeing Miles was to think to himself how ridiculously white Miles's teeth are. He was also surprised at how young Miles looks, unlike Atticus, who despite being put through his paces by British Army gym instructors on a regular basis, looks every one of his fifty-seven years. Atticus looks at Miles and can't help but wonder … if he, too, had partied hard for all of that time like Miles had, maybe he would have fared better in the ageing-face department. But when Miles leans over the table to pot an easy red, his dress shirt becomes loose from his dinner-suit trousers, and – woo hoo! – Atticus notices a distinct layer of fat around his hairy midriff. He glances down to check out his own washboard stomach and suddenly feels more than a little better, but only for a moment, because self-doubt begins to crawl back up his legs – the self-doubt that is the niggling taunt of the middle-aged man. Watching Miles as he moves to pot a more difficult pink, Atticus thinks that perhaps it is better after all – as one grows grey and visibly aged – to look after the face rather than the stomach, it wasn't like he got any luckier with women – hadn't had any luck there in years. Maybe he should have married that woman he met in Cyprus, who loved him, when he had the chance, rather than expecting a supermodel to walk his way. The army had brought prestige, danger, and inadvertently via (he had to admit) somewhat nefarious means, money. But what was the point of a strong body and quite a bit of cash if you were pushing sixty and sitting alone in the evening? Wouldn't he be happier these days if he spent the evenings lounging on the sofa with his wife resting her feet on his legs, while drinking a nice real ale and chowing his way down a carton of Pringles, taking it in turns with his wife to fart while she drinks cheap wine and binge-watches *Happy Valley*?

Yes, he would. But old habits die hard, and a quick swim in the bitterly cold sea tomorrow morning wouldn't do any harm, it might even tighten the face up a bit…

'Man! How did I miss that?!' shouts Miles, who pours himself a second glass of Lady Helen's whisky.

Atticus picks up his cue, applies chalk and assesses the table as if he's at the Crucible. He fails to follow through and fires off a skew shot when Rupert walks in. Rupert is holding his phone in the air and heading straight for Miles. Atticus is about to say something like, 'Ah, Rupert! Long time no see!' but notices that Rupert's face is a mangled mess of pent-up emotion, which is the opposite to the expression Miles has adopted, which is more along the 'smugly satisfied' line.

'What the hell is this, Yank?' says Rupert, still holding up his phone and marching up to him, despite the gammy leg. 'Some mate you are!'

In an obvious attempt to appear unfazed, Miles picks up the chalk and begins to apply it to the end of his cue.

'I see it like this,' says Miles, as Atticus, who is trying his best to act as if there is absolutely nothing to see here, takes another shot. 'If you don't want people to know about your sordid little love affair, then you shouldn't hang around the local beaches forcing a lip lock on your latest squeeze.'

Rupert fronts up to Miles, nostrils flaring. If Atticus isn't mistaken, despite the bravado, Rupert is shaking, but then Miles does have at least five inches and twenty pounds on Rupert, and two, fully functioning legs.

'You have no idea about my life,' says Rupert, who pushes his phone in Miles's face. 'And who the hell blackmails their own friend for a bit of measly cash.' He turns to Atticus. 'He wants money to keep quiet. If not, he tells my wife!' Atticus has no idea who Rupert is playing about with these days and quite frankly does not want to know. He takes another shot and reacts in no way whatsoever to what he regards as playground politics, being not in the least bit surprised by the behaviour of the two men. They were always undisciplined idiots in one way or another, but then neither of them were army officers, and that said everything to Atticus.

'You have absolutely no scruples, no sense of loyalty!' bellows Rupert. 'I set up this reunion in good faith – as a friend!'

Miles laughs and pushes him away.

'Bull. Shit,' says Miles, noting that Atticus missed his last shot and begins to assess the table.

'We all have a reason to be here, and that reason isn't about wanting to reminisce about old times – ain't that right Buddy?' He addresses this to Atticus.

Atticus doesn't respond but hands his pool cue to Rupert. It appears as though he's offering up his next shot, but really, he's just trying to even them out on the weapons front in case this thing gets nasty. Rupert pushes the cue aside and storms out of the room muttering something about revenge. Then a gong sounds.

'Great start!' says Miles, throwing his cue on the table. 'Always good to get things going with a bang!'

Chapter Ten

DONNA

'What a *lovely* bunch of people!' I say, walking into the kitchen and carrying an arm full of dirty plates.

Lamorna follows on behind me carrying yet more plates and places them on the worktop. She flops down on a chair at the table. 'They certainly do appear to be,' she says.

She's got to be joking.

'I was being sarcastic,' I say.

'You're glowing, by the way,' says Lamorna, the sarcasm forgotten.

'It'll be the heat in here,' says Jago.

'No. It's because Joe is here,' says Lamorna.

'No,' I echo. 'Maybe it's all the nipping up and down the servant steps like Daisy in *Downton Abbey* that's brought the glow on?'

Joe walks in looking dapper in his waiter's tails and without a glow in sight. Jago sprinkles hundreds-and-thousands on top of two enormous trifles.

'That went well,' says Joe, also dropping an armful of plates on the worktop. 'I thought they'd be a bit uppity, but they're not a bad bunch at all. I think even Pinky is growing on me.'

'And not a murderer in sight!' says Lamorna. 'Although Donna thinks differently. She doesn't think they're very nice, and she usually has a nose for these things – character profiles, and so on. That's why she's such a good detective.'

'She absolutely does not have a nose for these things,' murmurs Jago, smiling down at one of his trifles with obvious pride while adding some final sprinkles with a flourish. 'I can count on, oh, two hands, the number of times she's brought some unsuitable oaf home as a new friend, thinking they're the dog's whatsits, only to discover not long afterwards that they were absolute wastrels. I mean to say ... look at that Cat woman she brought home last year. She turned out to be some kind of mafioso drug runner! And she wasn't even called 'Cat', she was called Susan!'

'*And* she was a murderer,' adds Lamorna.

'Well, quite,' says Jago, who glances up at Joe and turns away, blushing.

I would argue my case, but he has a point. The waif and stray-type human has always seemed appealing to me.

'She's too trusting, that's all,' says Lamorna, offering me a smile.

I fill the kettle and pop it on the Aga to prepare coffee for the party. 'I can't put my finger on it,' I say, turning to face Joe. 'But I'd swear they're putting on a grand show up there and have been waiting for us to leave the room before digging their claws into each other. Mark my words. There's just something ... odd, about them.' I glance at an empty coat on the floor by the Aga. 'Where's Patch?' I ask, glancing around. 'Patch? Patch?' I shout, bending to look under the table.

'He must have nipped out when Joe came in,' says Jago, flopping down on a chair, the trifle masterpieces now complete.

I turn to Lamorna, who has begun reading Joe's palm and muttering something about a shorter life than he might have hoped for.

'Oi, Mystic Meg!' I say. 'Go out into the castle and find our dog, or *you'll* have a shorter life than you might have hoped for!'

An endearing smile later, Lamorna skips out of the room.

Chapter Eleven

The dining table at the Mount is heavy oak and baronial. The room has the vaulted ceiling of a church and the size of fireplace befitting a castle. The roaring fire, stoked by Perkin who has been making the odd silent – and somewhat menacing – appearance now and again, fills the room with an aroma consisting of that heady mixture of woodsmoke and burning peat. Lady Helen doesn't usually burn peat as she's trying to be eco-friendly, but Rupert ordered it in to add authenticity, meaning that, as is often the way when weighing up eco-friendliness with Insta-friendly living, Lady Helen has had to leave her principles at the same door she closed firmly behind her the moment she legged it to Antarctica. The dining table can seat twenty-two, but tonight there are just seven, with Atticus sitting at the head. Three guests line either side, facing each other.

Sienna leaves the dinner table, makes sure the doors at each end of the room are closed and crosses to a side table to pour herself a brandy.

'Right,' she says, turning towards them. 'Now that the staff have gone, let's get to it. You've all seen this year's accounts for the consortium, so let's go around the table for thoughts.'

'Now?' says Dr Jane, glancing at Pinky for support. 'We're here all weekend and we haven't had dessert yet. Why the rush?'

Sienna glances at Atticus before sitting down. 'Because there's a lot to get through and I should imagine difficult decisions have to be made. Nadine, we'll start with your thoughts, please.'

Pinky is about to open her mouth when a voice murmurs, 'Why her? She already thinks she's the queen of the frigging world!'

It's Miles. Sienna clocked that he was drunk before they finished the starter, which was surprisingly delicious – and familiar. A Nigella speciality, if she's not mistaken. Miles pushes his heavy seat backwards allowing it to scratch along the wooden floor. He also crosses to the drinks table and pours a brandy before leaning against the fireplace like a catalogue model and saying, 'What is there left to say, anyhow? It's time to stop being soft and take more money out of the accounts. I'm sick of losing money.' He raises his glass. 'Here's to the Pimpernel Club! From huge success to abject failure in one lousy year! Cheers!'

'Don't throw this at our door, Miles,' says Matt. '*You* were the one who introduced us to that Saudi guy. *You* were the one who said it was time to pull out of Iraq and move into other avenues. And where has that left us? The account in Jersey is empty, and if the Nasdaq crashes next week after the election, then we're all screwed, especially Jane. And all because we listened to nothing but a drunken waste of breath.'

'That's you, by the way.' This is directed to Miles from Rupert who has been knocking down the booze and been awkwardly quiet all evening.

After a moment's silence leaving both Miles and Matt without anywhere to go other than for one to challenge the other to step outside for a duel (anything less in this setting would be an absolute travesty), Sienna turns to Pinky in the hope that she will recover the situation, but Dr Jane, looking pointedly at Sienna, says, 'Look. There has to be a way to solve this, and we will.'

Dr Jane glances around the table but is offered not one scrap of support, as counsels are being well and truly kept.

'We did always say that there would be a right time to walk away,' says Rupert.

'That might not be necessary,' says Atticus, looking a little smug. 'I've found an opportunity here in Cornwall that I can get us into early, but we'll need to act quickly.'

'Here we go…' says Miles. 'More bullshit.'

Atticus pauses. Jaws are clenched.

'Ignore him and carry on, Atticus,' says Dr Jane, throwing Miles the disparaging glance of a schoolmistress.

'Basically, the whole county is sitting on a gold mine. Actually, that's not far from the truth, because it is a mine of sorts, but it's not gold, it's—'

'—Lithium,' cuts in Sienna, who read an article only last week about global shortages of the stuff and how there's more lithium in Cornwall than in the whole of China (or something like that).

'That's right, lithium,' says Atticus, who is looking, Sienna realises, a little put out that his thunder was stolen. 'In the not-too-distant future, Cornwall will see its mining heyday return again, only this time it won't be about tin with a bunch of Poldarks running around mopping up the profits – *we* will be the new Poldarks. I think that we should rebrand, too. I thought we'd call it the Poldark Project.' He holds up his hands. 'That's if we all agree to invest, of course.'

'I agree already,' says Matt. 'Except for the name, which is naff.'

Atticus leans under the table and removes a briefcase. He flicks the locks and takes out a pile of plastic files and passes three down each side of the table.

'It's all laid out in here. Initial investment, timescale and returns. This isn't a quick turnaround, guys, but it has legs. As usual, there may be a little trickery pokery involved to protect the identities of some of you.'

'We're all grown-ups. Say it how it is,' says Matt.

And Atticus says, 'I mean that we may need to utilise the rules of business and commerce to our advantage. I suggest that you all take a look at the proposal in the morning, and we can iron out the details tomorrow afternoon.'

Miles is already flicking through the pages. 'It says here that we'd be investing in a company called Warleggan Holdings. Never heard of 'em. Who are they?'

Atticus looks at Pinky. 'It's us, actually,' she says.

'Us, as in the Pimpernel Club?' asks Jane, who is glancing around looking a little confused.

'Us, as in Atticus and myself,' says Pinky, smiling at Jane across the candelabra-lit polished oak. Sienna notices a flash of something that might be regarded as genuine hurt cross Jane's watery eyes.

'That's bullshit!' says Miles.

'It's business,' says Atticus, calmly. 'We all have separate interests, and this is one of mine.' He smiles at Pinky. 'Ours.'

Many voices become raised. Sienna bangs her glass on the table.

'Order! Order!' she shouts, as if she's morphed into a county-court judge. 'Let's all read the report overnight and see what's on offer. I don't think we should allow the fact that Pinky and Atticus have taken the initiative to do something for themselves to cloud our judgement. Business is business, and if the lithium thing is sound, I'll be in. Anyway, there's a more urgent matter that we need to discuss first, because something has been brought to my attention that—'

'Brought to my attention?' repeats Miles, with a faux English accent. 'Brought to my attention? What are you, a ninth grade schoolteacher about to give us an intervention? Who made you spokesperson anyhow?'

Sienna is unmoved, as is the rest of the party. She's also trying to ignore Matt who's giving her the 'Not now, surely?' stare.

'—brought to my attention,' she continues, 'that is very concerning. And as you have the floor, Miles, I'll hand over to you, especially as you think that discussing the accounts is pointless, but maybe that's because you've found another income stream, and a very lucrative one if you get your way…'

Glances are exchanged but Miles simply shrugs and knocks back his drink before throwing Sienna an icy glare.

'I suppose you mean my book?' he says. 'Some pal you are.'

Miles's words bounce off Sienna like a ricocheted bullet. This is a woman who has stood only feet from exploding buildings and has outstared more than one evil general before being thrown out of their country. An icy stare from Miles is child's play.

'That's the one,' she says.

'What book?' asks Jane. 'Does anyone else feel like they've turned over two pages at once?'

'A tell-all book about his time with the British Army in Iraq,' explains Sienna. 'It's called – can you guess everyone? – *Spies, Lies and Videotapes – Corruption and Espionage in Iraq*.'

'What the actual fuck!' Rupert stands so rapidly that his chair falls over, and that's a heavy chair. 'I'll bloody kill you,' he shouts. 'You absolute piece of shit!'

'Sit down, Rupert,' says Atticus, calmly.

As for the others … mouths are open, eyes are wide, all except for Pinky, who's smiling, wryly.

Jane finds her voice first. 'How could you come here, Miles, and spend a weekend with us all, knowing all along what you're intending to do?'

Miles shrugs. 'Dunno. A total lack of scruples, I suppose.' He takes a pack of cigarettes and a lighter out of his jacket pocket and allows a dramatic pause while he lights up. 'I was going to tell ya'll about it this weekend anyhow – not until tomorrow night, when we'd all at least pretended to get along and have a good time. But, hey! I might as well tell you now.' He takes a long drag. 'Fact is…' He leaves his position of loftiness by the fireplace and crosses to stand behind Rupert's chair, blowing the smoke downwards towards him. 'I've made some risky investments that haven't paid off and my income is down to nothing – zilch. With our investments bringing little in these days and with *quite* a few unpaid debts chasing me down, I've had to think of other ways to make money. The book seemed like the obvious choice. I'm just surprised no one else has done it before me – especially you, Sienna, but then that's what this is all about, isn't it? You're just miffed because I've beaten you to it, old bean. It's a great read… You've all got some *really* cracking secrets!'

'But we all agreed,' says Jane, glancing around the table. 'I specifically remember on the roof at the airport in Basra – we were drinking the gin that Rupert's godfather had sent him – and we swore to never speak a word of the things we told each other.' She looks at Pinky imploringly. 'My research, Nadine?!'

Miles, quite unnecessarily in Sienna's opinion, turns his chair around to sit astride it. Sienna allows herself a smile as the ridiculous gesture falls flat as it's a very heavy chair and if the reason for doing so was to display some kind of masculine dominance, he has failed on all counts. She'll definitely put *that* in her own book!

'If you're broke, get a real job,' says Matt. 'The rest of us have.'

'That's right,' says Jane, who is becoming increasingly wired. 'We all said that we'd have other jobs – that we wouldn't rely on the consortium for money.'

'Real jobs are for losers,' says Miles. 'I've had a damn good time with my cut of the money, and I'm sorry, but if y'all can't say the same then you're the dumb fools, not me. Truth is, if you want me to keep silent, pay up. I want a million to put the thing through the shredder – and that's pounds, not dollars.'

At this, Atticus stands, walks around the table, puts all of his weight behind his right arm, and throws a punch that catches Miles with a satisfying thwack right on the side of the face. He flies backwards and lands on the floor.

Sienna stands and glances down at him. 'Turning that chair around came right back to bite you on the arse, didn't it?' she says.

Cheers go up. Pinky says, 'Time for pudding, I think.'

Chapter Twelve

DONNA

Lamorna has just dashed into the kitchen with Patch in her arms and is speaking ten to the dozen in what Jago would regard as the glorious language of Dante – aka Italian. This change of language would appear odd to outsiders (it certainly does to Joe, who's looking at her like she's certified) – and it is – except that when Jago taught Lamorna how to speak in Italian, he said that if ever she got into an argument, or had something to say that required great drama, then she should say it in Italian, because only the majestic and expressive language of the Roman Empire could suffice at such a moment: like now, apparently.

'Good, God!' says Jago, who is the only person in the room to understand her because he gave up trying to teach me any language years ago 'And you say that he punched the American right in the face?!' he adds.

Lamorna nods enthusiastically and puts Patch down, who gets straight into the job of running his nose around the kitchen floor looking for titbits like a snuffling pig.

'Well, well. It looks like Donna was right after all,' says Jago. 'I did say that she had a nose for these things... Maybe Lady Helen was right, too, and there is going to be trouble at the mill – or the Mount, rather – after all!'

Joe takes Lamorna by the arm, leads her gently to a chair, and, as a father will speak calmly to an overly excited daughter says, 'Take a deep breath and tell us what you know ... in English.'

'Well,' begins Lamorna. 'I went to look for the dog as you know, and I found him in the foyer – he was cocking his leg against a rather large pot containing an aspidistra. To be fair, he probably thought it was a tree.'

'Right,' says Joe, giving his temple a quick rub.

'I picked him up and he farted – the dog did – so I thought I'd pop him outside to see if he needed to empty his bowel, so to speak, and of course, Patch being Patch, he legged it. But as luck would have it, the exterior lights had been left on (someone might want to turn them off when we go to bed because they'll cost a fortune with the rise in energy prices these days), so I dashed after him, around the rocky bit that's just outside the main door, and he was doing his business on a bit of grass that he found, so I didn't disturb him because that can lead to constipation, and after a bit of cajoling, I managed to pick him up and we headed back towards the door. Those trifles look amazing, Uncle! I hope you've saved some for us.'

Joe's temple is really starting to throb now.

'And...?'

'And what?' says Lamorna.

Joe looks at me. His expression is painful to look at. Right. My turn. 'What Joe wants to know is ... where does all the excitable talk and the punch that Jago mentioned come in? Basically. Get there faster.'

'Faster. Right. The thing is, when we were outside, I noticed that one of the big windows was open – the dining-room windows. They're very grand, aren't they?'

'They are,' agrees Joe.

'And they're also quite high up ... you can't just peer through them like you can with normal windows, what with it being a castle and all...'

Joe bites his lip.

'But here's the thing...' Lamorna leans towards Joe, adopting her best, conspiratorial expression. 'I heard loud voices – an argument type of thing – coming from the window. Well, not *from* the window, that would be silly, windows can't speak, but from the people in the room behind the window. And guess what...?!' She glances around. We wait for her to speak until I realise that she actually wants us to guess. OK, I'm game...

'Someone got thrown out of the window?' I suggest, thinking, I bloody hope not. Jago will go mental if they aren't all alive enough to appreciate his trifle!

She shakes her head and frowns. 'I'm afraid not, no. But worry not, because just my good luck there was a ladder propped up against the wall under the very window that was open – I mean, what were the chances of that?'

'*Almost* negligible,' says Jago.

'Exactly. I climbed up the ladder, which was awkward I can tell you, what with holding Patch under my arm – he's a bit of a wriggler. And when I got to the top and looked in the room and saw what a lovely scene it was, with the dinner table set and the fire roaring and the candles and the guests all dressed up in lovely dresses and dinner suits, I was surprised to see that they were all having the most almighty row, well, a couple of them were anyway.'

'Which two?' asks Joe.

'You'll have to wait, Joe, or it'll spoil the finale.'

'That's my girl,' says Jago.

'So anyway. From what I could gather from the conversation, it seems like they're all in some kind of money-making scheme together and have been for years, something to do with Iraq. Only it's kind of gone belly up and one of them – the American – is going to write a tell-all book about it and make millions!'

'Oh dear,' says Jago. 'That's never good.' He shakes his head. 'I remember this one time, sitting in the House of Lords, there was this duke, odd chap, he smelled like gutted herring, well he did a similar—'

Joe looks at me pleadingly.

'And that sounds like a great story, Uncle,' I say, feeling bad about interrupting him mid-flow, but Jago's stories can be all-night affairs, and we simply haven't the time or those trifles will start to go off. 'But maybe tell us later. Go on, Lamorna.'

'Right,' says Lamorna. 'Well, you can imagine, I nearly fell off the ladder because the front edge of the storm is just arriving by the way and it's blooming windy out there, although it's not snowing or hailing yet, thank goodness.'

'But returning to the dining room,' says Joe. 'And the guest's antics…'

'Ah, well. When the American told them what he intended to do – the thing about writing the book – that was when the older one – the tall dark one, the one with the scar on his face – got up, walked around the table as calm as you like, and punched him – the American – and he flew right off the chair! The doctor lady dabbed his face a bit and checked him over and then they all sat back down again like nothing had happened and the Home Secretary announced that they were ready for pudding. Which is quite weird behaviour, but I suppose they are war veterans who have seen a lot worse.'

I look at Joe.

Joe looks at me.

'The game's afoot then,' says Jago, before adding, 'But as a point of interest, I'd like to point out that Lamorna said all of that far more succinctly the first time in Italian, which I think proves my point rather. I also think that you should listen to my story about the man in the House of Lords at some point…' He glances at me and then at Joe, pointedly. 'Old sins cast long shadows,' he says. 'Remember that.' Jago subsequently hands Joe a trifle and wipes the rim of the bowl with his apron to clear a smudge of cream. 'Drop that and I'll kill you,' he says, before glancing up and blushing, then scuttling off to the fridge in a fluster to take out a little dessert bowl made of cut glass. He hands it to Lamorna.

'A special trifle just for you, Honeybunch,' he says, handing her the bowl. 'You're officially the best detective of the family.'

I *would* be cross, but she probably is, to be fair.

Lamorna takes a seat at the table and beckons Patch to sit on her knee. Jago grabs two spoons and takes a seat next to her. He glances up and nods towards the door. 'Off you two trot with those puddings,' he says. 'Lamorna will pop up with the coffee and mints in ten minutes. And do try to find out exactly what's occurring up there. Lady Helen will want to be kept abreast of things on the old satellite phone!'

Glances are exchanged.

'What satellite phone?' Joe and I say in unison.

Jago shrugs, a spoon hovering by his mouth. 'The one Helen left for us in the booze cupboard. Emergencies only, though, because calls cost an arm and a leg, apparently.'

'Do you think we might have to use it,' asks Lamorna, licking the back of her spoon. 'Because I can't really spare an arm – what with the harp – but I might be able to offer half a leg?'

'I should think it will be an absolute certainty with this crowd,' says Jago. 'And the building storm is a lovely – if predictable – touch for such a weekend. Cornish weather really does know how to turn on the drama for such an occasion. It's uncanny really. But then, Lady Helen has always been a good planner of events.' He glances up again. 'Off you pop!' he says, 'and if you could, would you try to postpone any murders until tomorrow morning at the earliest, because there's a programme on Radio 4 about the science behind conjurers later tonight and Perkin and I are desperate to catch it.'

'Oh, I nearly forgot!' shouts Lamorna as Joe and I head out of the door. 'When I was in the hallway looking for Patch, I think I saw – well, heard and smelt – Lady Helen's ghost. If you catch a whiff of Marc Jacobs *Eau So Fresh* then you've found your man, or ghost, rather.'

I hear Joe giggling to himself as he turns to walk through the door.

Chapter Thirteen

DONNA

That was three hours ago, but something unfortunate has happened since then, and that something unfortunate is what Lamorna has begun to describe as 'The Defining Event' or, as Uncle Jago refers to it, 'An absolute and total bloody nightmare that was categorically not my fault!'.

Where to begin? With the delivery of the trifles to the dining room, that's where.

When Joe and I entered the dining room carrying the enormous trifle bowls (the size of these things should not go understated) we felt like eighteenth-century serfs who were displaying their finest creations to their lords and masters. There were at least two 'Oohs' and perhaps even a couple of 'Ahs' as we placed them on the table. All were smiles and not for one second did the group appear to have had any kind of altercation. As they each in turn came to the serving table to help themselves to a satisfying bowl of England's finest dessert, the whole crowd were nothing but politeness and manners, all except Pinky, who declined to tuck in, but as she looks like the kind of woman who has the iron will to always forego pudding – even Jago's trifle – this was not a surprise.

Joe whispered, 'I know Miles has a black eye, which I'm sure he didn't have earlier, but do you think Lamorna exaggerated the story, and more than a little bit.'

To which I replied, 'Lamorna never lies.'

To which Joe said, 'Hmm.'

Over the following half hour, coffee was called for and subsequently delivered by Lamorna, while Joe obliged by nipping downstairs for the cheese and biscuit selection and the port. More food and drink were enjoyed while Lamorna sat in a corner and played a selection of folk songs, sometimes on her Cornish harp and occasionally on the piano. Jago did not leave the kitchen because, while he was perfectly prepared to cook for the gathering, he was not prepared to belittle his noble status by appearing in public as 'staff'. He did, however, join us for my Ella Fitzgerald tribute performance, with me singing, and Lamorna and Jago playing various instruments; backing tracks were courtesy of my iPad and an amplifier did the rest. At 10pm Miles retired to bed, the mood definitely lifted, and the party really got started because Pinky kicked off an impromptu karaoke session. She sang, 'Killing Me Softly', followed by a rip-roaring rendition of 'I Will Survive', which I thought was a little predictable. It's clear that Pinky is nothing short of a party animal once she's had a drink, but then she *is* in the Cabinet and so no doubt has had plenty of practice when it comes to boozy parties. Even Dr Jane took a turn with the mic and pulled off a cracking rendition of Dusty Springfield's, 'You Don't Have to Say You Love Me', followed a little later with the classic Lily Allen number, 'F**k You'. Sienna sang the old Spice Girls number, 'Who Do You Think You Are' and had all the right moves to go along with it, too.

For his part, Joe has played the waiter brilliantly, making sure that the drinks were flowing while nipping off to do an occasional sweep of the castle. By 11pm Jago and I were ready for a bit of a sit down and a gin and tonic, which left an opening for Lamorna and her guitar. She positioned herself by the fire and with the guests gathered around she brought down the tempo by singing a few old-time acoustic favourites, such as Shakira's 'Chantaje' (which she sang in Spanish) and also, 'Rolling in the Deep', by Adele.

Eventually, Lamorna slowed things down even further by channelling her favourite artist, the Cornish singer, Daisy Clark. Lamorna has a beautiful voice, softer than mine, which is deeper. At a suitable juncture, she said, 'The following songs are for Donna and Joe – I love you, guys'.

Somewhere a pin dropped, and everyone heard it.

Lamorna cracked on with her cover of Daisy Clark's 'Complicated'. At the point where she moved onto the opening lines of 'Battle Scars', Rupert stood, offered his hand to Pinky, and smooched her around the floor. By the look of Dr Jane's desolate face as she watched them dance, I think that I can safely conclude that Dr Jane is in love with Rupert.

Eventually, Lamorna moved onto her (and my) favourite Adele song – 'When We Were Young'. Which was when Joe appeared in front of me and offered his hand.

Joe Enys.

Standing in front of me.

Asking me to dance to a smoochy song.

It's clearly a defining moment. But what was I to do?

Stand, that's what I was to do. And let him hold me in his arms, and dance. And I bloody loved it. When Lamorna moved on to, 'Hopelessly Devoted to You', however, we both became terribly awkward and shuffled away.

At eleven-thirty, with the musical entertainment complete, Lamorna packed away her guitar while Joe and I began to tidy away the detritus of the dessert table. Most of the party were sitting around the fire reminiscing about the war, which was nice. Rupert stood awkwardly, raised his glass and said, 'To the fallen', and the room fell quiet. Which was when I remembered that although this lot could be a bit odd, they had served their country in the ultimate way, and that was worth remembering.

It was just after the toast, however, that the defining moment happened. With the last of the food almost cleared away, Pinky sidled up to Joe, who had an outsized trifle bowl in his arms, and declared that she perhaps ought to try the delights of the, now infamous, trifle for herself. After confirming that, no, there was no trace of any kind of nut in there and no, absolutely no nuts whatsoever had travelled across the sea and manoeuvred their tricky little way onto the island (a lie, clearly) Joe scooped out the last dregs of jelly, cream and custard and tried his best to make the subsequent mess look presentable in the bowl. Like a lion on feeding day, Pinky tucked in.

A minute or so later, the bowl had fallen to the floor with a clatter, and so had Pinky, who was holding her throat while semi-convulsing and kind of frothing at the mouth. It was only when Joe said, 'Shit' and Dr Jane rushed up and said, 'Nuts!' that we realised what must have happened. Calling 999 would be useless. Not only was the tide in but the approaching storm had begun to rattle at the windows, the lights were starting to flicker, and we were up one of those creeks without any kind of paddle. The good thing about hosting a party for a group of war veterans, however, is that they are pretty much unrufflable, are all trained in battlefield first aid, and we had a doctor amongst the party, which, as Lamorna said, was incredibly handy. No sooner had Pinky spluttered out the word, 'EpiPen', than Dr Jane had grabbed Pinky's clutch bag, taken out the aforementioned cure-all and administered the required antidote. Lamorna, steadfast as ever, returned to her harp to provide a musical accompaniment.

Pinky was revived fairly quickly, which was a mixed blessing, because the first thing she said once she'd stopped convulsing was, 'I want the chef sacked and I want him sacked now!'

And that is why I have left Joe and Lamorna on dining-room duty and hotfooted it to the kitchen because Jago is doing the wall of death and is saying things like, 'I'll tell you this, Donna Nightshade! If the nuts don't kill her, then *I* will'. Which isn't helping.

Joe has remained in the dining room because he doesn't want to leave Pinky's side in case Penworthy goes bonkers with him. As for Lamorna ... she doesn't want to miss out on any further action because she is of the definite opinion that the introduction of nut products into the trifle must have been a murder attempt, and let's face it, it could have been. Jago, having been asked (calmly) how nuts could have got into the trifle, has gone absolutely apoplectic and has apparently never been so insulted in all of his life, which I doubt.

'I'm leaving this cursed island right now!' says Jago, turning his attention to a spot of vigorous washing up. 'Well, right after I've finished this, because Lady Helen will not thank me if she has difficult-to-remove grime on her oven trays.'

'But you can't leave, Uncle,' I plead.

'Why?' he says, turning away from the sink to look at me blankly.

Why?

Think, Donna.

'Well, for one thing, because the tide's in. Aaand there's a storm raging.'

'A storm? Nonsense!'

He returns to the scrubbing of the tray. The lights dim and flicker.

'See!' I say, looking up at a row of lights hanging down above the table. 'That's the storm doing that.'

'Nonsense,' he says again – it seems to have developed into his favourite word. 'Any flickering lights will simply be the work of the ghost of the samurai soldier, because if I know anything about ghosts – and having lived at Penberth all of my life, I certainly do – then I know that our samurai friend will be mightily annoyed by the damn woman's shenanigans, especially as Helen and I are good friends. The affrontery! That damn MP needs putting over her mother's knee and giving a good hiding!'

'Firstly,' I begin, 'you're not allowed to say things like that anymore.'

'Who says?'

'Some people.'

'Which people?'

'I've no idea. The people who decide these things.'

'Pah!'

'And secondly, since when did *you* ever give any of *us* a good hiding?'

He holds up a wooden spoon that's dripping in Fairy Liquid suds and says, 'There's always a first time, Donna Nightshade.'

I sit down at the table and drum my fingers while Jago continues to wash, dry and put away all the implements he brought from our own kitchen into plastic boxes ready to take home. It seems he means it – this going-home threat – and I can't blame him. Pinky's demand to sack him was a little harsh, but she had just escaped death, so…

'I wish you'd reconsider, Uncle,' I say, adopting my best cajoling face and voice. 'She was in shock, that's all. Joe is going to escort her to her bedroom and explain that it couldn't possibly have been anything to do with you and that one of the guests must have somehow contaminated the bowl. It *had* been sitting there for an inordinate amount of time before she deigned to eat any.' (I do realise this broke health-and-safety guidelines for the amount of time it's safe to leave unrefrigerated dairy products on display, but that's the least of our problems right now.)

Jago remains unmoved. 'My mind is made up. I will not

cook for such a bossy, arrogant, self-important woman who collapses after only two mouthfuls of trifle! Nuts or no nuts!'

OK, so he means it, which leaves me well and truly scuppered because if there is one thing that neither Lamorna nor I can do, it's cook.

Chapter Fourteen

When Joe knocks on Pinky's door just after midnight, it takes her a while to say, 'Enter,' but eventually she does. On stepping inside, he sees that she has already changed into silk pyjamas and has applied a beauty mask to her face.

'Before you say anything,' says Pinky, lighting up a cigarette and offering him the stool by the dressing table, 'there was absolutely nothing suspicious about that trifle. It only takes a trace of nuts to hit the food or the bowl and I'm a goner. That chef is a blundering old menace and managed to cross-contaminate the thing, that's all.'

Joe opens his mouth to speak, to say in fact that Jago, despite his country-squire demeanour, is only sixty-five and that sixty is the new forty; but it's difficult getting a word in with a woman whose nickname is the 'Mouth of Westminster'.

Eventually, Joe says, 'There were no nuts in the trifle when it left the kitchen, so unless you believe that either me or Donna slipped them in there on our way to the dining room, you're going to have to face the fact that the trifle was tampered with in situ. And when you add that to the death threat...'

Pinky perches herself on the edge of the bed and says, 'I'll remind you of my office, detective sergeant, and that I am not in the habit of being told what to think by a country policeman.'

And Joe says, 'It is my awareness of your office – your status – that leads me to the conclusion that I have no choice but to inform my DCI about this event. The tide will be out and the causeway clear by five in the morning and I strongly suggest that you leave the island then.'

There's a knock at the door.

'Piccadilly Circus,' says Pinky, flicking ash into a glass before shouting out, 'Come in!'

As the door opens an image of a samurai soldier wielding a crossbow flashes into Joe's mind, only leading him to wonder if a samurai soldier would choose a crossbow as his weapon of choice. All of those thoughts happened in the millisecond before the door fully opened, however, and Dr Jane walked in.

'I've come to check on the patient,' says Dr Jane, cheerfully. She's carrying her doctor's bag and is still wearing her dinner dress. Donna told Joe that it was an old one from Coast

Dr Jane takes out a blood-pressure monitor and Pinky rolls up the sleeve of her dressing gown more obediently than Joe would have expected.

'This idiot thinks that one of the old gang has tried to murder me,' says Pinky. 'What do you think to that, Jane?'

Dr Jane glances awkwardly at Joe.

'He's under the illusion that one of the gang slipped nuts – probably ground – into the trifles. He'll no doubt think that they tampered with both of them, just in case.'

'I see,' says Dr Jane, who is slipping a monitor collar over one of Pinky's hands, while Pinky continues to draw on the cigarette held by the other.

'Tell me, detective,' says Pinky. 'What's the motive? Why would one of my long-term friends want to kill me?'

Joe opens his mouth.

'Don't worry. I'll tell you now to save you the bother. There isn't one. A motive. I know for certain that not one of my friends in this castle is in league with the people who are out to get me, and I know this because my people did background checks on all of them before I agreed to come. I'm not a complete imbecile.'

Dr Jane, who had begun to squeeze the blood-pressure puffer, pauses for a moment.

'You're going to have to accept that there's been a tremendous cock-up by those Nightshade oddballs… Either that, or it was *they* who slipped the nuts in on purpose, while all the time making a big deal about not having any nuts on the premises. It does, after all, have the amateurish feel of a faux-pirate fiasco about it – and yes, I had checks done on them, too, and I know that they don't exactly have a squeaky-clean track record. Quite the opposite, in fact. What was it that I found in their police files – plural, by the way – again? Piracy, attempted murder, ankle monitors? The list goes on. I have to hand it to them, though, they put on a cracking evening's entertainment, so we'll let it slide.'

Joe has nothing to rebut this with, because, to be fair, tonight does have the amateurish feel of the Nightshades about it, but only if you don't know the Nightshades. Because after last year, Joe is more than aware that if any of them had wanted to murder Pinky, they would have worked out something a darn sight more twisted than nuts in a trifle… Or would they?

'One of the aunties is still in prison for attempted murder, is she not?' says Pinky.

Ah.

Joe blushes.

Pinky helps him out. 'Look. Don't worry about it. I've sacked more chefs than I've had hot dinners.' She giggles at her joke. 'All I ask is that you get rid of the uncle, and we'll draw a line under the matter and salvage the weekend, and we'll also thank our lucky stars that we had Jane here to look after me.'

Joe isn't so sure. 'Even so,' he begins. 'I would like to…'

'Call your boss? Cover your arse?' Pinky flicks more ash. 'Grow a pair! And if you don't – if you *do* insist on investigating this non-event, then I hope you will investigate your own people, and by that, I mean the whole Nightshade clan. I wouldn't want to have to report back to your boss that you've been remiss in this. And do remember, DS Enys, that I'm the Home Secretary, which means that I'm your *ultimate* boss and that *my* say is the final one, not some DCI from Truro. Savvy?'

Joe, rather than reverse out of the room bowing, isn't quite ready to play the role of the country copper just yet. Joe doesn't care about promotion, or whatever the Home Secretary might do to his career if she's angry with him, because he has no intention of being promoted and thereby leaving Penzance ever. It's perfection. He's just about to buy a cracker of a house, too. He walks slowly towards the door before turning around for his big finale.

'Your blood pressure is fine,' says Dr Jane, stealing his thunder.

'One last thing, Home Secretary,' says Joe. 'What was the argument about earlier? The one before dinner, in the dining hall, when Atticus Black punched Miles Johnson – I noticed a trace of a black eye before he disappeared to his room.'

Dr Jane begins to faff with the blood-pressure sleeve and doesn't look up. Pinky adopts a blank expression.

'Nothing but a harmless scuffle between old friends,' she says. 'They were always sparring like a couple of mad March hares, those two.'

'They were indeed,' agrees Dr Jane, shaking her head.

'But what do you expect?' adds Pinky. 'One an ex-special forces operative, and the other an ex-US marine…' She turns her head away from Jane and blows out cigarette smoke. 'Remember that time in Iraq when Miles got Atticus in a headlock, Jane?'

'Do I ever,' says Dr Jane, rolling up the monitor cuff. 'I thought Atticus was going to kill him.'

Joe notices Pinky throw Dr Jane a bit of a look.

'Well, quite. But it was all in the spirit of the thing, Jane. I don't believe he actually meant it.'

'Oh, yes, of course,' says Dr Jane quickly. 'There *was* a war on.'

'If you don't mind, detective sergeant,' says Pinky,

throwing him a glare. 'I'd rather like to go to bed ... unless you're so worried about me that you'd rather sleep on my floor all night? But I warn you, I snore like a Royal Navy stoker after a run ashore.'

'That won't be necessary,' says Joe, who couldn't think of anything worse than spending a night on Pinky's floor, snoring or no snoring. 'I'll be sleeping in a cottage by the harbour.' He takes out his card and hands it to her. 'Phone me if you need me, or send someone down to the cottage.'

Pinky laughs. 'Need you? I have a special-forces soldier in the bedroom to my right and a doctor in the room to my left. Why on earth would I call out for you? Now off you toddle, officer. Toodle pip!'

As the door shuts behind him, Joe decides that it would be wisest if he wandered around the castle interior and carried out a final set of security rounds – just in case. Maybe he'll go and get Donna first (she's bound to still be up and drumming her fingers on the kitchen table) because ... well for a start, it's a blooming spooky castle and although he's no scaredy cat, he'd rather not patrol it alone. And also ... it might be nice to spend a bit of private time wandering around the castle at night with Donna, just like the old days before it all went wrong. His phone pings. It's Demelza.

How's it going, Sweetheart? Anyone dead yet? Miss you. x

Timing.

Is everything.

Joe is sure that the woman has some kind of AI set up wired to his brain.

He fires back a quick, *All good here* text, before heading off to do security rounds, choosing to go it alone this time, after all.

Chapter Fifteen

DONNA

It's 6.30am on Saturday morning and I've woken up, not in the cottage that the Nightshades were allocated for the weekend, but in Joe's cottage next door and I appear to have spent the night in a bed. I'm alone, but I'm also practically naked, so…

I take a moment to straighten out my mind (and my hair) and put the cogs of the last seven hours or so in place. Ah, yes. I remember now. What happened was…

A little after midnight I was sitting in the kitchen at the Mount with a bottle of gin in front of me while eking out some comfort from listening to the soothing sounds of Patch as he slept, when Joe wandered in.

He wandered in.

Joe did.

Joe is actually here.

I still can't believe it.

Despite the fact that the woman he'd been placed on the island to protect had almost died from suspected nut-poisoning just a couple of hours before, Joe smiled his lovely smile, looked really quite happy and refreshed despite the time of day, glanced at the bottle of gin in front of me on the kitchen table and said, 'Is there a drop in there for me?'

On reflection, this was the moment when we should have made the sensible decision of retiring to our separate cottages and not downing a bottle of gin. That is, we should not have morphed into teenage Donna and Joe by sitting up talking and slowly getting smashed.

The conversation began in a benign enough manner:

Me (pouring gin): 'Joe Enys, drinking while on duty? Wonders will never cease.'

Joe: 'Pinky has declared me as being most definitely *not* on duty, and she's Home Secretary so sod her. If she dies, she dies.'

Me: 'I'll drink to that!'

Chink.

Joe: 'I've just done security rounds. Bloody hell, this castle is spooky!'

Me: 'Did you sweep the whole castle?'

Joe: 'Yep. I nearly shit myself in the church. A bat flew in!'

More is said about the Mount and its nooks and crannies, leading us to freak each other out about the presence of the samurai ghost, whom Joe thought he heard moving about in the library – something about the curtains moving, etc. More booze is poured.

Me (being sensible for a moment): 'Are you going to tell the high-ups about the trifle incident?'

Joe: 'I'll wait until morning and tell Penworthy then. Demelza reckons she went on a date tonight and I don't want to spoil it, just in case, you know…'

Me: 'She got lucky?'

Joe: 'Exactly. That's unless she's dead before then.'

Me (joking): 'Penworthy? No such luck.'

Joe (not joking): 'No. Pinky. The Right Honourable Pain In My Arse.'

Me (tittering): 'I wish there really was a right honourable Pain In My Arse. That would be hilarious.'

Joe: 'It would! They'd be told off by The Speaker for having too much cheek!'

Laughs.

More booze.

Me (realising that somehow our chairs are now touching): 'Do you think the nut thing was a murder attempt?'

Joe: 'No idea. But she's been sent death threats recently – one arrived at her office this morning.'

Me: 'Do they know who sent it?'

Joe: 'No, but she's got this international crime ring after her.'

Me: 'Maybe they've infiltrated the castle and there's an assassin in our midst? Because if there is, I need to go and get Lamorna up here sharpish as she definitely wouldn't want to miss out.'

Joe: 'Infiltrators are unlikely. But if anyone did put nut products in the trifle—'

Me (interrupting): 'Which they did, clearly, as *we* definitely didn't do it.'

Joe (twitching in his seat): '…Then it had to be one of the reunion party, unless – and don't shout at me for this but remember I'm a copper – unless they paid Jago to do it. Have you noticed him flush with cash lately?'

Me (remembering that he's just bought a couple of new pigs and I definitely didn't notice any money go out of the account to buy them): 'Jago?! You can't be serious? I know he hates her politics, but he's no murderer.'

Joe (looking into his glass): 'Which means that it must have been one of the reunion party, but it's so amateurish.'

Me: 'Maybe it was *meant* to look that way, or maybe this wasn't a murder attempt at all. Maybe one of the crowd just doesn't like her and wanted to, I don't know, get their own back for something, or freak her out. They must have known she'd carry an EpiPen with her – and that Dr Jane would be around.'

Joe: 'That's the thing, though. I need to find out who amongst them knew about her allergy, because she wasn't allergic to nuts in Iraq – I heard Rupert asking Dr Jane about it. It's an age onset thing, which can happen in later life, apparently.'

Me (downing my glass): 'Well, who knows, but I'm too wired to go to bed. Fancy doing another set of security rounds? We could look for that ghost!'

Joe (hesitantly): 'I would, but…'

Me: 'Come on! When else are we going to get the opportunity to roam this old place at night? I say we start with the library, because – and I don't want to frighten you or anything – that's where Lady Helen thinks he hangs out…'

Joe: 'Who?'

Me: 'The ghost. He likes to rattle the curtains.'

Joe (swallowing and turning pale): 'You're shitting me! But that's what happened to me, Donna!' His shoulders relax suddenly. 'You're winding me up.'

Me: 'I'm not. Scouts honour. Dib dib. That's why she knows he's on the prowl again – because of the library curtains. I say we start there.'

Joe (standing, after also downing his gin): 'Do you ever get the feeling that we're in a real-life version of Cluedo, only it's a mash up with Jumanji and we're about to walk into the seven rings of hell?'

Me (loving it because Joe's face is a picture): 'God, wouldn't that be great?! Just like the old days, eh?'

Joe (holding out his hands to help me up and smiling): 'Old days? You hated me in the old days.'

Me (let's face it, flirting a bit): 'That's why they're called the old days and not the present days. Come on, let's go and catch that ghost!'

Joe: 'You'll be the death of me, Donna Nightshade.'

Me (slapping him on the arse as we head out of the kitchen): 'But you'll enjoy the ride anyway?'

Joe: 'Every. Single. Time.'

To my dying day I will never understand why, sometimes carrying Patch under an arm and sometimes letting him scurry ahead of us, we walked around the whole castle carrying a torch (Joe) and a lit candle (me). We could have simply put the lights on as we ventured from room to room, but as I said to Joe, my candle was the equivalent of the canary in the mine in that I could use it as a kind of warning system to show us that the ghost was there, because everyone knows that a candle will flicker when brushed by a ghost. This theory proved baseless, of course, what with all the draughts

'Or maybe because there are simply too many ghosts all around us to prevent it from flickering…' I said to Joe as we tiptoed into the library. He gulped just as the battery on his torch went dead, leaving us with only the candle to navigate with. Again, we could have put the light on, but we were quite tipsy (drunk) by then and let's face it, feeling sixteen again, so we took a seat in the library and waited for the ghost to appear.

Fifteen minutes later, with Patch lying on my knees and snoring away, we realised that the only thing moving in the room was the flickering candle.

'Those curtains definitely swished when I was in here before,' said Joe. 'And they look like really heavy curtains! They even moved a bit on the rail.'

'You didn't think to have a look behind them?'

'Not a chance.'

'Even though you were doing security rounds and an assassin could have been hiding behind them and the whole point of touring the castle was to find and apprehend such a person?'

'You've got a point,' he said. 'But I'd become preoccupied with the ghost theory.'

Which caused us to laugh out loud. We soon stopped laughing, however, and started sweating because suddenly they moved. The heavy curtains did. They actually moved – a proper swish!

Now, the best thing to do when stumbling across a suspected ghost is simply call him out on his behaviour because, come on, when did you last see the headline '*Woman Murdered by a Ghost!*'? I do it all the time at Penberth and it works a treat. They *hate* being tackled head on. I said as much to Joe, who was less than certain.

With tentative steps, we stepped towards the curtains and, blimey! they moved again. A big swish this time. Joe screamed, I dropped the candle, Patch barked (it was more like a howl, really) and all three of us legged it.

The corridor was as black as night, but somehow – like bats using echo sounding – we ran down it straight as arrows. We stopped running and started panting, and then panic set in. Not because of the ghost, but because of the candle. Candles don't mix with old houses that are full of wooden flooring and wall panelling, so I explained (in a whisper, because ghosts can't hear you if you whisper) that we really did need to go back to the library and pick up the candle. Not only did we need light to navigate by, what with the torch issue, and the refusal to put on lights, but we would be excommunicated locally if we burnt down the Mount – and Lady Helen wouldn't be too impressed, either. Joe agreed to go back for the candle, but whispered, 'I think we'll put some lights on this time...'

And that's when it got really freaky, because to be honest I damn well knew that it was just a strong draught acting on those curtains, so I wasn't expecting what happened next to happen ... and when it did, I completely poohed my pants, because just as we rounded the corridor to step towards the door to the library, we caught a glimpse of a figure about twenty paces away down the hallway.

'Jesus Christ! Did you see what I just saw?' said Joe, no longer bothering to whisper.

'If you saw a samurai warrior running down the corridor, then yes, I saw what you just saw.'

And then we started to laugh – absolute belly howls of laughter – because we were quite tipsy (OK, drunk) after all.

Having tiptoed into his cottage, we sped through the house like maniacs shouting, 'Be gone, dark spirits! Be gone!' After checking under both beds (it's a two bedroom gaff) and then inside every wardrobe (again, two), Joe lit the fire in the lounge despite the very late hour (because by this time we were far too wired for sleep) and for the first time in years (nineteen, it's been nineteen years), we talked – properly talked – and drank lots of water (to rehydrate, because we're not sixteen anymore). And it was exactly like the old days, sobering up together in the skate park on the prom.

'Not including today's events,' said Joe, 'which have been unusual, or the murder of your Uncle Jack last year, which was bonkers, what have your first six months as a good old-fashioned detective been like?'

I looked at him. 'Are you being sarcastic?' I asked.

He shook his head. 'I'm not.'

'In that case … they've been rubbish. No murders, no burglaries, no missing husbands or cats. Penzance has been nothing more than a sleepy hollow of benign good-doers.'

Joe raised his brows. 'Not for my constables, it hasn't. Regrets?'

'Oh, Joe,' I said, nestling further into the sofa and tucking my legs underneath my bum. 'You have no idea. You?'

In a heartbeat, he said, 'Not taking you to the love seat at Newlyn Cinema when we were sixteen. That's my regret.'

There was a moment. I look down at my glass of water. 'I always wanted you to take me – asked you to, I seem to remember,' I said. 'But you didn't want your mum to find out that you'd been spotted smooching with "that Nightshade girl".'

'I know,' he said. 'And that's why I regret it.'

Another moment.

I wanted to say, 'OK, let's do it then. Let's dump Demelza and Jase (although, you can't really dump a man who's never here) make up for lost time and book tickets for the love seat at the cinema and let's show the world (OK, Penzance and Newlyn) that we mean it this time.' But I didn't say it; I just sat there until eventually I said something else – good, but not quite as good.

I said, 'I've missed you.'

And he said, 'I missed you too.'

And I said, 'Music?'

And he said, 'Adele?' grabbing his phone.

And eventually, just as I started to fall asleep with my head on his shoulder to the classic song 'When We Were Young' (which I reckon Joe selected on purpose) he said, 'Come on, let's get you to bed.' And after escorting me up the stairs and depositing Patch on the bed first because Patch was far too tired to walk, Joe asked me if I wanted him to turn the bedside light off before he left, to which I said, 'Yes,' because I'm not really scared of ghosts, it was all fakery on my behalf.

Then he said, 'Goodnight, Donna Nightshade,' backed out of the room and disappeared into the shadows. And now my watch tells me that it's 6.30am, and after only two hours of sleep I need to shake my tired backside, clear my baggy head and get to my own cottage next door because my breath is rank, there's work to be done and Jago has pulled a blinder on me good and proper. On knocking on Joe's door, I find that there is no answer, and on pushing the door open I also see that the bed has not been slept in. Pretending not to be disappointed, I stir my stumps, decamp next door to my family and prepare myself to not look the least bit sheepish when I explain why I didn't sleep in my own bed last night. Lamorna will be delighted, of course. She'll also wet herself when I tell her about the ghost!

Chapter Sixteen

It is still dark outside when, at 6am Joe Enys pauses halfway up the steps towards the Mount and, standing in the pouring rain and leaning into the ever more powerful wind, catches his breath.

He didn't manage one iota of shut-eye after leaving Donna tucked up in her bed (what a feat of iron willpower that had turned out to be) and for two reasons: firstly, although the drunken Joe Enys had genuinely believed that the ghost of a samurai soldier was wandering around the hallowed corridors of the Mount, sober Joe Enys remembered that ghosts are a fabrication of the highest bullshit and has cottoned onto the fact that there must be an actual real person, an alive one – wandering the castle's corridors in disguise, which is not a good thing when he's got a Right Honourable to keep alive. Secondly, he just spent a whole night with Donna Nightshade, and there's just no way of entering into a world of slumber after that kind of experience.

What the hell had he been thinking of having a drink with

her? A drink! With Donna Nightshade! That kind of malarkey has never ended well because her blood is genetically infused with a heady cocktail of rum and derring-do. And why the hell didn't he chase after that samurai person, either? (Donna was going to poke fun at him about that one, no question!) But most importantly, why had he let Pinky rile him so much to the extent of abandoning his post? He should have spoken to Perkin (*where is Perkin, by the way?*) and asked for a bedroom to be made up close to hers – even a mattress on the corridor outside of her room would have sufficed. He was here to protect her, not dash about the castle with Donna Nightshade, pretending to be Shaggy to her Velma, with Patch playing Scooby-Doo.

No, all he needs to do now, he thinks to himself while dashing up the final steps (steep, slippery ones etc.) is to storm the citadel and check that Nadine Pinkerton is still alive and hasn't been run through with some form of medieval weaponry in the night. Forget about the wrath of Scotland Yard, or the Home Office, or even the Prime Minister bearing down on him if anything happened to Pinky because his real lord and master, DCI Penworthy, will have his guts for garters, or 'balls on a platter with some fava beans and a nice Chianti' as she likes to word it herself.

When Joe reaches the castle entrance, he finds that not only are the heavy doors ajar but that a man in yellow oilskins and carrying a lantern is standing in the doorway cursing the fact that the front door was left open all night. It's Perkin, and when he sees Joe he fixes his expression into disappointed-teacher mode, nods towards the open doors and says, 'Was this you, sir?'

Joe over exaggerates his thinking face, adds an associated, 'Erm,' and leaves it at that. No point letting word get around amongst the local chatterboxes that Joe Enys left the front door to the castle open all night.

Perkin sighs but says no more and starts to force himself outside, his aged, tanalised-looking face standing up well against the horizontal rain.

He turns to face Joe and shouts. 'I'm going down to the harbour buildings to batten down the hatches.' His voice is barely audible above the waves which are rhythmically crashing against the rocks below. 'The full brunt of the storm will be here mid-morning so I'd better do what I can while it's relatively calm.' A gust catches both men out and Perkin falls on Joe, who props him upright again.

'Relatively calm?' repeats Joe. 'Just how bad is it going to get if this' – he nods towards the great outdoors – 'is relatively calm?'

'I believe it's developing into what's known as a superstorm,' says Perkin. 'The BBC are expecting it to be the worst storm since that fiasco in '87.' Perkin turns away but quickly turns back again. 'Oh, and could you possibly advise the guests that the causeway will be unpassable by around ten-thirty, so if they want to leave the premises, leave now or forever hold their peace, so to speak. Anyhow, I'd better be off to lash down the chicken coop. Cheerio now!'

'Cheerio,' repeats Joe, quietly and half-heartedly, while watching the lantern swing its way down the rocks. He subsequently does what he should have done a few hours before and puts the might of his weight behind one door and then the next, to close them. Up and around the inner workings of the castle Joe sprints, leaving a trail of wet footprints and an excessive number of lights on as he goes – there is no way he's repeating the error of last night's candlelit adventure, rising energy costs or not. With his heart pounding and a vision of Penworthy cutting off his testicles in some kind of bizarre police demotion ceremony flashing across his mind, he clenches his fist to knock on Pinky's bedroom door, just as it opens and Pinky appears wearing a Dryrobe and flipflops.

'Good morning!' she says, with one eyebrow raised quizzically. 'Don't tell me you've been here all night?'

Joe can't answer for a moment as he's out of breath. 'On and off,' says Joe, wiping the rain and Pinky's sarcasm from his face. 'You off out?'

'I'm going for a morning dip,' she says. 'Want to come? Although by the look of you, you've been for a swim already.' She steps past him and begins walking down the corridor, her flip-flops clap-clapping as she goes.

'A dip?' repeats Joe, following her along the corridor. 'I don't think that would be a very good idea. The sea is up to a force six at least, and it's raining – sleeting, in fact – quite heavily now.'

She stops walking, turns around and sidles up to him. Joe gulps.

'You know, you're really quite attractive when you're wet,' she says. 'Are you sure you don't fancy a dip?'

'I'd rather you didn't take a dip at all,' says Joe, trying to look like a really cool copper, rather than how he really feels, which is like a teenage kid talking to Stifler's mom in *American Pie*.

'Spoil sport!' she says, playfully bopping the tip of his nose with a finger. 'I'll be perfectly safe in the harbour. Cold water swimming is all the rage these days, you know…'

Joe does know. One of his constables was the first on the scene of an incident with a middle-aged woman just last week whose heart and lungs packed up when she opted to jump straight into Mousehole harbour and was blue-lighted to Truro hospital.

He continues to follow her along the corridor. She stops again. Her tone changes. The woman can flip moods in a heartbeat.

'Look. If you're swimming, come with me, if not, off you trot and do some waiter-type duties. The others are all still under the illusion that you're actually a waiter, except for Jane who I had to tell. So, you'd better keep up the charade, hadn't you?'

Joe isn't going to be riled again.

'No, ma'am, I hadn't,' he says, grateful that he grabbed his weatherproof coat before he ran up the hill. 'If you're determined to swim, then I'm going to sit on the rocks nearby and wait for you. Trust me, I'd rather not, but you leave me no choice.'

She shrugs. 'It's your funeral,' she says, before turning on her heel.

'But not yours,' murmurs Joe. 'Not on my watch, at least.'

Atticus Black is standing by the harbour wall and is also wearing a Dryrobe®. He's freezing his balls off but being of a special forces background (long time ago now but he clings on to the kudos of past glories) he's attempting to look as hard as nails.

It was the oddest request from Pinky last evening, to meet him here in the cold and the dark of the early morning with a storm building. But that was Pinky for you. Odd.

'That's just the point,' Pinky had said. 'Absolutely no one else will be up and about, lurking in the shadows.'

No. There was something afoot with Pinky, he knew it. Most likely she wanted to speak to him about that damn fool Miles. The Pimpernel Club certainly had a great deal to lose from this so-called tell-all book of his, but none more so than Pinky; and by God, if she fell from grace this time she would surely never stop falling. A book like that wouldn't do his own reputation much good, either. He would be dismissed from the army in disgrace for a start and, therefore, lose his significant army pension. And all because that damn fool Johnson has blown all of his own money and the weasel has come back for more. Only he wouldn't be getting a penny – or a dime in his case – from any of them, Atticus would see to that. And so would Pinky, by the looks of things. The punch in the face was a nice bonus, but a black eye wouldn't stop a man like Miles from getting his own way, it would simply spur him on. No, if they were going to shut Miles up for good, then the very best person to work out how to do it, was Pinky.

He glances upwards towards the castle steps and through the low cloud and rain he sees Pinky working her way down towards him, in flip-flops of all things. And wait a minute? Why the hell has she got that waiter fellow with her, what's his name? John? Jacob? Joe? Atticus waits for the perfect moment to unzip his own Dryrobe in order to reveal to Pinky what he believes to be the body of a man still in his prime. Pinky, focused as ever, fixes her eyes on his and doesn't give him the satisfaction of a sneaky once over, but then he is turning a darker shade of blue.

'What's the waiter doing here?' he asks, nodding towards Joe who is huddled inside the gift shop doorway. Pinky quickly unzips her robe and slips it off, showing not one hint of a shiver.

'We've got six minutes, give or take a few seconds, in this temperature of water, before we venture into hypothermia territory,' she says. 'We'll get in at the far end of the harbour and swim back to our things. And Joe is not a waiter, he's a policeman.'

Atticus glances up at Joe, who throws him a mock salute.

'After you,' says Atticus, who cannot help but admire Pinky's form as she slips out of her flip-flops and starts to trip along the harbour wall like a gymnast on a balance beam. Christ, she would have been a good filly to harness and take for a romp across the downs when they were younger – still would be; not that you could ever harness a woman like Pinky, no one had, not for long, anyhow. Maybe it wasn't too late to have a go? With a renewed spring in his step, and without much thought or process, he dashes after Pinky and follows her into a perilous sea.

Professor Jane MacAvoy has woken early feeling odd. She's not ill or discombobulated from the events of the night before – she's a trained battlefield surgeon, after all – but quite simply annoyed. Rupert didn't knock on her door last night, and his sharp words to her as they had left the Godolphin Hotel still rang in her ears. It was such a sudden turnaround. How could a man go off a woman so quickly – in a matter of seconds, even? And then there had been his behaviour at dinner. Barely giving Jane a second glance and yet flirting with every other female in the room. Was he trying to throw out a smoke screen? If so, it was a pretty cruel trick to play, especially when she'd been so adventurous in bed the night before. She sighs and throws her suitcase on the bed. She's not happy at all with her choice of clothes for the weekend (walking trousers, T-shirts and a fleece) and had no idea that Sienna and Pinky would go all-out glam for the weekend. This was a veteran's reunion, for goodness' sake. They had all been friends at a time when a shower was impossible, when they struggled to wash out their one spare uniform, when they would barely bother to put a brush through their hair of a morning (except for Pinky, come to think of it; Pinky always looked spotless). But dressing up for each other this weekend seemed, well, utterly fake.

Pulling one item after another out of her suitcase, Jane realises that she needs to up her game on the dressing up front if she is going to keep Rupert interested. Smiling suddenly, she remembers the Agent Provocateur underwear she'd worn the night before when they had been on the sleeper train. She smiles. No, if she's going to keep Rupert then she needs to do something about it. The lacy knicker-and-bra set is draped over the Victorian radiator in her room, having given it a quick rinse in the sink when she arrived. Jane rushes over to the radiator and finds that both are still a little damp, especially the knickers in the crotch area. But that doesn't matter – she won't have them on for very long anyway! Throwing off her off-white M&S pants and sports bra, Jane quickly shaves her legs in the sink, slips on the silky underwear and a little make-up, dons her off-white towelling dressing gown and, barefoot, slips two doors down to Rupert's room with her mind firmly set on having a quick romp between the sheets this morning, and even if he subsequently ignored her all day, at least she would know that she'd been close to him that morning and that his coldness was all just a silly ruse.

After gently knocking on his door and at the sound of footsteps approaching from within the room, Jane opens her dressing gown and adopts a seductive pose. When the door opens, she says, 'Did someone call for a doctor,' before noticing that despite the early hour Rupert is dressed, shaved and ready for the day – he's even got his shoes on. Her pose melts into an awkward gait and the dressing gown, sensing Rupert's indifference, chooses to close itself across her frame.

'What do you want?' he says, nudging his head forward to glance up and down the corridor.

What did she want? Jesus.

'I … just wanted…'

Rupert shakes his head and sighs. 'Just go back to bed, Jane. You're a fifty-year-old woman and this isn't appropriate behaviour. I'm a married man, remember?'

The door closes on her face.

Jane bites her lip and fights back a truckload of mixed emotions – shame, disappointment, disgust in herself… She's a distinguished medical professor for Christ's sake, how on earth had she fallen to this? And then all those old, long-buried emotions began to rise again – obsession, jealousy and hatred –

and what a time for them to bubble up to the surface, especially when she had so much to think about today. She blinks back the tears and dashes back to her room, not knowing that as her door closes, another one, or possibly two, open.

One of those doors belongs to Rupert who is dressed in the type of smart-casual gear that befits an off-duty celebrity weatherman who's come away for the weekend – designer jeans and a good quality woolly jumper. There had been a note pushed through his door last night insisting that Rupert report to the Mount's church at 6.45am the next morning. It was in his interest, the note said, to make sure he attended the meeting.

Rupert, having a certain familiarity with the Mount, knows that the church at the Mount is an impressive affair – more of a tiny abbey really – and is accessed from the outside. As Rupert dashes across the castle's battlements towards the church door, he wonders why he's surprised at the severity of the weather this weekend, after all, he doesn't remember forecasting such a strong wind. It's probably because, other than London where his celebrity friends live, his hometown of Marlow is the only place Rupert concentrates on weather-wise and has been reprimanded several times for standing in front of Cornwall on the green screen weather map. But yes, thinking about it, he did often comment that there was yet another fresh wave of heavy weather rolling in towards the area he referred to as 'The West' i.e., Cornwall, Devon and the bottom bit of Wales. His director had once told him that his forecasts were becoming a little bit London- and the Home Counties-centric. 'And don't forget about Shetland,' she had said to him, waggling a finger. 'That's part of the United Kingdom, too!' After which Rupert had had to google the exact location of Shetland and subsequently decided that it was so far north that it was practically in Scandinavia and so the Norwegians were best placed to cover it.

Despite the Mount's church being an impressive affair, Rupert, having seen it all before during visits to see his godfather, takes no notice and marches straight down the aisle to the alter as fast as his one good leg and one not-so-good leg can carry him. Miles is waiting for him, leaning against the font, looking smug.

'I knew it would be you,' snarls Rupert. 'Out with it, then. How much do you want, you slimy bastard?'

'Fifty grand,' says Miles.

'Fifty grand!' The figure echoes around the rafters leaving Rupert devoid of further speech. He was expecting two thousand as an appropriate bribe, five at the most, especially as they were in Iraq together and – hello – part of the same friendship group and surely there was a kind of protocol to follow for the bribing of friends. A cap on the amount, perhaps? But fifty grand?

Rupert finds his voice. 'Dream on,' he says. 'You're not the only one to have blown this year's dividend. My wife and kids cost me a fortune.'

Miles selects a YouTube video on his phone (one he prepared earlier, clearly) and the music to *Strictly Come Dancing* comes on. He holds the phone up to Rupert who sees an image of himself strutting his stuff to the *Dirty Dancing* theme tune. His wife had been right. That particular sequinned top they insisted he wear really didn't do anything for him, despite the fake tan and the chest wax.

'You got a hundred grand for doing the show,' says Miles. 'And that was less than a year ago, so I think that you do have the cash.'

Rupert starts to walk away down the aisle. 'You're wrong,' he says. 'I paid off some of the mortgage and the rest went on my daughter's school fees. There's not a penny left so you can swivel, Johnson.'

Miles reads out a series of numbers; numbers that Rupert recognises as his wife's mobile-phone number. He stops walking but doesn't turn around.

'You've got a week to pay up,' says Miles. 'If not, the wife gets an eyeful of your antics with our good doctor. I'll WhatsApp you my bank details later.'

'Does camaraderie mean nothing to you?' asks Rupert, finally turning around, his voice wrung through with resignation.

Miles has the good grace to think about it for a moment. 'Yes, I should say that it does. And if you were under fire then I'd risk my life to cover you. But this is business, man. Plain and simple. I've told you before, don't take things too personally. Some you win, some you lose.'

'I genuinely don't have the kind of money you want,' says Rupert.

Miles walks towards him. 'Then find it,' he says. 'Or Mrs Pendleton gets an eyeful of your infidelity.'

'If my wife ever catches sight of those photos, Johnson,' snarls Rupert, fronting up to him, 'then you're a dead man.'

But Miles simply laughs and steps backwards. 'You're forgetting that I know the truth about your leg – your unfortunate negligent discharge? A bullet from your own gun! Jane covered that up for you nice and sweet, so don't come the innocent with me. Roadside bomb, my ass. And whaddya mean, kill me? You haven't got it in you, Pendleton, and you never had.'

With a purposeful bash of shoulder on shoulder, Miles walks away.

Sienna Blackville is also up and about at this early hour, wrapped in a thick, complimentary dressing gown and pacing the floor of her room while sucking on an e-cigarette. On pulling back the curtains she can just about make out the faint lights of Penzance twinkling through the murk across the bay. What a day for it, she thinks. A raging sea and storm-force winds. If there was ever a fabulous story to break to mainstream media it was this one, that's if she ever wrote gossipy journalism, which she doesn't, because Sienna is purely hard-core news. But even Sienna could abandon her journalistic snobbery for this kind of gossip. She had asked herself over and over why she agreed to help Matt this weekend – to keep his secret safe for him until the perfect moment arose to spring his surprise and say, 'Ta-da! Let's see how you wriggle out of the shit this time, Nadine!' She knew the answer of course; it was partly because of her deep and enduring sense of justice. But also – and she couldn't help but admit it while pausing in her pacing for a moment – there was something deliciously dramatic about Matt's plan for this evening – his big reveal. Pinky was also looking far too good for her age. *Botox your way out of this oncoming shit show,* thinks Sienna, before chiding herself for being such a bitch. No, she had to admit it, she had simply not been able to help but get swept up in the theatre of it all, not that she didn't have enough of her own issues to think about – to act upon. There was the issue of Miles and his book to consider… Damn the man! How the hell could he even consider bringing the Pimpernel Club into disrepute after all they had been through together; after all they had collectively achieved. His book wouldn't exactly do the sales of her own memoir any good, either. But, poor Jane… She would be affected by the scandal the worst of all, of course. Even more so than Pinky…

Sienna sucks on the cigarette even harder. Her karaoke song last night should have been 'One Way Or Another' by Blondie, but then, why foreshadow to the others the fact that she had come to the island with an agenda? Why give the first glimpse of her own particular plans? Pinky and Atticus hadn't. Miles hadn't.

She hears a knock at the door. She knows it will be Matt, and it is. He dashes in and quickly closes the door behind him.

'How's it going?' he asks, looking far too excitable for Sienna's liking.

'To plan, obviously,' she says, nodding towards the bathroom door. 'If you want to know where your little secret is, it's in there, but I'm starting to feel really disloyal to Pinky, so you need to find another hidey-hole – right now, preferably.' She puts down her e-cigarette and softens her expression. 'Don't you think we've all got enough to think about this weekend with this lithium deal in the offing? I've been reading through the file, and it could be a massive boost, Matt. And you know how vital that is for the project. Don't you think we should be concentrating on that – and on quashing Miles and his damn book – rather than this … revenge project?' Sienna places a hand on Matt's arm. 'You can't see it, Matt, but you've become obsessed with Pinky.'

His stare turns to iceberg levels of coldness, a really cold iceberg that is right at the top of the world. She removes her hand.

'There's room for both things,' he says. 'My plan with Pinky *and* the lithium deal.' He marches across the room and knocks on the bathroom door.

'It's Matt,' he says. 'You can come out now. The coast is clear.'

Sienna takes up her e-cigarette, just as Miles's so-called package walks out of the bathroom, looking awfully similar to a samurai ghost.

Chapter Seventeen

DONNA

It takes me about two minutes to close the door to Joe's cottage, give Patch the opportunity to go to the loo against an obliging post and then quietly nip into my own cottage. I expect my family to be in bed still, enabling me to behave as if I slept in my own bed all night. And yet I see a crack of light under the kitchen door and find not two but three people and a bird of paradise sitting around the kitchen table and tucking into one of Jago's breakfast specials. Patch, who is used to enjoying our quiet mornings together at Penberth (my family are not early risers) glances up at me with an expression of surprise as we walk in. Ruby, our macaw, lets the cat out of the bag by shouting, 'Shiver me timbers, look what the cat dragged in!'.

It's such an ordinary sight – the three of them around a table – that I almost don't react to it, until I remember that I left Ruby at home under the tender care of Aunt Kerensa, who is now sitting at the table, eating a bacon sandwich. All of this would be acceptable except for the fact that Kerensa is an unswerving vegetarian, and so the woman sitting at the table can't be Kerensa, it must be…

'It's Auntie Donna,' says Lamorna, reading my thoughts. 'She's swapped places with Aunt Kerensa for the weekend and has come to help out. Isn't that nice?'

Lamorna pushes her chair back slightly and beckons Patch to sit on her knee by offering him bits of bacon. Jago turns towards the bubbling coffee machine and starts to hum. I keep my position by the door. This is all I need.

'Auntie Donna,' I begin, but she looks at me and I stall. I was going to try to hang a few more words onto the greeting to complete a sentence, words along the lines of, 'What the hell are you doing here?' I change my mind, however, because Auntie Donna is a bit of a badass sometimes and she gets very cross if we converse in what she refers to as 'banalities' and I simply cannot cope with a cross Auntie Donna this morning, what with her being the volatile sort. Instead, I take a seat and hope to Christ Almighty that she doesn't guess that I've been shacked up with Joe Enys all night, because Auntie Donna despises the police, especially Joe, who is the person who arrested her back in the day when she tried to kill Uncle Jack and ultimately went bonkers.

'Surprise!' she says, throwing a beaming smile in my direction.

'We told Auntie how you spent the night on guard up at the Mount,' says Lamorna, looking up.

Auntie Donna adopts an over-the-top concerned expression. 'It's no wonder you look like rat shit, Darling,' she says. 'No wonder at all.'

I try to brush my hair with my fingers while Auntie turns to

Jago and says, 'A full fry-up this morning for this one, Jago please. She needs to keep her strength up!'

My gin-lined stomach hears this and starts to dance a tango. Uncle Jago, like a painter of faces who knows my every drunken colour palette, places a cup of black coffee in front of me and says, 'I, er, called in the cavalry.'

'So I see,' I say, feigning joy at the sight of Auntie Donna.

'What happened was,' continues Jago, 'last evening, what with being more than a little upset at the Home Secretary's treatment of me, I phoned home expecting to speak with Kerensa – for a little sympathy and spiritual guidance, understandably. But of course, not knowing that the two of them had done one of their swaps yesterday, I found myself telling all of my woes to Auntie Donna here, and well, as you can imagine, Auntie Donna is not too pleased with what the Pinkerton woman said about sacking me as chef, what with me being a noble Nightshade and so on. She offered to come over herself, to take over kitchen duties… And here she is.'

'Here she is, the old boot. Here she is,' squawks Ruby. (Ruby absolutely hates Auntie Donna. It must have been a real battle to force her into the cage to bring her here. Is that a peck mark on Auntie Donna's cheek?)

Patch jumps from Lamorna's lap straight onto Auntie's because Patch, conversely, loves Auntie Donna, but only because she feeds him with all kinds of unsuitable titbits that dogs absolutely should never eat. Auntie begins to stroke him in the way that a supervillain would stroke a cat.

'And of course, having learned to cook in prison,' continues Jago.

'To cordon bleu levels,' adds Lamorna.

'I'm simply perfect for the job!' finishes Auntie Donna.

I look across at Jago, who has taken a seat at the table and has the good grace to look sheepish.

'I've met that mad bitch before, of course,' says Auntie Donna.

Pinky. She must mean Pinky.

'She came on a visit to the old homestead…'

'Homestead' is what Auntie Donna calls prison.

'She stopped to have a chat and we had a bit of a row about her voting record on women's rights. Honestly, Darling, if only Jago had managed to polish her off last night, then we'd all be the better for it – the whole bally nation! She'll probably die soon anyhow, so not to worry.'

This statement is concerning.

'Why, Auntie? Why might the Home Secretary die soon?'

'Why? Isn't it obvious? Once Jago told me of his humiliation, I put her name in our *Ye Deadliest of All Curses* book. And unlike you, Donna Nightshade, I wrote her name in my own blood.'

'But Sister,' begins Jago. 'I couldn't have, "polished her off" as you put it, because, as I told you, I absolutely did not poison that woman.' He enforces his point by jumping up, grabbing a tea towel and carrying out some aggressive drying up.

'Whatever you say. Whatever you say,' says Auntie Donna, before adding, 'You know, it really is a shame we've had this bust-up with her – because of family honour and all that – as the Home Secretary and I have a lot in common.' She looks at her fingernails. 'Kind of.'

The only thing to do when this kind of conversation raises its head within the daily machinations of my family is to nip it in the bud or we'll be here all day. I move us on by saying, 'And what will *you* be doing, Uncle dearest, while Auntie Donna is busy in the kitchen? Are you going to act as her helpmeet?'

'He is not!' says Auntie, spitting out the last of her breakfast. 'I work alone or not at all. He's going to bunk up in Perkin's quarters because – and you all need to remember this – he's got his book to finish.'

This perks Jago up. 'Perkin has a fabulous library of his own here at the Mount, Donna,' says Jago to me, putting the tea towel down. 'Did you know?'

I did not.

Auntie Donna has more. 'I have to say, Donna, that I am slightly annoyed that you dragged him away from his work in the first place. Jago's book will be the financial making of us all. It's got bestseller written all over it. Kerensa says so.'

'Great work cannot be rushed,' says Jago, sipping on his milky coffee.

'No, it can't,' agrees Auntie Donna. 'But if you *could* get your arse sufficiently into gear to go at a pace slightly faster than glacial, that would be helpful, because the roof at Penberth is in a shocking state and I fancy a spell in Bora Bora once I'm released.'

About Jago's book:

Five years ago, Jago walked into the kitchen at Penberth and declared that he finally understood 'life'. When we asked him exactly what it was that he understood he said, 'everything'. This wasn't a particular surprise because for several months previously he had been arguing the toss about quantum theory with an old mate who happens to be an

Oxford don, and after much toing and froing and many previous years of academic study concentrating mainly, but not solely, on physics, Jago announced that he was retreating to his study to write his 'great work' which is to be called, *I Am Universe.*

Whenever I ask what *I Am Universe* is about, he says, 'About? About?' and looks at me like I'm a Neanderthal. I have a hunch that 'the great work' is quite simply about the interconnectedness of all life which of course, to any person who gardens, or walks, or wild swims, or does any of those outdoorsy things on a regular basis, already knows about instinctively. It can't be a coincidence that once Jago declared that he finally 'understood everything' he began to take a regular sauna, consume a daily multivitamin and a home brew of trace minerals. He eats food that is grown only in genuinely nutrient-rich soil and will not drink cheap wine, which has put the off-licence bill up somewhat as I'm now banned by him from buying wine when it's on offer at Co-op and Sainsburys. It is possible that once he has completed his life's work and readers finally get to immerse themselves in, *I Am Universe,* that after wading through five-hundred pages of a merging of physics, biology and spirituality, they will realise that all they needed to do rather than read the whole book was a) skip to the annexe, which will no doubt suggest a health regime to adopt and b) accept that death is a part of life and that melting back to the earth isn't death, it's life. The end.

If I know Jago, and I do, then he will definitely dedicate a chapter to (b) as he bangs on about the never-ending cycle of life so often that I could write the book myself in a fraction of the time and save him the bother.

Because his great work isn't finished, however, we remain skint, which is why Auntie Donna is nagging him about it, not that she's remotely interested in the scientific and spiritual workings of the universe, but because her twin, Aunt Kerensa who is a Buddhist, believes one hundred per cent in Jago's project and has persuaded Auntie Donna that once it is released it will be a tome adopted by humanity on a scale not seen since the Bible and – most importantly – we will be rich again! Which kind of goes against the ethos of the book in the first place but what can I say other than that we're the Nightshades.

'And I'll tell you this Donna junior…' This from Auntie Donna again. 'If that bitch of a politician even thinks about criticising *my* cooking, starting with this morning's breakfast, which I'm about to go up to the Mount and prepare, then she won't have to wait for some lightweight international espionage mercenary psychopath to kill her off, because I'll do it!'

Auntie Donna throws the dog off her knee unceremoniously and stands. My forehead drops to the table with a thud. Joe is going to do his absolute nut when he finds out that we've brought a bona fide villain – with a history of knife crime – to the island.

'Never mind, sis,' whispers Lamorna, patting me on the back. 'At least she doesn't know about Joe.' I glance up and Lamorna makes an eek face. 'Yet…'

Ah. Right.

'Now, Auntie Donna,' I say, sitting upright and trying to hide the nervousness from my voice as she turns around from the sink murmuring something about 'what kind of a place has no dishwasher?'.

Lamorna and Jago both flash me 'Don't go there,' glances from their respective seats. But it's no good, I have to.

'Yes, Darling?'

'The thing is, there's someone else here for the weekend, helping us out … as a waiter. He's staying in the cottage next door.'

'This is a mistake,' murmurs Jago.

'The thing is, he's here because he's been asked to keep an eye out for any possible threat to the Home Secretary.'

Her eyes light up. 'Is it that Interpol sex bomb you've been having a good time with because I've been desperate to meet him?!'

'Not quite.' Here goes. 'It's actually the local detective sergeant, Joe Enys.'

Not one muscle on Auntie Donna's face moves. She says nothing.

'And I know you two have a bit of a history…' I say.

'A bit?!' scoffs Jago, before remembering to keep schtum. He looks down at his cup.

'Aaand I would just like to remind you that we ought to be nice to him because he knows all about the fact that you and Aunt Kerensa swap places now and again, and he also knows all about Uncle Jack, too…' I offer her as hard a stare as I dare.

Many moments of silence follow – aching, cavernous moments – until Auntie Donna eventually says, 'And he is more than welcome here, isn't he, children?' She offers smiles all round.

What. A. Relief.

'So long as he keeps away from my kitchen,' she adds.

Ah.

'Won't that be a little difficult, Auntie,' offers Lamorna. 'Only, he'll have to collect the food, what with being a waiter – it's his cover story.' Lamorna turns to me. 'With the benefit of hindsight, he should have chosen another name rather than Joe – like an alias.'

'Speaking of which,' says Jago. 'We need to remember to refer to Auntie Donna as Auntie Kerensa when we're in company. Loose lips sink ships and all that, and what with the actual Home Secretary being around…'

'Good point, Uncle,' I say, before turning my gaze to Auntie Donna. 'From now on, even to Joe – to all of us – you're Kerensa, OK?'

'No,' says Auntie Donna. 'It's messy and you'll forget. Just call me Auntie.'

'Just "Auntie"?'

'Correct.'

Auntie takes a packet of cigarettes out of her left bra cup – the lighter is in her cleavage. She lights up and takes a drag before saying, a little too sweetly to be a comfort, 'I'll be sweetness and light to this police person, promise.'

I would feel relieved, but her words drip with a twang of sinister foreboding.

'Anyhow, thank you for coming, Sister,' says Jago, standing. He grabs his coat off the back of the chair and heads to the door. 'And if there's nothing else for me, I'll be off to find Perkin.' I notice that he is practically skipping by now. 'Toodle pip!'

'Toodle pip!' repeats Auntie, the epitome of joviality. 'And don't forget to write that damn book!' she shouts after him, before turning to me and saying, 'Time to feed the animals, I think. Now then, where did I leave those nuts?' She laughs her supervillain laugh and Lamorna flashes me her well-practised, 'oh, dear' look, because when it comes to jokes, you never can tell with Auntie.

Chapter Eighteen

DONNA

Breakfast carried off without a hitch – thank God! It's now 10am and I'm walking through some of the deepest and darkest corridors of the castle towards the Garrison Room. I am not alone.

The Right Honourable Pinky is by my side and I'm trying to explain to her that what we're about to do is more than a bit daft. It seems that she received a note under her bedroom door while she was swimming first thing this morning – swimming! In this weather? – inviting her to a rendezvous with a friend who has something to discuss with her to 'their mutual benefit'. When Pinky grabbed me by the arm after breakfast, showed me the note and said, 'And you're coming with me. But don't tell anyone else, especially the copper – and that's an order,' of course, I said yes straight away because I got carried away with the drama of it all and when all is said and done, this is the Home Secretary, and I can't help but be a little smug that she chose me as her confidante and not Joe.

As we approach the door to the Garrison Room, I can't help

but imagine that there's a big neon sign above the door – a pink one – with TRAP written on it and an arrow pointing into the room. I place a hand on Pinky's arm to put a check on her actions.

'On reflection,' I begin, whispering for no apparent reason. 'We ought to have told Joe about this.'

She looks down at my hand in a way that leaves me under no illusion that I need to remove it.

'I told you,' she says, also in a quiet voice, because, you know, there be monsters ahead. '*No* police.'

'But this is really weird, and someone ought to…'

She cuts me off. 'On your website you brag about being the descendant of genuine pirate stock and that you singlehandedly caught a drugs ring last year. You also advertise the fact that you're a kickboxing femme fatale who's up for a bit of action. Are you telling me now that that's all bullshit, or what?"

It does say that. More or less word for word.

'No, it's not. I am and I do,' I say while reminding myself that I'm not one of her Westminster cronies and that her snarky glances are starting to jar. I *should* tell her to sod off and storm away while making a quip about there being a difference between bravery and stupidity, and that most pirates weren't necessarily super-brave, they simply had bigger swords and guns than the next guy … but I *really* want to see who's behind that door, even if we are walking into the lion's den like lambs to the slaughter and will soon find ourselves up shit creek without a paddle.

'Look, all I want you to do is wait at the door,' says Pinky. 'I know exactly who is in there – well, I'm pretty certain – and all they want to do is talk about a little unfinished business we have between us – unfinished on their behalf, not mine. This person is a pussycat really, although admittedly they're a little … confused.'

With a heavy heart, I nod my acquiescence and she opens the door.

Chapter Nineteen

While Pinky is turning the handle to the Garrison Room, Joe is in the library alone, trying to keep his eyes open while drinking very strong coffee and reflecting on his morning so far, which as mornings go has been odd.

The first odd turn of events happened when Joe walked into the Mount's kitchen to find Donna's Auntie Kerensa standing over a pan at the Aga having stepped in to save the day. Joe generally feels a little uneasy around Kerensa because he's never sure which Kerensa is going to be on parade that day – free and easy yogi, or edgy psychopath. Last year, during the investigation of Uncle Jack's murder, Donna had told him that her twin aunties often traded places at Bodmin Prison and were sharing the burden of 'doing time', hence their change of behaviour. But Joe never bought this story. And when he'd phoned the prison and asked if it was possible 'hypothetically speaking' for identical twins to trade places there, the prison officer had laughed so much that she'd started to choke. Joe, therefore, came to the conclusion that Kerensa was most likely schizophrenic, but harmless enough. And yet... The guest breakfast was superb – those scrambled eggs were perfection – and Joe specifically remembers Lamorna saying that the three Nightshade women (not including the mad auntie in prison) would be scuppered if not for Jago, because not one of them could cook – could barely boil an egg. So maybe, just maybe, the two aunties were somehow pulling the wool over the guards' eyes, or had paid them off; and maybe, crazy as it seems, they are regularly trading places after all? Joe shakes his head and realises that he'll never understand the inner complexities of the Nightshade family.

The second odd thing of the morning occurred during Pinky's early morning swim, which was really quite revealing. Atticus Black had been standing by the harbour wall in the dark, lit only by the one old-fashioned streetlight and clearly waiting for her. She tried to feign surprise that he was there and after the brief and bitterly cold swim together, as Joe escorted Pinky up the path (steep, slippery, etc.) back to the castle, she had said, 'And don't read anything into the fact that Atticus was at the harbour when I arrived because it was pure coincidence'. She must have thought that Joe had just fallen off the nearest gullible tree to believe that one, especially as he had ducked down to dash along the harbour walls when they had swum away and had listened to their conversation which had been about a business venture concerning the search for lithium in Cornwall. They had big plans these two, that was for sure. Both had assumed that the St Clements family would be at the castle this weekend, and Pinky had intended to use her weight as Home Secretary to smooch them into selling land to her and Atticus. Since great swathes of Cornish land is owned by just a few families, it made sense to Joe that if a person wanted to start mining for lithium, then they needed to either own their own land or have access to a great deal of it. Hence the smooching of the St Clements clan, except that Lady Helen had scuppered things by jetting off to Antarctica.

'We'll keep it between the two of us this time,' Pinky had said through shivering teeth as they slowly edged through the water. 'They've all had their pound of flesh for very little input as far as I can see.'

'What about Miles?' Atticus had asked.

Joe couldn't see Pinky's expression, but it didn't take her long to say, 'Leave Miles Johnson to me. Oh, and should something untoward ever happen to me, you'll sort everything out, just as I asked, won't you?'

'I will, but it won't happen,' Atticus said.

'I wish I had your confidence,' said Pinky. 'But in my profession, you can never be too sure.'

They turned around and swam back.

Joe takes out his notebook and writes down the conversation as he remembers it before sipping on his coffee and shuffling to get comfortable on a nineteenth-century sofa. The thought strikes him suddenly that this whole weekend feels like some kind of elaborate performance – like one of the outlandish plays Donna puts on at the Minack Theatre. Yes, this weekend definitely has the feel of an amateur Nightshade production about it, not that Donna would be plotting to kill the Home Secretary, obviously. Joe has the distinct impression that the Pimpernel Club are all just players on a grand stage and that the audience for the production – the carefully prepared audience, perhaps – is the Nightshade clan, not that the guests could possibly have known that Lamorna would walk the dog in the dark, climb a coincidentally placed ladder and look through the window just at the very moment Atticus threw a punch. He would have to think that one out. And as for Pinky, she's a cabinet minister, and most of the others are very well connected and don't need to perform for anyone. Joe sighs and reminds himself that he has just spent the evening with Donna Nightshade, and her mad, exotic, wide-of-reality imagination has simply rubbed off on him and that this whole 'plot to kill the Home Secretary' threat is nothing more than fiction. But still … there was that weird thing at breakfast.

The door to the library opens and Lamorna walks in wearing her trademark dungarees, ankle boots and chunky jumper. Her copper hair is tied in a loose bun on the very top of her head. She throws herself on the settee next to him like the fun younger sister he's never had.

'Did you clock that weird thing at breakfast,' asks Lamorna, sotto voce.

'I did,' says Joe, tapping his nose.

Lamorna, Joe and Donna had served a full English breakfast of scrambled eggs, sausages, bacon, beans and black pudding. 'And they can like it or lump it,' was Auntie's advice as the three of them headed out of the kitchen carrying lidded serving dishes and placing them carefully on hot plates in the dining room, hot plates pre-positioned by the indomitable (and disinterested) Perkin, who conveniently pops up now and again. It was very much a self-service affair with the 'staff' subsequently hanging around like wet weekends and lurking in the shadows. Donna made her excuses early to see if 'Auntie' needed any help preparing lunch, which was a ruse to escape the dining room that Joe saw through immediately – Donna Nightshade is not a woman who tolerates being treated like a serf, and some of this crowd were definitely on the self-important side of hoity-toity.

'Yes,' continues Lamorna. 'That argument at the window between Matt the pilot and Pinky was very suspect.'

Joe has to digest this for a moment because Lamorna's 'weird thing at breakfast' is different to Joe's 'weird thing at breakfast'. His face betrays his confusion.

'Didn't you notice that Matt fellow follow Pinky when she took her cuppa to the window seat? He whispered something only she could hear, and her face turned to thunder. I've never seen anyone go so red – red with anger, you know, not embarrassment. Embarrassment tends to be more crimson than red in my experience. Didn't you notice?'

He hadn't. So much for protecting the MP, but then he had been dispatched to fetch a fresh batch of scrambled eggs by Atticus, who wouldn't have needed to eat so much damn protein if he hadn't been pratting about in the sea at six o'clock that morning.

'It must have been when I went off to replenish the eggs,' said Joe. But Lamorna simply batted that back by saying, 'No. You were definitely there, but you were daydreaming staring out of the other window looking down towards the harbour.' She shuffles towards him and grabs his arm. 'Were you thinking about Donna? Did you spend the night together – you know, making love and all that? Because Jago and I haven't had time to ask her yet.'

Joe goes red and unlike Pinky, this is definitely the embarrassment shade of crimson. 'We didn't ... it wasn't ... we just talked – and went to bed completely and totally separately.'

But Lamorna just smiles her knowing smile, the smile that Joe became so familiar with last year when he was interviewing her as a murder suspect. She pats his hand and says, 'All in good time, my friend. All in good time.' And then she rewinds the conversation and adds, 'So, what was it that you noticed that was weird, because I've got a feeling it was that Matt fella who spiked the trifle with nuts. He would have had a handy stash of them on him, what with being a pilot. They have loads of nuts floating around on those big aeroplanes and he could have just grabbed a load from the hostess. I wonder what his motive is?'

Joe is trying to process this when she adds, 'But, anyway, don't answer that. Go on with *your* weird breakfast story… Ooh! Is it the fact that the only one who didn't show for breakfast was Miles the American?'

It wasn't. But she has a point.

'It was the thing Jane said about—' But Lamorna cuts him short.

'About orphans needing to stick together!' she exclaims, and this time she's correct. 'How weird was that? Do you think they're actually a secret society of orphans, because *I* could join!'

Lamorna's expression is so open, hopeful, heartbreakingly innocent, that Joe's heart can't help but fracture just a little. Joe doesn't, on a day-to-day basis, see Lamorna as an orphan – the Nightshades are a close bunch, after all. But the bottom line is that her mother died in childbirth and her father, the grotesque Jack Crowlas, was murdered last year (thank God), not that

Donna knows that Jack was Lamorna's father, so he'd better not let that slip out. (It's complicated.) He decides to step over the orphan thing.

'You know, maybe we're seeing intrigue where none exists,' he says. 'Maybe Jago *did* accidentally contaminate the trifle – he did have nuts in the kitchen after all, and it only takes a trace. Maybe this whole attempted murder theory – vehemently discouraged by the woman herself – is nothing but hot air.'

Joe stands.

'Mark my words, Lamorna. The Pimpernel Club may have many secrets and lies between them, but the Honourable Pinkerton-Smyth is as likely to get murdered as I am!'

'You're the boss,' she says, following him to the door. 'Fancy a game of snooker before lunch?'

Chapter Twenty

DONNA

As Pinky turns the door handle to the Garrison Room (think whitewashed dungeon), I consider abandoning my post as her confidante and bodyguard (pirate ancestry or no pirate ancestry) because I suddenly remember that I've been in the Garrison Room before, on a school trip to the Mount twenty-five years ago, and it strikes me as more than coincidental that a woman who has had death threats, and perhaps even an attempt on her life last evening, should be invited to a secret rendezvous in a room that is literally dripping with lethal weapons.

I say as much to Pinky, but she just winks at me and pulls a pistol out of her handbag – so much for her expecting to be greeted by a pussycat. She puts a finger to her lips and steps inside, leaving the door ajar enough for me to see that the light is on. Through the crack in the door, I watch her walk to the end of the room. 'There's no one in here,' she shouts out, before disappearing behind a display case.

Relieved that we haven't been ambushed, I'm jolted back

into fight-or-flight mode when I hear a gunshot echo from within the Garrison Room. I'm stunned for a moment, leading to a second or two of indecision, until I realise that the person with a gun is Pinky, who is on my side, so I edge slowly into the room, just in case Pinky has gone full Total Recall on me, to see what she's playing at. But she isn't playing at anything. She's been shot and is lying on the floor with her gun abandoned next to her. She's holding her side and blood is beginning to seep across her beautiful cream-silk blouse. My first thought, I'm ashamed to admit, is, 'she'll never get that stain out'. My second thought is to grab the gun for my own protection while glancing around in full Charlie's Angel pose ready to take a pop at the murderer before they take a pop at me. But there's no one here, and the only sound in the room is coming from the wind rushing in through a medieval (bows and arrows) sized window that has been left open. I fall to my knees. Pinky is barely conscious and thick, dark blood is starting to trickle from her mouth.

'Get Jane,' she manages to say before closing her eyes. And then again, quieter, almost inaudibly, 'Get Jane.'

It's only as I'm dashing along the corridor with a cocked gun in my hand that I realise how this might look…

Having hidden the gun in an aspidistra pot in the foyer (because a gun is never a good look on anyone, especially someone maligned as an ex-con like me. Old sins etc.) I see that Dr Jane is walking down the stairs between the library and the guest bedrooms. There is no time to explain in depth, I say, but

Pinky has been shot and is calling for her to come, what with being a doctor.

Down through the castle we run, and on reaching the Garrison Room, Dr Jane takes a cautious approach to entering it. Once she's sure that there's no one in there, she approaches Pinky. I follow a few paces behind.

'She's dead,' says Jane, turning to face me.

There is a moment of quiet, of disbelief. Eventually, Jane stands, takes on the expression of unemotional practicality that I assume a battlefield surgeon must be well-versed in, and says, 'I'll stay with her. You go up and gather the others; in the dining room, perhaps. Ask your staff to prepare drinks and perhaps a sugary biscuit or two.' Jane takes off her long cardigan and drapes it over Pinky's face while I grab my phone out of my jeans pocket – it's easier to phone Joe, after all, than to search for him.

No signal.

Bollocks.

'You shouldn't stay here alone,' I say, turning towards the door. 'We should go upstairs together. I'll find Joe and perhaps you could gather the others. The news would be better coming from you.'

Jane takes a moment to consider this but agrees before crossing to the window. I join her and we peer out. There's at least a hundred-foot drop down to the rocks below the window. And as for the weather? There she blows!

'Who else was in the room with you when it happened?' she asks, her hair catching in the wind.

I shake my head. 'That's the thing. Absolutely no one. I … I can't understand it.'

'Then I hope you've got a good lawyer,' she says, looking straight at me before heading to the door. 'Because with no other exit and stone walls at least three-feet thick, the only person who could possibly have done this – other than Spiderman – was you.'

With that little bombshell released into the ether, she walks away, leaving me hoping that no one finds the gun in the aspidistra. It's got my fingerprints all over it, after all.

Chapter Twenty-One

'If she's been murdered, where's the body?'

These are the first words out of Detective Sergeant Joe Enys' mouth as an astonished-looking Donna turns circles like a dog who is looking for a suitable spot to lie down. Furthermore, at the end of the Garrison Room is a raised display case and within the case is a mannequin that should be, but isn't, wearing the suit of a samurai warrior. Joe would assume that this is all an elaborate Nightshade joke, but Donna's mouth is opening and closing like a line-caught cod, and although Donna is a good actress, Joe knows that she's not kidding.

All of this means that he's got a dead Home Secretary on his patch (location to be determined) and someone is running around the place dressed as a samurai warrior. He follows a trail of blood from where Donna says Pinky fell, to the door, where it peters out.

'Honestly, Joe. She was right here,' says Donna, finding a few words. 'One minute she was an everyday normal person, and then there was a gunshot, and I ran in, and then she was lying on the floor, asking me to get Dr Jane, which wasn't an easy conversation for her to have, what with the blood coming out of her chest. And that's what I did. I dashed out to find Jane. And when we came back, which was only a few minutes later – five or six at the most – Pinky was dead. Properly dead. Confirmed dead by a doctor. And now ... no body.'

Joe kneels down at the spot.

'She's been dragged,' he says. 'Don't step on the blood,' he shouts. 'Forensics will want to examine it. Where is Jane now?'

'She went to gather the troops; to tell them what's happened, under the impression that Pinky is still here, lying on the floor with her cardigan over her face.'

'Who's cardigan?'

'Jane's cardigan, the one she was wearing. She wanted to cover Pinky's face. It wasn't a great cardigan, to be honest. Bobbly. She won't miss it.'

Joe sniffs the air like a dog who's on the scent of a squirrel. 'I can still smell the gunpowder,' he says, looking up from his kneeling position. He takes in the missing costume of the samurai warrior, thinks about last night, thinks about Donna's last comment, and begins to laugh, even though he's got:

1. A missing dead corpse hidden somewhere on the island – the corpse of the actual Home Secretary.
2. A murderer on the loose.
3. A high tide.
4. A storm ravaging the island (more like a hurricane) and there's absolutely no way he can call for backup.

He can't think of an 'e' by now, but pound to a pinch of salt there will be one.

It's just Joe, the Nightshade clan, a butler, a dog and, oh yes, a bloody parrot (macaw).

Joe explains why he's laughing, and the laughter becomes contagious. After a couple of minutes of hysterics, Donna rests a hand on his arm, tries to contain her laughter and says, 'And don't forget about the Auntie Donna situation!' before laughing again.

Joe finds his composure. 'What Auntie Donna situation?' he asks, his laughter subsiding.

Donna stops laughing. 'You know… The fact that Auntie Donna is filling in for Auntie Kerensa…'

And then Atticus Black skids in through the doorway, looking rather pale. He runs into the room looking all around the place while shouting, 'Pinky! Pinky?' Joe and Donna leave him to shout himself hoarse until he eventually says, 'But, Jane said—'

'That the Home Secretary is dead,' says Donna, finishing his sentence.

'Well, yes.'

'I'm afraid she's right,' says Joe. Donna nudges him and he adds, 'And we're very sorry for your loss, Mr Black, aren't we, Donna?'

Donna nods profusely.

This exchange does not seem to have helped Atticus to understand the situation, which is understandable, given the lack of a body.

'So … where is she?' asks Atticus.

'Now that …' says Donna, glancing at Joe and shrugging

'… is a mystery. But I don't think she can have got far, what with being dead.'

Joe bites his bottom lip.

Atticus opens his mouth to speak, and yet it is not his deep, barking voice that suddenly rings out into the eerie, weapon-lined Garrison Room, but the far sweeter voice of Lamorna.

'Thank God, I've finally found you, Joe!' she shouts, running up. 'I've been looking all over for you.'

'Why? What's wrong?'

Lamorna grabs Joe's arm and starts pulling him towards the door.

'You need to come. There's been some kind of explosion in one of the bedrooms!'

Chapter Twenty-Two

'Whose bedroom?' asks Joe, whose brain simply cannot process any more unfortunate news. 'And answer me in English please, Lamorna. Not Italian!'

'The American chap's,' says a breathless Lamorna. 'I was chatting to Matt the pilot as we were walking along the corridor together and we both distinctly heard it – the explosion. We tried the door but it was locked, then Perkin came along the corridor playing the spooky butler thing so we asked him to go get a crowbar so we could break down the door. But Perkin said that maybe we should simply try to find the American first, rather than assume he's inside, so that he could let us in without causing any damage, but we can't find him. Our deduction is that a gas pipe has blown up, or something like that. Why are you down here, anyhow? Is it an impromptu party?' She glances around.

'Pinky has been killed,' says Donna, who makes an eek face.

'No!'

Lamorna's face fills with … what? Horror? It's delight, Joe realises.

'Properly killed?' she says. 'Not just poisoned by Uncle Jago?'

Donna nods enthusiastically.

Lamorna hits Donna playfully on the arm. 'Wow! A proper case for you! That'll pay for the roof! Is she in here, then?' Lamorna asks Donna for her phone and walks into the Garrison Room and starts looking around.

A ridiculous farce, thinks Joe. *Once again, I'm with the Nightshades and I'm caught up in a ridiculous farce.*

He grabs Lamorna by her dungaree strap and ushers everyone out of the Garrison Room. After closing the door on the crime scene, he asks why there is no key or secure keypad for a room that is literally dripping with weapons. Probably because there are weapons dripping from every wall in every room in the castle, thinks Joe, receiving only shrugs from everyone else. The Mount is basically a supermarket for murderers.

Lamorna tugs on his sleeve to 'Come check out the explosion!'.

Joe gathers his wits. 'Listen, guys,' he says. 'We're best travelling in threes until we know what's going on and I've done a sweep of the castle and grounds. Atticus? Can you go to the library please and wait with the other guests.'

Noticing the confused and somewhat distraught expression on his face, Joe shows Atticus his police warrant card and explains that he, Detective Sergeant Joe Enys, is now in charge of the situation.

'What about Uncle Jago and Auntie?' says Donna to Joe as they begin to hurry down the corridor on Lamorna's heels.

'The brigadier could go look for them,' says Lamorna. She turns to Atticus to explain as they run. 'Jago is in Perkins' quarters and Auntie is in the kitchen. Don't be offended if she tells you to fuck off. She'll only be joking with you.'

'In fact, you'd probably be better just leaving her where she is,' says Donna. 'She can kind of … look after herself, our auntie.'

She certainly can, thinks Joe, who is forcing other – darker – thoughts from his mind.

At Lamorna's insistence, they all speed up while running along the cream-painted, arch-ceilinged stone corridors, up the twisty, stone staircase and into the foyer, at which point Joe turns to Donna and whispers, 'Don't let the guests leave the library. I'll see you in there when I've found out what's happened upstairs.'

But Donna doesn't follow Atticus as he begrudgingly heads towards the library. She continues up the stairs dashing after Joe and Lamorna. Joe stops on the stairs and throws her a look that says, why are you still here?

'Lest we forget, but *I'm* the actual detective Lady Helen hired for the weekend. And if the guests are dropping like flies on us, there's no way on earth I'm missing out on upping the fee!'

Joe has no answer to that.

Chapter Twenty-Three

DONNA

Matt the pilot is waiting by the door to Miles Johnson's room when we arrive at the scene. He's leaning against the door examining his fingernails so I think my hypothesis about Lamorna's imagination working overtime is probably correct. As weekends go, it's a bit of a belter and the raging storm is such an atmosphere-inducing bonus. Yes, it's praying on my mind that I've hidden a gun with my prints on it in a plant pot (I'll dispose of that later). And Pinky's demise and subsequent disappearance within twenty-four hours of Joe coming onto watch isn't a good outcome, either. Looking at those drag marks, my bet is that she's been dragged out through the family's quarters and will be shark food by now. And as for this reported explosion? I think Lamorna's imagination has been running on overdrive again. I bet it was just Miles the American sneezing loudly. Men of a certain age often do that.

Perkin has arrived holding a crowbar and I remember that Matt isn't aware that Pinky is dead, because if he was, I doubt he'd have been strolling along the castle's corridors talking about navigating his Boeing 777 via great circle routes with Lamorna. Now, however, is probably not the best time to tell him about Pinky.

'I'm back!' says Lamorna, striding up to Matt. 'This is our very good friend, Joe, who was once Donna's childhood sweetheart but now they're just friends … although after last night, who knows. He's a policeman – the waiter thing was a ruse – so he's allowed to break down doors without getting into trouble with Lady Helen. He was put here to watch over the MP, although that's a bit academic now – and that's why I was a bit longer than I expected – because there's been some kind of death on the premises – and it was a gun issue rather than a nut issue this time, if you know what I mean.'

Matt looks at the rest of us in turn before adopting an expression of disbelief. He says, fairly quietly, 'You don't mean…?'

'Nadine is dead. Yes,' says Lamorna excitedly.

I step forwards. It's time for a little damage limitation.

'I'm afraid Nadine was shot in the chest just a few minutes ago. She was declared dead on the scene by Jane MacAvoy.'

Matt slumps against the wall, which is a better – more human – reaction than Jane's at least.

'She was in the Garrison Room at the time of the shooting,' explains Lamorna, who loves to clarify. 'Oh, and I should say that we're very sorry for your loss,' she adds, resting a reassuring hand on Matt's arm. An oil painting depicting the Battle of Waterloo wobbles as he tries to gather himself. He's ashen.

'I'm sorry…' he says. 'I just can't … I can't process this. I need to find my…' He stumbles and starts to breathe heavily.

'Wits? Marbles? Feet?' asks Lamorna, wafting her hand in front of his face.

'Lamorna,' I say quickly. 'Take Mr…' I pause, having no idea of the man's surname.

'Lewis,' says Lamorna. 'But we just call him "Matt the pilot".'

'Take Mr Lewis down to the library where the others are gathering. Put his head between his legs and then perhaps get him something to drink.'

'I'll try but he might not be that bendy,' says Lamorna. 'And what about Joe's rule that we're only to walk around in threes?'

We look at Joe, who shrugs. Lamorna takes the shrug as a green light and places a supportive arm around Matt's waist. She helps him along the corridor while Perkin hands Joe the crowbar.

'That door is six-hundred years old,' says Perkin, who looks at Joe as if to say, 'So if I were you, son, I'd just ignore the possible explosion and deal with the other shit you've got going down,' which makes Joe hesitate.

I don't.

I take the crowbar and, while wedging the pointy bit between the door and the frame, say, 'Only six hundred? That's nothing. The front door at Penberth began its life on the *Mayflower* and I'd still smash the shit out of it if I thought there was a spot of trouble inside.'

With one strong heave-ho, the wood splinters with a delightful crack and the door opens.

I take a moment to look around the room. After a cursory glance, and even ignoring the unmade bed, it has to be deduced that there has been no explosion. All is not wasted, however, as I love old castles, old rooms, old beds, old curtains, and this one doesn't disappoint. There is the must-have four-poster bed, a small sofa at the foot of the bed, an upholstered window seat and beautiful drapes which, if I'm not mistaken, are made from a William Morris fabric. I have a look for the maker's label on the inside of the curtain lining and smile. They have been made by a friend of mine, Louise Thomas, the ex-stage manager at the Minack Theatre, who kicked that job into touch a few months ago and now does a very nice line in high-end curtains. I make a mental note to compliment Louise on her hand stitching next time I see her while Perkin stands staring at the broken door with a scowl on his face. Joe heads towards the en-suite bathroom still searching for the yet unaccounted for explosion.

It doesn't remain unaccounted for, for very long.

'Jesus. H. Christ!!' shouts Joe as he opens the bathroom door. He rushes a hand to his mouth and retches a bit before committing to vomiting on the bathroom floor. He grabs a towel to wipe his mouth, steps backwards out of the bathroom and closes the door behind him. I rush to his side and say, 'What on earth?'

Leaving his hand on the door handle, Joe turns to Perkin and says, 'Make sure all the CCTV footage for the past twenty-four hours is available for me to look at – is it saved on a loop, or…?'

'There is no CCTV footage,' says Perkin.

Joe looks like he's trying and failing to formulate words.

'When the tide is in, we always turn it off – energy saving. You can blame the cost-of-living crisis for that.'

'Right. In that case ask Dr Jane MacAvoy to come up to see me here please.'

'Directly?' asks Perkin, obviously wanting more information from Joe, which, I can tell from his face, will not be forthcoming.

'Yes, please. Directly.'

Perkin harumphs. 'And shall I tell her to bring her doctor's bag?' he asks.

'I think we're a little beyond that,' says Joe.

Chapter Twenty-Four

DONNA

Joe's first words of explanation once Perkin's footsteps have echoed down the corridor are, 'I think we can safely say that this is one body that *won't* be disappearing on us.'

'Is it Miles?' I ask. 'Has he been shot too, or…?'

'Not shot, exactly, more … obliterated. Lamorna was right about the explosion – the body parts are in the bath, although there is an arm on the floor.'

I turn the handle, because even though this is surely the grimmest thing I'll ever see, I simply have to see it to believe it. I look inside and manage to keep my breakfast down, but only just. It is a literal bloodbath. I close the door and look at Joe. Neither of us laughs this time. Suddenly the bedroom is full to the brim with the noise of the storm. One of the iron-framed windows is rattling and there's an associated tap on the window, like the ghost of Cathy is trying to summon Heathcliff; although if I were Cathy, surely I'd be clambering to get out of this hell hole rather than in it.

'Was it suicide, do you think?' I ask.

Joe shakes his head. 'I doubt it.'

'Was there a hairdryer plugged in, did you notice? Because he really was quite vain, and they do say not to use electricals in bathrooms?'

Joe opens the door a crack and looks in. 'No,' he says, before closing the door again promptly, because make no mistake, every time that door opens from now to eternity it will feel like the opening of the portal to the seven circles of hell (although there are eight now, clearly).

'What about some kind of elaborate masochistic sex play that went wrong?' I ask, sitting on the edge of the bed to gather a little strength.

'What the hell kind of sex play do you know about that would lead to this kind of shit storm?!' asks Joe, looking at me oddly.

'I have no idea, Joe! But some people get a kick out of near-death sex acts, and maybe he wasn't alone in there? The bathroom door wasn't locked, so maybe he was in a relationship with one of the other guests and it all went a bit … far. I'd start looking for someone with a bit of charred skin and burn marks if I were you…'

We sit on the bed in silence and yet the whirring cogs of our collective consciousness are deafening.

'Let's go through this logically. The bedroom door was locked,' says Joe, rushing over to the door that Perkin left half-open, on account of the frame being damaged. 'And the key is still in the lock on the inside,' he adds, just as the window rattles itself open and the full power of the storm blows in. Joe darts across the room again and puts the weight of his body behind the window to close it. I join him and we both glance down at the rocks below, rocks being pounded by what is surely the worst storm I have ever known. We return to sit on the bed, which feels safe.

'So, we've got a missing but definitely dead MP,' I say. 'And a dead but not missing American. Where the hell do we even start?'

Joe puts his elbows on his knees and rests his head in his hands. He takes a moment before looking up.

'We start by keeping the remaining guests and staff safe and accounted for, which we're doing, kind of. When did the causeway become impassable?'

'Just before Pinky was shot,' I say. 'Around eleven. And it won't be open again for another eight or nine hours, maybe even longer, given the storm.'

Joe crosses to the window again. That run of carpet will be worn out by teatime. 'No boat will cross to the Mount with this swell,' he says. 'And it's too rough for a helicopter. Which means we're stranded on the island without backup until at least seven or eight this evening.'

The electric lamp on a side table flickers.

'Stranded in a castle with a murderer,' I say quietly.

'Unless the murderer is holed up in one of the harbour cottages,' says Joe, trying to console me.

I finally let out a little laugh, although it's more of a low-energy titter, really.

'Well, God help him if he is,' I say. 'Because he'll rue the day he ever stepped one toe on the island if he disturbs Auntie Donna while she's cooking!'

The door opens and Jane walks in.

'What is it now?' she asks.

Joe sighs before crossing to the bathroom.

'I'm sorry to tell you this,' says Joe. 'But Miles seems to have been blown up. Prepare yourself.' Joe rests a hand on her arm as she approaches. 'What you're about to see will shock you.'

She looks at him. 'Trust me, detective. When you've seen what I've seen over the years, nothing can shock anymore.'

Joe opens the door, Jane steps into the bathroom and retches.

'Sweet Jesus,' she says, her voice echoing around the tiled room. 'What sick fuckery is this?!'

Chapter Twenty-Five

While the Pimpernel Club gather in the library, Joe asks Jane to leave the bedroom and puts in the necessary but dreaded call to Penworthy. He's sitting with Donna on the edge of Miles's bed, the door to the bathroom remaining well and truly shut. Joe would prefer it to be hermetically sealed and never opened again. In fact, he'd like his *life* to be hermetically sealed and not opened again if that meant not having to put this call through. His finger hovers over Penworthy's private number. They have an agreement that if a dodgy call needs to be made then they are to phone each other on their private, rather than work phones. 'And don't WhatsApp me and don't even *think* about using the police radio,' she once said. 'We don't want the whole bloody world to know!'

Where should he start, he wonders. How about, 'Hi, ma'am, the thing is, the Home Secretary is dead. In fact – and try not to laugh – she's not just dead but her body is missing.'

No, that won't do.

How about a bit of a lie to save his own skin? 'Ma'am. Enys here. About the Home Secretary. She's done a runner. But she left a note that said not to send anyone looking for her because she's nipped off to the Maldives and isn't coming home.' Actually, that might just work. Donna puts up both thumbs in encouragement and quickly presses 'call' on the phone on his behalf.

'Jesus Christ on a bike!' shouts Penworthy once he's explained that the Home Secretary is both dead and missing. Despite the hurricane, she's gone to Truro on a shopping spree because her daughter wouldn't stop pestering her for a trip to TK Maxx. 'I gave you one job,' she shouts. 'One bleeding job! All you had to do was keep the woman alive for forty-eight hours! Wait a minute, Joe – I said no crop tops, Keris. No, not that one. Absolutely not. I don't care if Sennen wears the same thing or what her mother lets her do, I want that belly button covered up. What did you say? Right. One more dirty look from you, young lady and you can forget Boardmasters this year. I'm back, Joe. The tide's in at the moment, you say? When does the causeway open again?'

'Eight-ish, although with the storm, it might be later, depending on the swell. It closes again at midnight.'

Penworthy takes a very deep breath. 'That might be just the thing that saves us. Except that if you've got a rampaging psycho on your hands over there, you might be screwed. Maybe one of them has gone mad, PTSD type thing? What the hell happened, anyway?'

Joe explains as much as he can with the limited knowledge he has, keen to point out that he carried out security rounds on a number of occasions last night (missing out the detail pertaining to the samurai ghost), watched over Pinky while she was swimming, and that he did all of this despite her having ordered him to leave her alone. He also explains that as he was put on the island as a waiter, he had actually been required to do some legitimate waiting duties to keep up the ruse, and it was in fact while carrying out these duties that she was shot. (This is an absolute lie, of course, but after last year's reintroduction of the Nightshades into his life, Joe's moral compass has gone slightly off-kilter.)

'And she went alone to this bizarre weapon-heavy museum room thingy…'

'The Garrison Room,' confirms Joe.

Should he lie, or…?

'She asked Donna to go with her.'

There's silence, but not for long. 'Donna bloody Nightshade?!' shouts Penworthy. 'The Home Secretary attended a secret rendezvous in an armoury with an ex-con and you knew nothing about it?'

Joe turns away from Donna and reduces the volume setting on his phone quickly.

'That's correct, yes.'

'Have you lost all the sense you were born with? Tell me this: why is it always Donna Nightshade that is the first person on the scene of a murder?'

'Not *always*,' offers Joe, albeit in a murmur.

'And you say there was no one else in the room, no other way in, no other way out. And when Donna was standing at the door, she heard a shot and Pinkerton-Smyth fell to the ground.'

'Yes, ma'am.'

'It all sounds very convenient to me. Why the hell did Lady Helen ask her to be there anyway? I knew it was a damn mistake. Putting the Nightshades in charge of someone's welfare is like asking a Tiger to mind a baby – I told you, Keris! You need to find something that covers your arse! The only two people who should ever be that familiar with your undercarriage area are your lover and your gynaecologist! Find some bloody trousers!'

Joe looks at Donna and smiles. Donna puts her thumbs up again. She wouldn't if she knew she was Penworthy's number-one suspect (again).

'Look, the way I see it is this,' says Penworthy. 'Either one or more of the guests did it, or one or more of the Nightshades did it, or it was this Perkin fella. The butler. What's he like?'

Joe thinks hard about this and can only think of one word…

'Gothic,' he says.

'Gothic?' repeats Penworthy. 'That's all we need. I thought he was posh?'

'He is. And gothic.'

'Right. What would be his motive?'

'What would be a motive for the … other people?' asks Joe, defensively.

'The Nightshades? They don't need one,' scoffs Penworthy. 'They have form, reputation and can probably be bought. It *could* have been someone who came onto the island and is hiding; someone we don't know about yet. But bearing in mind what you've told me about the nut in the trifle incident the night before, that possibly rules out the last two, not that we should let something that might have been a simple error send us in the wrong direction … so watch out for that. My instinct says that you've already met the murderer or murderers, so nail them. My money is on a Nightshade. Start there.'

Joe isn't going to ask how much money. He's done that before and, yes, he won, but only by nefarious means.

'The causeway is clear again at 20:30 you say?' she asks.

'Yes, ma'am.'

'In that case, we never had this phone call, understand me? I'm keeping the whole thing quiet until the tide goes out. Tell all the guests that there's a media ban. Take their mobile phones off them and keep them huddled. Have you done an initial search yet – dead woman's room, a sweep of the castle, that kind of thing?'

'No, I phoned you first.'

Penworthy chunters to herself before saying, 'OK, so here's what I need you to do…'

'What's that?'

'Solve the damn thing before you contact me again when the causeway opens.'

Joe's head drops. Solve it? She doesn't even know about Miles yet!

'And if you can't solve it properly, pin it on a Nightshade until you can. But in no circumstances whatsoever do I want to be in the situation where I have to be arsed bringing a team of detectives over for a full-on murder investigation for the Home Bloody Secretary. It's the weekend and I've got Zumba later. Parking in Marazion is bad enough at the best of times without the world's press taking all the spots. You've got eight hours, Enys, or you'll be back working as a community copper before you can say *Donna Nightshade is a complete psycho*!'

Another smile from Joe to Donna.

'Start with the search and the interviews and take it from there. Use Donna to help you if you must, but don't trust her and keep a beady eye on the lot of them. Something smells fishy to me and pound to a pinch of salt there's a Nightshade involved somehow. Right, I'm off. Anything else?'

Joe looks up to the heavens, presumably hoping for an angel to pop down and whisk him away.

'Kind of,' he says. 'It's just the small matter of it being a double murder…'

Penworthy is silent. That is never good.

'I was waiting for the right moment to tell you,' he says. 'But one of the other guests is dead. We're not sure if it's murder, or suicide, or a dodgy sex act…'

'How?'

'Blown up.'

'Shitting hell. Where?'

'In the bath.'

'Who was it?'

'The American.'

'That's all I need. Repatriating bodies is a right pain in the arse.'

'There isn't much left to repatriate … perhaps an ear or two. An arm. A few teeth embedded in the ceiling.'

'The deaths are probably linked but concentrate on Pinkerton and the rest should follow. I'll send a clean-up team in tomorrow. Phone me back when the causeway opens tonight, and Enys…'

'Yes, ma'am?'

'Don't cock it up!'

The phone goes dead.

'Did she send me her love?' asks Donna. A thin veil of sarcasm floats across the room.

'She wants to keep it quiet until the causeway opens, to give us time to get to the bottom of it, so we need to make sure that we put a blanket of silence across that lot downstairs. We'll have to take their phones, give them to Perkin to keep safe. They don't seem the type to want any adverse press attention so you should be fine.'

Perkin appears at the door holding two sets of Marigold gloves and an assortment of different-sized sandwich bags.

'I thought you might need these,' he says. 'To search the room without leaving any more fingerprints… And the guests are all assembled in the library. The doctor lady has told them what's happened, and Jago has telephoned down to his sister– the new chef – who's staying in the harbour cottage. He's asked her to pop back up.'

'What did she say to that?' asks Donna, sounding nervous suddenly.

'She said that she will be up when she's good and ready and that she'll have to prepare lunch anyway, so if you want to see her she'll be in the Mount's kitchen. Jago did explain that it's highly likely that there's a murderer on the loose and apparently, she just laughed.'

Joe's heart sinks. His theory about Auntie Kerensa being schizophrenic seems unlikely now. He turns to Donna who makes a shape of a gun with her hand, puts her hand to her head and pulls the trigger.

It's time to fire off a text to Demelza.

Joe: *Get me a full character profile on Pinkerton-Smyth. Birth, childhood, marriages, affairs, the lot. I'm going to send you another message with a list of names – ex-army types. See what you can find out about them, too.*

Demelza (answering immediately): *OK. Why?*

Joe: *I'll phone and tell you when you get to the station. And I need you to stay in the office all day. Totally hush hush. Message me when you get there.*

Demelza: *No Probs.*

Joe puts his phone in his pocket and tiny but sharp pangs of guilt dance across his chest and work their way down to his gut, where all such emotions dwell and do irreparable damage. Perkin hands over the gloves.

'Any idea what we're looking for?' asks Donna, pulling on the Marigolds.

'No idea. You'll know when you find something.'

'Like this, you mean?' she says, taking a piece of plastic out of her jeans pocket. 'I reckon it's the top piece from the heel of a stiletto.'

'You're right,' says Joe, who is struggling to open a sandwich bag with rubber-gloved hands. 'Where did you find it?'

'It was by the bathroom door. I noticed it when I was staring at the carpet waiting for Penworthy to stop telling you that I'm the chief suspect – again.'

Joe is about to protest, but Donna's no fool, and it doesn't matter how much you turn down the volume on an iPhone, every man and his dog can hear the conversation, especially someone as shouty as Penworthy.

'All you have to do is find the Cinderella whose shoe that fits,' says Donna, 'and you've found your murderer. Told you I was good at this.'

Joe finally opens the plastic bag.

'Correction,' he says. 'What we will have found is someone who came into the room and who *might* be a murderer. Miles may have been in a relationship with one of them for all we know … and the murders might not be connected, which would be very unlucky for us – to have two murderers loose on the island at once. But it's a possibility.'

Joe notices a look of uncertainty on Donna's face, which is surprising as Donna would rather lop off her own arm than appear to be on the back foot or, God forbid, nervous.

'This is really serious, isn't it?' she says.

Joe nods.

'We're in danger, aren't we? Stuck on the island – no way in; no way out…' She glances towards the window because Catherine Earnshaw is still rattling the thing, trying to get in.

Joe wants to step up and put his arms around her and tell her that everything will be all right, that Joe is here to protect her – to protect everybody. But he can't, partly because that would be a lie – he's crapping it himself, after all – but also because if he puts his arm around her surely she'll be able to tell that he's still, after all these years, a crazy fool in love, and what if Donna Nightshade isn't in love? He'd feel like a bit of a tit, and also … there's Demelza to consider. There's always Demelza to consider.

'Eight hours isn't very long,' she says encouragingly. 'And we'll be fine so long as we stick together.'

Joe smiles.

Donna smiles.

Perkin, who is hovering at the door, coughs and the door swings lopsidedly open. Lamorna dashes in singing 'It's Raining Men' and carrying a knight's shield. She's strapped a thick belt around her waist and stuffed a sword *and* a machete between the belt and her dungarees.

'I *know* you said we were to walk around in pairs,' she says,' but that lot down there are getting edgy and argumentative, and Jago has gone off to search the castle for murderers because he's been on the blower to Lady Helen – satellite phone – and she's gone apeshit. Oh, and "Auntie" has just pitched up to make lunch. I thought I'd come and hurry you two along a bit before nipping back down to resume guard duties. What happened to Miles, by the way?' she asks, making her way towards the bathroom. 'Was it deliciously gruesome?'

Joe looks at Donna, Donna looks at Joe, and both lunge forward to shoo Lamorna away from the eighth circle of hell.

Chapter Twenty-Six

DONNA

A search of Miles's room produces a number of items, some interesting, some not so much: a phone, predictably locked but with a picture of Jane and Rupert standing together on Marazion beach in a lip lock set as the screen saver. Joe and I file that little titbit away under the 'hmm, how very interesting' category. There are no credit cards and no photos of loved ones in his wallet, just two-hundred dollars, a couple of betting slips, and a lottery ticket, dated today, which I snaffle for myself before Joe sees. The most important item we've found is a file detailing the accounts of the Pimpernel Club, with an annexe for a company called Warleggan Holdings at the back.

'Right. Let's have a gander at this,' I say, flopping onto the bed. 'I'm good at accounts, well, magic balancing and a spot of money laundering if that helps…'

Joe throws me his schoolteacher glance.

'But all that's in the past now, obviously.'

He sits next to me, and I open the file.

After a cursory flick through, I can only conclude that what I've just gone through is, 'gobbledygook'.

'In what way?' asks Joe.

'Layers and layers of hiding the source of the money. You'd need the fraud squad to unpick it, and then I doubt they would manage it. I wonder what all the donations to these so-called projects are. It's been made to look like charitable donations, but I bet it isn't. Donations to the Oxford Foundation, whatever that is, run into millions.'

I turn to the annexe, which makes a little more sense.

'This is a basic analysis of investment by Warleggan Holdings in something called the Poldark Project showing projected returns for a ten-year plan. Part of the income stream is channelled off to the Pimpernel Club – fifty per cent by the looks of things. The reference "LWF" keeps coming up … any idea?'

'None.'

I close the file. 'I think this file is a catalogue of money laundering on an impressive scale. Is it OK if I keep it afterwards? A woman could learn a thing or two from this?'

Joe takes the file out of my hand.

'No,' he says, rolling it up and bopping me on the head with it before stuffing it under Miles's pillow. 'More of this later.' He jumps up. 'We need to go back to the Garrison Room. See what little secrets that holds.'

'None,' I say, following him to the broken door. 'It will reveal nothing. This has been a professional hit job, I reckon.'

'It doesn't hurt to quickly nip in there,' says Joe.

'Tell that to Pinky,' I say as we run down the stairs.

As suspected, the Garrison Room revealed nothing whatsoever that could even come close to a clue. No footprints, no snagged bits of clothing, nothing. Nothing except for the telltale trail of blood. It was simply impossible for anyone to shoot Pinky from within the room other than from the window because there was no one in there, and yet somehow, someone did. As for the question of how the body was removed in the few minutes it took me to find Joe after Jane and I had left the room … we have no idea. It's just a good thing that I didn't leave Dr Jane with the body as she'd be fish food by now.

Anyhow, I'm standing in a corner of the library watching the unbelieving faces of the guests as Joe confirms what Jane has already told them – that Pinky and Miles are dead. He's been vague regarding the finer details of the bloodbath, which is perhaps best, and skirted over the fact that Pinky's body is missing. As holding pens go, the library is ideal. There are enough chairs and sofas to seat a football team, lots of books to read and board games to play (although they may feel like doing neither), and a card table. Other than Matt Lewis, I can confirm that they are more upset that the weekend has been messed up than they are about the dead people, but as Lamorna keeps reminding me, they've all probably seen a lot worse. I take out my detective notebook, open it on a fresh page, rest the book against the wall and with a new Sharpie write the following:

Matt is the only one upset… Why?

It's not much, but it's a start.

My mind wanders to worrying about my family while Joe continues with his briefing.

Lamorna, I know, has gone down to the harbour cottages with her personal armoury scattered about her, because despite saying that we need to move about the island in at least pairs, the likelihood of Auntie Donna having taken Patch out to pee or having fed either Patch or Ruby is slim (non-existent, actually) and so I've dispatched her on animal-welfare duty. We worked it out that in normal weather conditions, it takes approximately half an hour for a person of Lamorna's fitness to dash down to the cottage and back. Allowing an extra ten minutes for battling through the storm force gales and a further fifteen minutes to spend with the animals, she should be back no more than an hour after she left. Which means that I expect her to walk through the library door in twenty minutes' time. I've told her to keep looking up to the sky in case of loose tiles, but not to look up so much that she trips and breaks her neck on the slippery steps and cobbles (truly, this place is a health-and-safety nightmare in a storm). If she's not back in this room exactly on the dot, then I'll be grabbing a few weapons of my own off the walls and heading out into the storm. She's going to bring my detective's bag of tricks from the cottage, which includes a set of two-way radios, or walkie-talkies, as Uncle Jago calls them.

Speaking of whom, Jago is officially missing in action. Having disobeyed police orders (he *is* a Nightshade to be fair) he disappeared off alone to do a search of the castle and grounds. Perkin was dispatched on an uncle recovery search and as neither has returned they are both AWOL, which is giving me an ulcer because the storm, far from abating, is gaining momentum. Hopefully, they are roped up and are not venturing down to the steeper and more exposed parts of the garden grounds. The only thing helping my anxiety is that Perkin also has walkie-talkies and his are professional ones not cheap ones like mine from Argos. According to Lamorna, Perkin left a radio with Auntie Donna, who he found in the kitchen, just in case of emergency. God help him if he sends out a distress call. She'll probably tell him to man up before turning the radio off, annoyed.

'The good news,' says Joe to the shellshocked guests, 'is that I'm not a waiter, I'm a policeman.'

'Tell us something we don't know,' scoffs Matt.

Joe steps over this as though nimbly stepping over a sleeping dog. 'And I've been tasked by my commanding officer, DCI Penworthy of Devon and Cornwall Police, to begin an immediate investigation before the causeway opens again in just under eight hours' time. I'm very sorry for your loss, but I won't apologise for insisting that you stay together here in the library and that you hand over your phones – media embargo, I'm afraid. Donna is going to pass a pen and paper around and I want your full names and addresses, please. Food will be brought to you.'

Atticus lets out a low moan.

'I'm giving my phone to no one,' says Rupert.

'You are and you will,' insists Joe. 'Being together in the library will give you safety in numbers and time to gather your thoughts.'

(Personally, I think it will give them time to sort out their alibis, but I'll keep schtum for the moment.)

'You will only leave this room for two reasons,' he says. 'To go to the study, to be interviewed, or to the lavatory. Either time you must be escorted, which is for your own safety as much as anything else.'

'Just to be clear,' says Sienna, who is sitting up ramrod-straight on a Queen Anne chair. 'I take it that you are treating us as suspects for murder, because if so, we're entitled to counsel.'

'I'm not ruling out any scenario at present,' says Joe, which must be the type of non-committal answer they're taught at police college, and I'll fix that sentence securely in my mind in case I'm ever put in a tricky spot in future investigations.

'But let's start with keeping each other safe,' says Joe. 'If you wouldn't mind, Mr Black, I'll begin my interviews with you. Would you step next door to the study with me please?'

A deep sigh that seems to go on longer than one of Aunt Kerensa's clearing yogistic breaths emanates from deep within Atticus Black.

'If I have to,' he says, pushing himself up from his chair, his maroon, corduroy trousers hanging crisply from his trim hips. He's the only one of the male guests who tucks his shirt into his trousers, the shirt being something that he must have ordered from a Scottish gentleman's outfitter. This is clearly not a man who is blessed with teenage daughters, because they would simply not allow their dad to dress that way.

Atticus doesn't have to open the door to the library because it flies open.

Lamorna has returned, breathless, wet through, with Patch at her feet and a rucksack on her back. The belt and weapons have been positioned around her raincoat this time. Oh, and she's carrying a bag for life. She opens the bag and Ruby, our macaw, flies out. She does two laps of the room then lands on an antique dresser that's full of the type of old books that absolutely no one ever reads.

'I've got your detective bag, Donna,' she says, handing me my black rucksack, 'And I thought some crisps might go down well.' She glances around at the astonished faces of the guests. Five tubes of Pringles are put onto the backgammon table. 'And as the sun's over the yard arm – just – I brought wine – and plastic glasses, too, just in case they get violent again and start smashing the place up.' She waves the glasses in the direction of the guests. 'It *is* supposed to be a party after all, eh, guys?'

I'm about to suggest to my sister that now might not be the best time for the guests to get rat-arsed when Rupert says, 'Nice one, gingernut.' (Which does sum up Lamorna perfectly.)

And Sienna says, 'Do you have a merlot?'

And Matt, who's cheered up a bit with the arrival of Lamorna, asks, 'Any chance of a G and T?'

Chapter Twenty-Seven

DONNA

'Before we start,' says Atticus, taking a seat in the study at an antique mahogany desk opposite Joe, 'I want to suggest – insist, even – that you go easy on Jane MacAvoy when you interview her. And Sienna, too.'

The desk is positioned in the middle of the small room (mahogany with an inkwell and blotting paper – proper job). I'm perched on the window seat with the storm raging behind me. When I suggest recording the interviews on my phone, Joe says, 'We simply can't do that, so don't.'

I said, 'OK, no worries, I won't'. But I've put my phone on the seat next to me and I'm recording the interview anyway, because one of these so-called guests is most likely a murderer and they can stuff their basic human rights where the sun don't shine.

'And why is that?' asks Joe.

'Simply because Jane is not as stoic as she seems,' explains Atticus. 'And she's just seen the dead bodies of two of her oldest friends ... that in itself should lead you to take sufficient care.'

Joe looks at me. The look, thinly veiled, says "Can you believe this idiot or what?" Joe Enys does not like Atticus Black. This should be fun.

'And Ms Blackville?'

'Sienna has a terminally ill daughter. This is a difficult time for her.'

I notice Joe's jaw soften, but only a little bit.

'Do the others know?' he asks.

'Nadine told me, so that's one who knows...' He looks to his hands to gather himself. 'Sorry, *knew*. Past tense. It's taking some getting used to... I just can't believe she's gone.'

Joe smiles but says nothing.

'And, Jane knows, of course, because ... well it's all so weirdly coincidental ... cruelly so...'

'What is?' I ask, because Joe is still offering nothing, just listening and waiting but I'm too impatient.

Atticus looks at me blankly like he's turned over two pages at once.

'What's coincidental?' I repeat, trying to jog him.

'Oh, just that Jane works at – is the head of department of – a medical institution in Oxford. It's crazy but she's the very person who might just be able to find a cure for Sienna's daughter. She's working on something at the moment and is incredibly close to a solution, but it's not looking as though she'll make a good enough breakthrough in time, which is dreadful. Just dreadful.'

There's a moment's pause to acknowledge the sadness of the situation, before Joe says, 'So, Mr Black.' He clicks the top of his biro. 'Talk me through your morning so far – from waking to arriving in the library.'

'I woke up at about five, five-thirty,' begins Atticus. 'Turned on the bedside lamp, grabbed a glass of water and went through my morning exercise routine, which takes about twenty minutes. Then – as you know already – I headed down to the harbour for a swim. Nadine was there and we swam within the harbour walls – the sea swell being greater than I expected. It was not a prearranged liaison.'

'Really,' says Joe. It's not a question, just a statement that lets Atticus know that Joe knows that he's lying. 'A brave move to swim in the dark when the front edge of the storm was arriving.'

Atticus does not respond. Joe is going to have to do better than that. A hard nut – something like a horse chestnut – gallops across my imagination.

'We have a weather forecaster in our midst,' says Atticus eventually. 'I had asked him about the sea state, and he'd predicted no more than a four.'

I laugh out loud at this. As a sea swimmer, a mariner and just basically Cornish, I know that this is absolute nonsense. Atticus throws daggers in my direction. (To confirm, they are metaphorical daggers, because you can't be sure who's throwing what around in this place at the moment.)

'What did you talk about?' asks Joe.

'We swam together to be sociable. We didn't talk much, what with the swell.'

Joe pauses and rolls his pen around in his fingers. He watches the pen for a while before saying, 'And after the swim?'

'I returned to my room, finished my morning exercises, showered and headed down to breakfast. That would have been at eight-thirty. I was in the dining room for say, an hour, then came to the library for a coffee and to read the paper on my iPad. After about an hour I returned to my room and didn't leave again until Jane knocked on my door with the terrible news. I'm not sure what time that would have been, but I went, as instructed, directly to the library to wait for you.'

'You have developed a limp,' says Joe.

'I have.'

'You didn't have one yesterday.'

'I bashed it against the harbour wall when getting out,' says Atticus.

'That'll be the swell,' I say.

'I thought perhaps it was a spot of arthritis,' says Joe. 'How old are you? Fifty-eight? Fifty-nine?'

Atticus tightens his jaw and just for a second, his left leg starts to twitch. Well played, Joe. You found his Achilles heel, all right.

'And did you see anyone else walking around the castle at any time? One of the house guests, any of the staff?'

'No one,' says Atticus.

'And where did you first meet Ms Pinkerton? Am I correct in assuming it was in Iraq?'

'Not quite,' says Atticus. 'We were in Kuwait at first. But I really got to know her – and the others, including Miles, before you ask – once we were established in Basra. A few of us used to gather on the roof of the airport for a smoke, mainly.'

'You don't seem like the smoking type, Mr Black,' says Joe.

'I'm not,' agrees Atticus, offering no more.

'You became good friends.'

'Difficult times pull people together.'

'A diverse group though,' says Joe. 'A met man, a political advisor, a doctor, a special-forces man like yourself… You seem like an unlikely friendship group.'

'Then you don't know the army,' says Atticus.

'And Miles Johnson,' says Joe, swerving off-route slightly. 'Would you regard him as a friend?'

'Not really.'

'Did you like him?'

'Not really.'

'And yet he was included in the group.'

Atticus shrugs. 'It wasn't for me to say who was in and who was out. There's always that one person in a group of friends or colleagues who grates on one.'

He's right there. I have to admit to having made a mistake or two on that front.

'It seems to me that you were a group of friends who for some reason named themselves the Pimpernel Club. That suggests a closed group with a common background or objective. You had no common background, so what was the objective, Mr Black?'

Atticus sighs and sends his eyes skywards before saying, 'To smoke, to talk and to stay alive. That's it.'

And then Joe surprises me by smiling at Atticus and saying, 'That will be all Mr Black, thank you.'

Even Atticus looks shocked, and a little smug, as if he's got the better of Joe, which is a mistake.

'You might want to ask something useful in all of this,' says Atticus, standing.

'Such as?' says Joe.

'Well, for a start, you might want to ask Rupert about his argument with Miles last evening.'

'Go on.'

'Miles and I were in the billiard room having a drink and playing snooker. Rupert burst through the door and started raging at Miles. I have no idea what about, but Miles just shrugged him off, as Miles would.'

'Playing snooker with Miles?' says Joe. 'I thought you didn't like him?'

'I don't – didn't. Weekends like this are full of bullshit. You just smile and get on with it.'

'That was quite a black eye Miles had last night,' says Joe. 'Any idea how he got it?'

Atticus laughs. 'After-dinner japes, that's all. A spot of mess rugby.'

'What is the Poldark Project, Mr Black?'

Atticus blinks a couple of times, purses his lips, then says, 'It's a private business venture. Why?'

'I'm simply following lines of inquiry. Close the door on your way out,' says Joe, deadpan, before adding, 'And while you're sitting in the library, do try to cure yourself of this shock-induced amnesia you seem to be suffering from, and try to remember why it was that your fist made contact with the dead man's face. And also remember that this is not the army, I am not your junior man, and this is a murder investigation. We'll speak again later. You can tell me all about the Poldark Project then.'

I've never seen this side of Joe before, but I like it.

Sienna Blackville looks fabulous considering her daughter is terminally ill and she's just found out that two of her friends are dead. Good on her, that's what I say. She's wearing a little make-up – mascara and a brightening foundation, such as Trinny London's BFF is my guess. Lady Helen said that Sienna was fiftyish, but she looks fortyish, with her highlighted blonde hair pulled into a ponytail and just enough wrinkles around the eyes to look older, but in a sexy way. I'll go firm on the statement that she has not succumbed to Botox and is a fan of those harsh facials that make a person look like a burns victim for two weeks but five years younger after that. She has a crisp, white shirt tucked into skinny jeans in a sexy but no-nonsense way, and the belt is good – no muffin top. She's wearing a cashmere cardigan over the top. Her boots have the look and breeding of Italian leather about them. Bravo, famous lady journalist! You nailed the 'spending the weekend away and looking fabulous but not trying too hard' look.

'Do you mind if I smoke?' she says.

Joe flabbergasts me by batting his hand in acquiescence. Lady Helen will go nuts! I dash to a side table and grab a handy ornamental bowl – Ming dynasty type. It's probably priceless but what the hell, I'll scrub it out later. I take an offered cigarette and we smoke together, mainly because I'm liking the vibe. Joe offers me a hard(ish) stare.

Sienna explains to us that she went down to breakfast late, at around nine. Atticus, Dr Jane, Pinky, Matt and Rupert were in the dining room already. Pinky was finishing up, but the others hadn't been in there for long and were still working their way through a delicious full English. There was no sign of Miles. After breakfast, she explored the castle, and then, at around eleven, she returned to the library to search out a book to read.

'The weather had already put a dampener on my plans for the weekend,' she says. 'It was already turning into a bit of a damp squib before … well, before the deaths.'

'What plans did you have?' asks Joe pleasantly. (He'd better not be going soft just because of the hair and the smile.)

'A little sightseeing? I thought I might walk along the seafront to Penzance.' She glances past me as if I simply don't exist and stares out of the window. 'Not today, though.'

Ash is flicked.

'Did anyone suggest saving a little breakfast for Miles?' asks Joe.

Sienna looks at him blankly. 'We're not that nice,' she says.

I think this is her idea of a joke, but with this crowd, possibly not.

'And were you intending to sightsee as a group or as an individual?'

'I was going to wander off on my own,' she says. 'Group gatherings need space, I think. And there's only so much reminiscing a person can do before becoming overly melancholic. The war was horrid. We all lost friends but we're not the kind of people to dwell too much.'

'Why are you all really here, Miss Blackville?' asks Joe.

She doesn't miss a beat. 'Not for the weather, clearly,' she says.

Joe waits. She's going to have to elaborate because Joe can

sit in silence all day, I know. He did it to me often enough as a teenager.

'We're here because Rupert thought it might be nice for us to get together,' she says. 'We all left Iraq at the same time and made a pact to meet up after ten years. That didn't happen, for one reason or another, so we've finally got together now. It's a bit awkward, to be perfectly honest. Twenty years is too long to be apart. Although in a way, it all feels like it happened yesterday. Such a sad time. And Rupert, of course … he has a constant memory of Iraq because of his leg.'

'How did that happen, do you know?'

'Roadside bomb. He was lucky. Miles was in another vehicle close by. He could tell you more if you…'

And then, finally, it all hits home. Sienna puts her elbows on the table and drops her head into her hands. There are no tears, no histrionics, just a deep, deep sigh of despair. She glances up.

'This can't be real,' she says. 'Am I in some kind of weird TV reality show?'

We both shake our heads.

'A nightmare, then?' she asks.

We shake our heads again.

'And they're both dead? Pinky is really dead? Because – and I know someone was out to get her – but she's not the kind of woman to get herself killed.' Tears well on her lower lids.

'I saw both bodies myself,' I say. 'Can you think of any of your friends who might prefer her to be dead?'

Her response is immediate and aggressive.

'No!' she says. 'Kill Pinky? No way! She could be a bit cantankerous – opinionated, that kind of thing. But none of us would want to harm Pinky, I'm sure of it. We all think – well, Atticus thought it first and we agree with him – that someone from the outside must have been hidden here already, at the castle, and they've chosen their moment and gone for it. It's a big castle. You could easily move about unseen.' She looks at me. 'Unless it was one of you lot.'

'There is the nutty trifle issue,' says Joe, no doubt noticing me assessing the walls of the room looking for a handy weapon.

'Which was either a mistake by the cook or put there deliberately,' she says, throwing another look in my direction.

I'm about to clasp my hands around her throat when Joe says, 'And all lines of inquiry will be followed, including the question as to how a stranger – as per your theory – would know which room was the Home Secretary's in order to slip the note under the correct door?'

He has a good point there.

'I have no idea,' says Sienna. 'But I'll tell you this; none of those people in the library are murderers. I know them. When you've been through a war together ... you know people. I have no idea how it was done – that's your job – but I do know that none of us did it.'

'And Miles,' says Joe. 'Doesn't his death strike you as oddly coincidental?'

'Coincidental, yes,' she says. 'Odd? No. You've jumped to the conclusion that it was murder. In my opinion, Miles's death was some kind of accident – no, I don't know how – but an accident, that's for sure. Yes, Miles was a Marmite character, and I should imagine he's made quite a few enemies over the years, but to blow him up deliberately? No way.'

'Was Atticus Black an enemy of Miles?' asks Joe, looking down to write something.

Sienna scoffs. 'You're referring to the scrap last night?' A hand is batted. 'That was nothing. Just a misunderstanding between two men who had had far too much to drink.'

'And what exactly was that misunderstanding, Miss Blackville? Do you know?'

'I have no idea. I was getting myself a drink when words were spoken. The next I knew a fist flew and that was that. Don't read too much into it. That's just how some men are.'

'And what about this?' says Joe, taking a small plastic bag out of the desk drawer. He pushes it across the desk. 'Yours, I believe. We found it in Miles's room. Should I not read too much into this either?'

Blimey, he's shown her the tip of the stiletto heel! I glance at Joe, surprised that he's gone in for the kill so quickly, especially as we haven't checked for sure that it's from one of Sienna's heels. Risky. He could easily look like a bit of a tit in a minute.

'It was stuck to the carpet outside the bathroom,' he says. 'Where bits of Miles's body are splattered around the walls as we speak.'

Sienna looks at me before closing her eyes and shaking her head with a resigned sigh.

'You were in his room,' says Joe. 'When?'

'Last night, before dinner. He pulled me in as I walked past.'

'Why?'

'Why do you think? We once had a bit of a … it wasn't even a proper snog, but a "thing" just before we left Iraq. He thought he'd try it on. I put him straight and I left. I'd gone to that part of the room to look through the window because his view is different to mine before you ask.'

'What exactly is the Pimpernel Club, Miss Blackville?' asks Joe.

'What it is, is none of your business.'

'There are two dead bodies floating around this castle. For all we know, *you* might be the next in line – *that* is what makes this my business.'

Sienna is unmoved.

'OK, we'll try this another way,' says Joe. 'Why did Atticus meet Nadine at six o'clock this morning – in secret. Was it to discuss their joint business venture?'

Joe seems to have forgotten about the 'go lightly on Sienna' advice, but fair play to him, Sienna's face has morphed into a picture of … is it surprise? Indignation? Annoyance?

All three, probably.

'I wasn't aware that they had,' she says.

'Is that right? I want to return to your earlier point…'

'Which one?' asks Sienna, boredom and disdain her constant bedfellows.

'You said that within the group you have discussed this morning's events. Have you reached any conclusions?'

'Only that the rest of us are in no danger.'

'How so?' asks Joe.

Eyes are rolled.

'As I *said*, the obvious answer is that someone broke in, killed her, and that person would have legged it just before the tide was fully in. She had been receiving death threats, according to Jane, who was closer to her than the rest of us.'

Is that a blush from Sienna.

'The tide would have been in already,' says Joe. 'And there is the storm to consider, of course.'

'I've seen people cross mined borders during hurricanes. Where there's a will, there's a way,' she says.

She's right there.

'And Miles's death?' says Joe. 'You can hardly account that to an international crime unit.'

'Anyone who wants Matt dead is unlikely to want me dead,' she says. 'And anyhow, I have a suspicion that he killed himself.'

'Why would he do that?' asks Joe.

'He was broke, lonely and desperate. He saw himself as a failure. People have killed themselves for just one of those things before now. He would have gone to bed last night feeling like the failure of the group. Miles committed suicide. That's what we think.' She scrunches the cigarette end into the Ming bowl.

Joe takes a moment. He twiddles his pen some more and asks, 'What do you know about Cornish lithium?'

I have absolutely no idea where Joe is going with this, but I'm blooming interested. Lithium in Cornwall? It would be easy enough to sink a mine, wouldn't it? Is that what the Poldark Project is all about because, if so, I want in. I visualise myself galloping across the moors on my trusty steed wearing a black cape and a tricorn hat. How cool would that be?

'I know nothing about Cornish lithium,' says Sienna. 'I *do* know, however, that there is a global scarcity of lithium.'

Is there now?

'If there is lithium in Cornwall then it will be worth a fortune if anyone can get to it,' she adds.

Better and better.

'I'll tell you what I think,' says Joe, leaning back in his chair. 'I think that the Pimpernel Club is a trading company established in Iraq in 2003. I think that Atticus and Nadine were about to venture out on their own – cut the club out of the profits. Is that what the row was about? Is that what a company called Warleggan Holdings was established for and why Nadine was killed? Embezzlement? Someone's desire to get out of the club? A juicy scandal that was about to erupt?'

Sienna laughs out loud.

'You have a wild imagination, officer. But I'm afraid our little friendship group is not so glamorous. Yes, we clubbed together after the war to make some investments. I have in-depth knowledge of the oil industry and so we invested accordingly and legally, as anyone else could have done at the time or any time since.'

'Isn't that what's known as insider trading?' I ask.

She fixes me a deathly stare. 'No. It's what's known as *using your initiative,*' she says, before shaking her head, sighing and coming out with, 'Look. The altercation last night was because Miles announced that he was going to publish a tell-all memoir, and let's just say that there are people amongst us who would rather he didn't do that – Pinky being one of them.'

Joe rips a couple of sheets of blotting paper from the pad and crosses to the window, which has started to rattle. He folds the paper and uses it as a wedge between the window and the frame before glancing down and offering me a quick wink. I usually abhor men who wink, but this wasn't that kind of a wink; it was a conspiratorial wink, and on Joe, it's super-sexy.

'And the other guests,' he says, returning to his seat. 'Atticus, Rupert and Jane?'

'What about them?' asks Sienna, her voice returning to the 'drenched through with indifference and annoyance' version.

'I should think that they're all in positions where bad publicity would topple them – a high-ranking officer, a TV celebrity, a top professor? What long-buried secrets do you all keep for each other that you wouldn't want raked up in Miles's book, and more importantly, are they juicy enough to murder for?'

'None whatever,' she says, and fair play, she's kept her composure, but then this is a woman who in her time has been stoned, shelled and shot at by some really nasty people, so a few questions from Joe is hardly going to crack her. 'Are we done here?' she asks. 'Only it's unlikely that I've got any other information that would help you out and do remember that I've just found out that two of my friends are dead.'

'I'm sorry if you've found me harsh,' says Joe, softening. 'I do appreciate that this is a difficult time for you, especially considering the distressing situation with your daughter.'

Sienna stands.

'My daughter has nothing to do with this. You know nothing about her or about my life, and I'd rather keep it that way.'

Joe gestures towards the door. The interview is over.

Chapter Twenty-Eight

'Two down, three to go,' says Donna, who has moved to sit on the witness seat opposite Joe. 'Thoughts so far, Detective Sergeant? Have we just interviewed a murderer, do you think?'

Joe rubs his chin, a delaying tactic he often adopts when he hasn't got a clue who's done what or what to say. He trusts neither Atticus nor Sienna: both have lied to him, that's for sure. But who or what are they protecting? What are they covering up? And beyond that – and something he needs to figure out quickly if he's going to even make a start on this case – how on earth were the two murders executed? There has to be a straightforward answer, but for the life of him, Joe hasn't a clue. He says as much to Donna, before adding, 'I think we need to get to the bottom of what this Pimpernel Club is really all about – this investment-portfolio thing. And I want to know more about Pinky and Miles, too.'

'You mean, understand the murdered and you might understand the murderer?'

'Exactly that.'

Donna smiles and leans forward. 'Hey, when we were kids would you have ever thought that we'd be doing this together?'

Joe smiles. He wouldn't. Donna was an absolute thug.

'Here's a theory…' says Donna. 'Maybe Atticus abseiled from the roof, stopped by the Garrison Room window, shot Pinky, then shimmied back up again – or he could have dropped down to the battlements, but then he would have needed an accomplice, to drop down the rope, or collect it up. If only I'd been more on the ball at the time she was shot, I would have quickly looked out of the window. I can say for certain though that there was no one on the rocks below or hanging off a rope outside of the window ten minutes later when I was there with Jane because we looked.'

Joe has a think about this… Atticus *could* have set up an abseil from the roof, shot Pinky, waited outside the window while hanging on the rope, then jumped back in when Donna left, grabbed Pinky's body (he'd be strong enough), throw her out of the window, lower himself down, throw the body in the sea, climb the rope and reverse the process. There was just about enough time between the murder taking place and Jane returning to the Garrison Room with Donna. And as unlikely as it was, it was possible, especially given his background. If only Joe had an army of police officers available to search every room and every inch of the castle, because if Atticus had indeed carried out some elaborate abseil murder quest, then there would be wet clothes somewhere … and a rope. Joe wonders how many people Atticus has killed over the years – admittedly in the name of King and Country, but he certainly must have form, just in a military way, which is allowed.

But if Atticus murdered Pinky, how was Miles killed?

Was it suicide as Sienna suggested?

Tiny steps, thinks Joe, *tiny steps,* before remembering that his eight-hour time window (now seven and a half hours) doesn't fit in with the tiny steps attitude.

'We need to keep a close eye on Atticus,' says Joe. 'And when Jago gets back – any sign of him, by the way? – ask him to search all the rooms in the whole castle again for wet clothes – and a rope. And he's to take Perkin with him.'

'What if Perkin is the murderer?' asks Donna.

'What if Jago is?' replies Joe.

Donna laughs. Her naïvety regarding her Uncle Jago never failed to astound Joe.

'Uncle?' she says, 'A murderer? Don't be ridiculous. Any particular reason for searching for wet clothes?'

'Just following on from your – albeit unlikely – theory about Atticus being an abseiling psychopath,' says Joe, before remembering that he's stuck in a castle on an island with the Nightshades, and so it's most likely that the most unlikely theory is the most likely outcome to expect. He's just about to say, 'Let's have Rupert in next,' when the door from the library opens with a bang and Auntie Donna wanders in carrying a large silver tray.

'Refreshments, darlings!' she says, placing the tray on the desk. 'I brought tea, miniature pasties, scones, jam and cream. And there's a tot of rum to finish off with.' She pats Joe on the back like she's trying to dislodge a nut. 'To keep your strength up.'

There is, Joe thinks, a bit of a snarky glint in her eye when she looks at him, but that could be the smoke from the fire. Auntie crosses to the said fire and stokes and reloads it with a couple of logs from the adjacent basket. She turns around. 'Well! It's quite the weekend you're having, Mr Enys. Any ideas on the identity of the murderer yet?'

'Not yet, no,' says Joe, before committing to a sniff and a seat shuffle.

'Isn't this lovely, Joe,' says Donna encouragingly, nodding towards the feast. 'You, er, you haven't let on to the guests or to Perkin that you're not Kerensa, have you, Auntie? Only, the police will be here once the causeway opens later, and, well, I don't think they'd take too kindly to the arrangement that you have going with Kerensa at the prison.'

'*Open* prison, Darling.'

'And Joe would get into a great deal of trouble if his boss found out that he knew…'

A trace of mischief crosses Auntie Donna's expression, Joe notices. She starts to pour tea. 'Of course, I haven't forgotten, sweetheart! I'm not a complete nincompoop! Come on, eat up. Lots to do today.'

Donna lets out a relieved sigh while Joe swallows back a bit of bile, because why why why didn't he believe Donna last year when she told him what her aunties were up to? He reflects that he's been in many interviews with wrong-doers over the years, and he can always trace their tragic fall from grace back to one decisive moment in their lives – that one moment at the very beginning of turning from the good to the bad when they came across a crossroads where they chose to go down a dodgy path rather than a sweeter smelling one. Joe had such a moment last year when he failed to believe Donna, and in doing so chose to venture down a very dodgy path indeed – the Knockturn Alley of paths. And now he was so complicit in Auntie Donna's wrongdoing that it was impossible to turn back. He just had to hope that nobody in authority ever found out that he knew, either that or find a way to get Auntie Donna released from prison early. He must have a think about that. Although … the thought of Auntie Donna on the loose on his patch brought up even more bile from his stomach.

Donna nudges Joe. She's telling him to relax and help himself to food and that it's not, as he's beginning to wonder, laced with poison. There's a third cup on the tray. Auntie Donna grabs an occasional chair from the edge of the room and drags it to the desk. Donna pours a third cup of tea.

'You'll be wanting to solve it before your boss lady pitches up, I should think,' says Auntie. 'Or else…' She draws a line across her throat and laughs. Joe gulps. Auntie then ignores the pasties and goes straight for a scone, plying it first with jam, followed by a huge dollop of clotted cream, which is the Cornish way, of course. She sits back in her chair and licks her fingers. 'They never get proper Roddas clotted cream in prison,' she says. 'It's always that awful squirty stuff. I must take some back with me when I go.'

'Which is when, do you think?' asks Donna.

Auntie glances at Donna. Joe simply cannot read her expression. 'All in good time, my love,' she says. 'All in good time. Anyhow, a little bird told me that you two spent the night together.'

'Where is Ruby, by the way?' asks Donna. 'And Patch?'

'Patch is sitting on the knee of the pilot – he's getting smashed – and as for the damn parrot … Lamorna has set her up on guard duty. She has instructions to attack. The doctor nearly lost an eye when she tried to go to the toilet just now. But back to you two love birds… Will we be hearing the pitter patter of tiny feet in nine months' time?'

Auntie Donna's expression remains unreadable, bordering on threatening.

Joe spits out his tea and starts to choke on the pasty crust he's just swallowed. Donna hands him a napkin and pats his back. That's the second hard pat he's had in five minutes.

'It wasn't that kind of night, Auntie,' she says. 'I was helping Joe with his duties, that's all.'

'Hmm,' offers Auntie Donna. 'We called it something else in my day. Now tell me, have you worked out how the Home Secretary was shot yet?'

Donna looks at Joe. He shrugs and takes another mouthful of pasty.

'Right. In that case, if I were you, I'd ask Jago,' says Auntie.

'Jago?' repeats Donna, and after a considered pause allowing her to drink some tea, adds, 'What does Jago know?'

'Know? He generally knows everything,' says Auntie. 'I should consult with him first. He's very good at puzzles.' Auntie looks at Joe. 'His MENSA score is off the scale, as you would expect with a Nightshade. But while I'm here I want to chat to you about the second death.' Auntie Donna puts down her cup. 'The chap in the bath. I've got a theory about him…'

But Joe and Donna don't have time to hear the theory because the door opens again and a very soggy and out of breath Jago appears, clasping his chest.

'I'm having a heart attack,' he says. 'And also, I have news of great import!'

He turns to stick his head into the library and shouts out to Lamorna – who by the sounds of things is playing the harp for the guests who remain trapped in there – to 'Keep an eye on those blighters'. He closes the door and collapses onto a chair by the door. 'We found a cardigan on the rocks! It's here, look!'

He holds out a raggedy, soddened cardigan and gasps for breath for a moment. Donna rushes over to inspect it.

'It's Jane's!' exclaims Donna.

'Careless,' says Auntie Donna, throwing in an exaggerated sigh.

'Careless?' repeats Joe.

Auntie Donna looks up. 'That looks like good quality wool,' she explains. 'Pretty daft of one of them to go losing it on the rocks. I hate waste.'

'But don't you see?' says Donna. 'This is the cardigan that Jane draped over Pinky's dead body when she pronounced her dead, so if it was found on the rocks, then the murderer must have thrown her body in the sea!'

'Or wanted it to look that way,' says Jago, who is beginning to get his breath back.

Joe gestures to Donna to hand him the cardigan, fingerprints or no fingerprints.

'I thought you said there was blood pouring from Pinky's chest,' says Joe, thoughtfully, turning the cardigan over.

'I did,' confirms Donna. 'It pooled across her blouse.'

'You would have thought the cardigan would have become stained. But there's nothing on here.'

Auntie Donna lets out a scoff. 'I would have thought it

quite obvious that any blood would have washed off by now.' She nods towards the window and says, 'The effect of the storm and the rocks are the equivalent of putting it through a sixty-degree intense cycle with an extra rinse!'

'Although with a sixty-degree cycle, it would have shrunk, being cashmere,' adds Jago, helpfully.

'Well, it's certainly food for thought,' says Joe, wishing the superfluous Nightshades would absent themselves – to the North Pole, preferably. 'Thank you, Jago,' Joe adds. 'Brilliant work. But if you wouldn't mind, I really do need to crack on, and I'd like you to do another job for me, please. I need you and Perkin to search the castle for any wet clothes that might have been stashed away, and a length of rope. It would be a wet rope, too.'

'Food for thought?' repeats Auntie Donna, ignoring Joe's instruction to Jago. 'Food for thought?' she says again. 'My brother just brought you all the evidence you need to show that the daft cow got herself turned into fish food and all you can say is, "Food for thought"?'

Joe looks at Donna. Donna looks pointedly at Auntie Donna. Auntie Donna rolls her eyes in Jago's direction. Jago looks at Joe and, circle complete, suggests they leave the two young ones to it.

Auntie Donna stuffs the last bite of her scone in her mouth and heads to the door, but not before saying, 'I'm only trying to help. Speaking of which, now's your chance to pick Jago's brains. I bet twenty pounds he can help with that Garrison Room mystery of yours, seeing as how your detective hasn't got a clue.'

'Joe has this all perfectly in control, thank you!' says Donna.

There is an uncomfortable pause; even Jago looks at his feet. But despite Donna's insistence that Joe has the thing in hand, Joe knows that he hasn't, and that one policeman solving a double murder in seven hours (six now) while trapped on an island with at least one murderer on the loose is simply impossible. He needs forensics. He needs sniffer dogs. He needs (and he hates to admit it) Penworthy.

'No, it's OK, Donna. Every little helps.' He turns to Jago, who is still sitting on a chair holding his chest. 'Mr Nightshade, has anyone explained to you the details – as few as there are – of the Home Secretary's death in the Garrison Room and her subsequent disappearance?'

'Lamorna gave me some brief details, yes,' says Jago.

'You can see why we're having a bit of a head scratch to see how it could have been done.'

'Why?' says Jago.

'Well… An empty room? No way in or out other than the door, which Donna was standing next to. Just the small window, which sits a couple of hundred feet above the rocks below. There was no one else in the room, and yet she was shot. So, the question is, how was it done?'

'I would have thought that was perfectly obvious,' says Jago, looking around at the group.

'I told you he'd know,' says Auntie Donna.

'It's not obvious to me, sir, no,' says Joe, who is partly hoping that Jago will hand the answers to him on a plate, preferably a gold-plated one, and yet simultaneously hoping that he won't because he doesn't want to look anything but sharp as a tack in front of Auntie Donna, who Joe knows is just waiting for him to trip up.

'The simple solution – the *only* solution other than a ridiculous hypothesis that some kind of abseiling, suicidal nutter shot her through the window,' says Jago, 'is that the murderer was standing in the far corner of the room – in the unlit bit.'

Confused glances are exchanged.

'But you must know … surely you know that it's an unilluminable room?' says Jago. 'One of Arthur's little experiments. He loves that kind of thing does Lord St Clement. It was the obvious place for a murder, really.'

'I didn't know,' says Joe, who's starting to think this case might not be so impossible after all and that with any luck he might be able to stave off being prescribed blood-pressure tablets.

'An unilluminable room? What's that?' asks Joe.

'It's exactly what it says it is, young man. It's basic physics. The room is designed in such a way that the light cannot find its way into every nook and cranny.'

Joe is none the wiser. His blank expression gives this away quite clearly.

'Arthur likes to stand in the unilluminable nook and scare people when they're looking at the samurai warrior. It's all in the design. Have you even a basic understanding of how light travels?'

Joe says that he does not.

'Right,' continues Jago. 'It's like this: the room *looks* perfectly rectangular, but in fact—'

'We don't need a physics masterclass, thank you,' interrupts Auntie Donna, who is hovering with her hand on the door handle. 'In basic terms, what you're saying, brother – and correct me if I'm wrong – is that the room is built in such a way that the light can't bounce sufficiently around the place to fill the room and so a person can stand in the room – in a dark shadow bit – and not be seen. They could then fire the shot, stay perfectly still and Donna would have had no idea that they were there.'

'Seems like the most obvious solution,' says Jago, glancing around.

Auntie Donna turns to the two detectives. 'That's that sorted then,' she says.

'Except that you're assuming she was shot,' says Jago.

'She was definitely shot, Uncle,' says Donna. 'I heard it with my own two perfectly serviceable ears. I saw the blood. The woman was a mess.'

'Fair enough,' says Jago. 'But Joe could be onto something on the blood front. It's like when I'm down in the valley looking for mushrooms ... I often think I've heard a shot and wonder what on earth my family are up to now, but in fact it's usually something quite benign, like a door slamming, or a bird-scaring cartridge, something like that. Never assume, little one. Never assume.'

'But if not shot,' says Donna, looking at Joe who is starting to get that familiar sinking feeling of utter despair returning to his stomach. 'How was it done?' Joe looks at Jago for an answer, no longer worried that the old oracle will solve it before he does, because frankly, any solution will do right now.

'Now that's a question for a better man than me, Gunga Din…'

Circles, thinks Joe. *He is going round in circles.*

Donna looks at her watch. 'I think we'd better show the next one in…' she says.

Joe takes a very deep breath and clicks the top of his biro. Auntie Donna throws him a wink as she opens the door.

'Tick-tock, constable!' she says. 'Tick-tock.'

Chapter Twenty-Nine

DONNA

Joe is sitting across from Rupert Pendleton and looking … relaxed, actually. Friendly.

'I understand that you're married, have two children and live near Godalming, Mr Pendleton?' says Joe, tagging a warm smile to the end of the sentence.

'Marlow, actually. And I am and I do,' says Rupert. He's adopted his BBC weatherman voice, I notice.

'I saw you on *Strictly*,' says Joe.

I force myself not to look at Joe askance because there's absolutely no way Joe's ever watched *Strictly Come Dancing* in his life, unless Demelza made him watch it. 'Great performance,' he says. 'Your wife seemed very supportive.'

'She was – is. I'm a lucky man to have her. We're very happy.'

'That's nice.' Joe takes a moment. 'And you're Lord St Clement's godson, which is how you were able to hold the reunion here? Quite an honour for you.'

'It is,' says Rupert, his hands crossed on his lap, offering no more.

'Your own parents were killed in a skiing accident, I understand; when you were quite young. That must have been traumatic.'

Rupert's brow furrows.

'It was, yes.'

'Down to business, then.'

Joe opens his notepad, and so do I, and notice a scribble I made earlier.

'Actually – sorry to interrupt, Joe,' I say, 'But I'm hoping you'll be able to answer a very quick question for me, Mr Pendleton, before we start.' I throw in a bit of a laugh. 'Only, I'll forget once we get going.'

'No worries. Go on.'

'I was wondering who the other orphans in the group are?'

'Other orphans?' says Rupert.

'Yes. Lady Helen mentioned to my uncle that some of your group are orphans.'

Rupert begins to rub his left eyebrow. I think in the trade they would call that a 'tell'. I'll watch out for it in future.

'I, er, I think Helen has remembered that wrong. I don't know of another orphan.'

'At breakfast, Jane mentioned to the group that orphans need to stick together,' says Joe, running with my thread. 'What did she mean by that?'

'I have no idea,' says Rupert. He pauses to look at his hands before adding. 'Listen, go gentle on Jane. She's not … well, she's not quite as robust as she appears to be. Nadine's death will have been more of a blow than she's letting on.'

'I'll bear that in mind,' says Joe. 'The Mount must have become a kind of sanctuary to you over the years. A second home with loving godparents, perhaps?'

'I wouldn't go *that* far,' says Rupert. 'But they've been very kind to me, yes.'

The words are out before I can button them in, but I can't help but say, 'Shame to repay them with this horror show of a weekend, then…'

Rupert looks at me, surprised and hurt.

I offer no expression of sympathy in return.

'It wasn't like I planned it this way,' says Rupert.

Hmm.

'And just to confirm, Mr Pendleton,' says Joe. 'You call yourselves the Pimpernel Club?'

'Yes.'

'And you're all present and correct. No one missing?'

'No.'

'Why the Pimpernel Club?'

Rupert flounders. He looks to the ceiling (oak beamed) for inspiration.

'I suppose it seemed jazzy.' Rupert leaves it at that.

Joe is silent. I keep schtum, too. Rupert is going to have to offer more, ticking clock or no ticking clock.

Rupert lets out a chuff of air, like a steam engine that's about to get going. 'OK, I'll tell you but it's nothing special and I don't suppose it breaks the official secrets act now to let it slip, but none of us, of our little group I mean, believed that there were any weapons of mass destruction in Iraq. We were all frustrated because Atticus's men were sent off day after day to search the western desert looking for WMD just to justify the war on a political front. Well, that's what we guessed, anyhow. The Pimpernel Club is a nod to the saying… "We seek them here; we seek them there" and so on. We all became very cynical by the end.'

I notice Joe's jaw soften, which is nice.

'I can understand that,' says Joe, gently.

'We were all really quite close back then,' Rupert adds, relaxing, beads of genuine wistfulness drip-dropping from every word. 'We would meet every night on the roof of the airport, chat about future plans – dreams, you know. It was special somehow. We trusted each other then.'

'But not so much now,' says Joe.

'Twenty years is a long time,' answers Rupert. 'People change. But I think the sentiment is the same.'

'*Lest you forget*,' I say, feeling bad to have stepped in on Joe's flow, but I suddenly remembered the invitation card and the words kind of fell out.

'Exactly,' says Rupert, who offers me a kind and knowing smile.

'Is that why you pushed for the reunion, Mr Pendleton?' asks Joe. 'Just in case you were all starting to forget.'

'In a way,' he says. 'Although it wasn't me who pushed for it, initially. It was Miles's idea to start with. He remembered that I'd jokingly said that if we ever had a reunion I'd ask Uncle Arthur if we could have it here. Miles had never been to Cornwall, and he was fascinated by the thought of a reunion on an island. He contacted me and asked if I'd organise it. I felt a bit of a chump asking Uncle Arthur, but the others quickly got on board and pushed me to ask him, so I asked, and he said yes.'

'And when did Miles suggest it?'

'Not long ago. A couple of months? I was surprised that everyone could clear their diaries in time to attend. We're a busy bunch.'

'You've all kept in touch over the years?'

'Not particularly; some more than others. I think the girls stayed in touch a little more. I should think that Atticus and Pinky stayed in touch, too, but I didn't see anyone socially, so to speak.'

'And yet Miles had your email address.'

'I guess so.'

'Is that because of the business syndicate you're all in.'

Is that another bead of sweat forming on Rupert's brow?

'You know about that?'

'Shouldn't I?'

'It's just that we don't tend to discuss the syndicate outside of ourselves.'

'Why?'

'It's private business.'

'But, you do keep in touch.'

'Yes, but not socially. That's what I meant.'

Joe opens the desk drawer and takes out Miles's phone – I *knew* he was going to do that.

'Can you explain this, sir?'

He pushes the phone, face up, across the desk. Rupert sees the photo of himself front and centre in an embrace with Dr Jane. One of Rupert's legs – the good one – begins to shake and his jaw tenses, but he doesn't seem surprised. He says nothing but takes on the expression of an insolent child.

'We have assumed that this was taken by Miles yesterday,

bearing in mind the view of the Mount in the background.' says Joe. 'Have you any idea why Mr Johnson would have a picture of you and Ms MacAvoy as the screen saver on his phone?'

Rupert shakes his head. 'Pass.'

'Were you in a threesome?'

Joe! You didn't go there!

'No.'

'Was Mr Johnson in love with or stalking either Jane MacAvoy or yourself?'

'No idea.'

'You're happily married, you said?'

'Did I?'

'It was implied,' says Joe.

Rupert leans towards Joe across the table and lowers his voice – it's going to be a man-to-man type thing.

'Look, these things happen,' he says. 'Jane's been very lonely, and she works incredibly hard. Her research is phenomenal.'

'How so?'

'Oh, she's doing research into certain – at present – incurable diseases. She's very close to finding a cure for one disease in particular. We bumped into each other a while back, and well, I suppose I felt sorry for her. She seemed so lonely, and she's not getting any younger. A few kisses never hurt anyone, did they?'

He felt *sorry* for her.

Sorry?

I visualise getting him inside a kick-boxing ring and beating the shit out of him.

'How much did Miles want?' asks Joe. 'For the photograph.'

'I have no idea what you mean.'

'Miles was blackmailing you or trying to.'

Ah, of course! Nice one Joe.

'Not at all. He was a friend – an old comrade. Comrades don't do that.'

'That's not what Mr Black told us,' says Joe. 'He told us about the billiard-room scuffle and I'm afraid he told us quite a bit more.'

No, he didn't. Ooh, Joe. You're a devil!

'OK, I give in,' says Rupert. 'He wanted money from me. So what? The man was broke, which is incredible, considering…'

'Considering what?' Joe and I say together.

'Look, you got me. I had a fling.'

'Had?' I say. 'But that photo must have been taken only yesterday.'

'It was,' confirms Rupert.

'But you just referred to your…' I hate to use the word fling, '… relationship with Jane in the past tense.'

'I did,' says Rupert, the left shoulder offering an involuntary shrug. 'It's over between us. Well, kind of. Maybe.'

Transparent. Utterly transparent.

'And by "maybe" you mean that you were happy to have sex with Jane until Miles called you out, at which time you dropped her like an oily rag to protect yourself. And now Miles is conveniently dead, you have a feeling that you might well take up with her again?'

Rupert looks at me blankly and says, 'Yes. So?'

No words. I have no words.

'Look. All I know is that Miles saw us, he took that photo and tried to blackmail me with it.'

'Tried?' says Joe. 'You weren't going to pay up?'

'I don't have that kind of cash.'

'How much did he want?'

'Fifty-thousand pounds.'

Right, we've got him! 'And because you couldn't pay, you decided that it would be easier to m—'

'Thank you. Mr Pendleton,' says Joe, stepping in. 'That will be all for now.'

Rupert looks at me.

I look at Joe.

Joe looks down at his notebook and writes something.

Rupert stands.

'I know what you're thinking,' he says, resting his hands on the table and leaning towards Joe again. Joe glances up.

'You're thinking that you've found a nice little motive for murder. But here's a few more for you to write in that handy little notebook of yours, and not just for Miles's death, either. Are you ready? One: did you know that Pinky got one of Sienna's TV documentaries cancelled three years ago? It was a documentary series about the international arms trade and was very, let's say, revealing. Mates in the BBC said that Sienna had put years of research and a lot of her own money into the project; it would have been a massive scoop. But then, suddenly, the Home Office did some leaning on the BBC high-ups – the honours list was mentioned – and before you knew it, the documentary was axed. It was all Pinky's doing and Sienna knew it.

And here's number two: if you think someone as brutal as

Atticus would ever let Miles write a tell-all book about the Pimpernel Club then you're completely mistaken. His career in the army is his life – and he's due a not insubstantial pension in a couple of years, which won't matter as much to him as his reputation, which over and above his greed – yes, he's a greedy man – is his entire life. Cut Atticus in half and like a stick of rock it will read "British Army" through the centre. As for Matt, there's something going on there with Sienna, so you might want to look into that because they've been having lots of cosy chats together. Basically, let's just say that I don't think any of us killed either Miles or Pinky, but if you're looking to pin it on one of us, then don't just look at me!'

He goes to the door.

'One last thing Mr Pendleton,' I say, crossing to stand behind Joe's chair. I look down at his notebook and see nothing but doodles … of samurai ghosts. 'You said earlier that we should tread carefully with Jane.'

'I did, and whatever you might think of me, I meant it.'

'And yet you flirted with Sienna and danced a slow dance with Nadine last night. Not once did you offer Jane any kindness or attention. Why did you behave that way? Because of Miles's threat of blackmail?'

Rupert glances at Joe as if to say, 'Women! They just don't get it.'

'A simple smokescreen,' he says. 'We wanted to keep it private for obvious reasons. Jane understood.'

'And would that obvious reason be because you're married or because you didn't want a motive for murder to be uncovered?'

'The first, obviously,' he says. 'And, oh, if you want to ask me anything else, I want my solicitor present.'

The door handle turns, Rupert slinks out and the soothing sound of Lamorna's harp drifts in.

Joe looks at me.

I look at Joe.

Smiles are exchanged.

Chapter Thirty

DONNA

With the clock ticking, Joe and I waste no time beckoning the penultimate guest into the study – Matt Lewis.

'You're a British Airways pilot, I understand,' I say, having swapped seats with Joe because the draught on my back from sitting on that window seat is seeping into my kidneys.

'I flew the red eye back to London yesterday morning.' He flashes me a full beamer. 'If I'm a little bit dazed, you'll know why.'

'Bearing in mind that two of your friends have just been killed, Mr Lewis,' I say, not returning the smile just so he knows I'm no pushover, 'I would be surprised if you were anything but dazed.'

The smile disappears.

He's fairly sexy is Matt Lewis, with blonde floppy hair and a boyish smile. There's a decent body under the jeans, shirt and round-neck jumper, which is light blue to match his eyes. I said as much to Lamorna last night, but she felt there were traces of a belly emerging about his midriff. She blamed it on airport/airline food and the antisocial hours of long-haul pilots.

'Are you married?' (I don't think it's relevant but I'm just nosy.)

'No.'

'Kids?'

'No, again.'

'Long-term girlfriend?'

'Are you coming on to me?'

'I like my men under forty. How old are you?'

'Fifty.'

'There you go.'

Joe coughs.

'Can you talk us through your whereabouts this morning, please,' I say. 'From where you were when you woke up to the moment you all gathered in the library.'

'I certainly can. I woke up – in my own bed – and alone. I was going to lie in, what with the jet lag, but decided it best to get up and get into the flow of the day. I must have rocked up at breakfast at around eight-thirty. We mulled over the old times and so on, then I went back to my room to get a book I'd picked up at the airport – the storm had put the kibosh on us doing anything really decent with the day, so I thought I'd set myself up in the blue sitting room in front of the fire and just relax. I was looking forward to it, actually. That's where I was when the commotion kicked off.'

'The blue sitting room is on the other side of the castle,' I say. 'How did you hear the commotion?'

'I didn't say that I *heard* the commotion,' he clarifies. 'It was Jane who found me.'

Maybe I haven't quite got him on the coals just yet.

'The others were all in the library when I got there, and Jane told us what had happened to Pinky, which seemed utterly unbelievable. I thought it was a joke at first and that Rupert had decided to turn the weekend into a murder mystery or something. Then Jane was summoned to Miles's room and the whole thing turned into a nightmare. It hasn't really sunk in yet, for any of us. Was Miles ... was it...?'

'He appears to have been blown up,' says Joe.

'God. It's just awful,' says Matt, who seems to be trying but failing to squeeze out a tear or two. 'Was it suicide, or...?'

'We're not sure at this stage. We'd like to know more about yesterday evening, after the meal. We know that Atticus punched Miles, and we know that Rupert threatened him following a blackmail attempt.'

'Blackmail? Christ. It's certainly a mess,' says Matt.

'You can see that we'd appreciate it if you could tell us what you know. Being a bystander in all of this you're probably in the best place to give us an unbiased point of view. Isn't he, Joe?'

I turn to Joe who's pulled up Auntie Donna's chair and is sitting next to me now (the window seat being a little draughty for him) and has started doodling a comedy picture of an exploding bath. (I think we Nightshades are having a bad influence on Joe Enys.)

'Yes,' says Joe, glancing up. 'The others have told us more or less all we need to know, but it would be good to have your take on it all, especially with regard to the consortium, the blackmail threat, Jane and Rupert's relationship etc.'

Matt glances from me to Joe and back again while biting his bottom lip. He's trying to suss out if we're bluffing, which we are, clearly.

'Look, regarding what you're calling the consortium, I never made as much money as the others because I didn't put as much in. And Miles had nothing on me because I'm not famous or a big shot like the others, so his tell-all book meant nothing to me. Write that down, please.'

'How did you find out about the book Miles was planning to write?' I ask.

'Sienna told us at dinner last night. He'd contacted her and asked her to put a word in with her publisher, which she refused to do, I understand.'

'I see. And what is it about this so-called consortium that the others wouldn't want to be revealed?'

Matt shakes his head. 'Look, we were in Iraq together, and believe it or not there's a bond; but really, I can't tell you these things because I'm not entirely sure. I just threw some money in and left it at that. And I'm not even sure how you'll find out, or if the consortium will just liquidate now because the person who knew most about it – the investments, the moving about of the money, about everything – was Pinky.'

'Not Atticus?' says Joe.

'He just likes to pretend it's that way,' says Matt.

'You think she might have been killed because of the consortium?' asks Joe.

'I didn't say that, but it's possible.'

'And what about Miles?' I say.

'Same answer.'

'Why?' Joe and I say together, leading to a fist bump, which we both regret immediately afterwards.

'Fewer people in the group means a greater share of the money for the rest, right? Or it might be a plan to collapse the consortium, and someone could take up this lithium thing alone…' He fixes his stare on Joe. 'Although my money would have been on Miles doing that kind of thing.' He stands. 'Well, you've got me to squeal on my friends, can I leave now?'

'Yes,' says Joe. 'And thank you.'

He turns to leave but I can't help but wonder if the blue-room story is a little too convenient. He could easily have asked the other guests their whereabouts and deduced that none of them were there this morning, thereby making it the perfect place to have pretended to be. Rupert had mentioned that Matt and Sienna seemed to be in cahoots about something, too… Maybe Joe is saving his breath to cool his pudding, but that ticking clock is getting louder, and I really don't want Joe to be demoted for this, or even worse, leave Penzance. Therefore, I have one final question.

'What book was it, by the way?'

'I beg your pardon?'

'This morning. What book did you take to the sitting room?'

'Oh, it was the new James Patterson,' says Matt.

'Which one?' asks Joe. 'The Alex Cross series or a Women's Murder Club thing.'

'The Alex Cross one,' says Matt, his hand on the door handle. 'Picked it up at the airport. Listen. When I said that the others were all there – when I arrived at the dining room at breakfast – thinking about it now, I was wrong. Atticus wasn't, he arrived later and, well, it's probably not relevant, but I noticed that his shirt sleeves were wet...'

'Thank you, Mr Lewis,' says Joe. 'That will be all for now.'

'What. A. Snitch!' I say as the door closes behind him. 'There's definitely a secret or two there. I just wish we had a tiny bit of a thread to go on so we could pull it.'

'Here's one. James Patterson hasn't had a new Alex Cross book out in years,' says Joe, leaning back in his chair to have a stretch. 'And our friend Matt could easily have gone to the Garrison Room and dashed back to the blue room in the allotted time without being noticed. The jury's still out for me but I need to think. Who've we got left?'

'Jane MacAvoy.'

'In that case ... show—'

But Joe doesn't finish his sentence because his phone rings. The ring tone is 'My Heart Will Go On'.

Joe fails to make eye contact and if I'm not mistaken, even in this low light of the castle on a grey day in a storm with only firelight and candlelight to go by (I couldn't resist the candles) he's blushing. 'Could you just...' He nods towards the door. 'Only it's Demelza and it might be confidential?'

Confidential, my arse. He just wants to speak to lover girl in private.

Chapter Thirty-One

Joe is sitting at the desk and staring at the notes he made during the half-hour conversation he just had with Demelza. It should have only taken fifteen minutes (tick-tock goes the clock etc.) but Demelza being Demelza (the most thorough policewoman in Christendom) she offered rather more detail on the Pimpernel Club than Joe was expecting, mainly because she has a pal from police college who's climbing the greasy pole at Scotland Yard who owes her a few favours. It turns out that the officer's sister is dating a computer technician who works for a publishing house. That publishing house is finalising the manuscript for a famous journalist who's been doing deep research into Pinky. Said journalist has written a tell-all book called, *Blood on Her Hands*. The publishing house's network crashed due to a bug being imported from the journalist's own memory stick and they got the tech guy (the one the sister is dating) to fix the system and in doing so he just happened to accidentally copy the manuscript onto his own hard drive. The information Demelza has provided is, in truth, nothing more than the bits of gossip her Scotland Yard pal could remember, but Joe is more than aware that many a difficult case has been cracked via such nebulous connections. The Scotland Yard pal was going to phone the sister and ask for greater granularity.

Joe, having put a very tenuous two and two together, has made a very shaky four by concluding that *Blood on Her Hands* might just be a tidy little sideline of Sienna's. He's based this on nothing more than the fact that Sienna is the only journalist he can think of who has the motive and the means to deliver the dirt on Pinky – the motive being nothing more than good old-fashioned revenge for having had her documentary cancelled.

He has to hand it to her though – Demelza's ingenuity knows no bounds, and not for the first time Joe realises that on a professional front he really would be lost without her. An image of Donna sitting on the sofa last night flashes into his mind and his heart fills with pure joy and fulfilment. Then he remembers that he's got himself involved with Demelza – he imagines a flapping fish caught in a net struggling to breathe – and he's got as much chance of clearing himself from this particular romantic net as that imaginary fish has from escaping the ropey one. He sighs and looks over the notes again. Demelza was certainly thorough:

> *Nadine Pinkerton was born in 1971 in a crack den in Bristol. She was registered at birth as Sylvie. There is no record of who the father was, and the mother moved from place to place, living off benefits and charity. There was one suicide attempt by the mother in 1973, and then another in 1975, between that time she had a second child*

with another unknown father. The three of them eventually settled in Oxford and the mother seemed to pull herself together for a while, until Nadine found her at the bottom of the stairs one morning, dead. The children were separated afterwards for reasons unknown, and they were put into separate care homes. Nadine was adopted by a family in Chichester, and she grew up as the privileged daughter of a Home Counties family who were the type who could afford to send their daughter to the best schools and meet the best people. It was ironic, Demelza said, that Pinky's voting record had always been against the benefits system, bearing in mind that it was the very same system that had kept her alive in childhood. 'Some people are just twats,' was Demelza's summary of the deceased Home Secretary. Nadine then went on to have the career that everyone knew about, except that the honours degree from Oxford was kind of a lie – she got a third class degree, not a first class one (as published on her MP website), because she spent the whole time either shagging her tutors or debating first-world issues with first-world dickheads (that was according to one fellow student that the 'journalist' managed to nobble). She married once – an investment banker called Jeremy Pinkerton. They divorced and she has been linked with, but not tied down to, a smattering of different tycoons ever since. Pinky has expensive tastes in men. There was a call recently for an enquiry into her personal, business enterprises – called for by a Labour MP who had been tracing her lifestyle and suspected her involvement in a 'money for parliamentary favours' scam, or one of those dodgy 'party donor' type affairs. This request was buried beneath a lorry-load of red tape when the Official Secrets Act was enacted by her lawyer and 'national security issues' were discussed in the House, and so the whole thing went away.

Joe isn't sure where this additional information about Pinky leaves him – clueless most likely – except for one key point: Is Sienna the journalist who wrote *Blood on Her Hands*, the tell-all book about Pinky? He says as much to Donna and explains his tenuous theory when he allows her back into the study.

'But even if Sienna really *is* the one who's written it,' says Donna, 'as a revenge thing because of Pinky quashing her TV documentary, that wouldn't actually give us a motive for murder on Sienna's part. She'd be better off if Pinky was alive and kicking, surely. If anything, the motive would be the other way around.'

'Pinky would want to bop Sienna off, you mean?' says Joe.

'Seems likely,' says Donna.

Joe feels as though Demelza has sent him down a rabbit hole that is so long and so bizarre that he'll probably bump into the Mad Hatter at the end of it.

'You're right. We need to concentrate on the here and now,' he says. 'The facts are that either an outsider has somehow got in and out of the castle and is long gone – despite the storm – or, one of the party did it. And we need to keep working away at the suspects until we find definite motives – and for *both* deaths, presuming they're linked, which I'm beginning to doubt.'

Donna slumps into a chair. 'If only we could have one chilling murder at a time to deal with,' she says. 'And dead bodies that stay where they're supposed to and don't go wandering off. Our lives would be much easier.' She chews on a pencil that Joe left on the desk before sitting up and saying, 'The interesting thing is that Pinky seems to have been a woman who had her fingers pressed in lots of hot pies, pies that possibly burnt her. We know that she had a troubled – hellish, even – early childhood, and you know, Joe, people like that often have troubled lives later on – look at me.'

Joe does, and often, and in ways she really oughtn't to know about.

'I think you should text Demelza and get her to double-check that the journalist is Sienna,' says Donna. Joe picks up his phone, grateful to be told what to do.

Joe to Demelza: *Ask your contact to find out for certain who the journalist who wrote that book is. And see if you can find out if Pinky's sibling is a boy or a girl – a name would be even better.*

Demelza to Joe: *Will do. Is everything all right over there? Be careful with that Nightshade woman. They're a right bunch of lying, murdering, pilfering gobshites!*

Joe quickly puts his phone away.

'Well, I suppose we'd better have the final suspect in,' says Donna, handing the pencil to Joe, who glances at the chewed end and smiles.

'I suppose we had,' says Joe, thinking: final suspect? What about Jago, not to mention the infamous Auntie Donna? And he doesn't know much about Perkin, either, who could be an international hitman for all Joe knows.

Donna slaps her cargo-pant-covered thighs, which Joe reflects is a new but nevertheless great look on her, and heads to the door. Joe, needing to stretch his legs, follows on behind because it never hurts to throw quick, beady-eyed glances at a room of suspects.

'Where the hell is everyone?' asks Donna, having found just Lamorna and Jago sitting at the games table playing chess. Patch is asleep on Jago's knee and Ruby is gazing longingly out of the window.

'I'm afraid we couldn't corral them any longer,' says Lamorna without looking up, her hand hovering over a bishop. 'People needed to pee and so on. They've gone off to the dining room for lunch. Auntie Donna said she'd keep an eye on them…'

'Which is like asking a man wearing a stripy shirt and an eye mask to watch your things while you nip to the loo,' offers Jago while concentrating on the game. 'But what were we to do?'

'And after that they're going to do their own thing,' concludes Lamorna. 'To be honest, we all got a bit bored in here – there's only so many songs about death one can play on the harp, especially ones Uncle Jago can sing to. We ventured into sea shanty territory, and they all started to complain. And that's checkmate, I believe, Uncle. Ha!'

Donna turns to Joe and shrugs. Actually shrugs, thinks Joe, who's beginning to wonder if the Nightshades are either… taking this thing seriously enough, or, have any idea what pile of crap he's in once Penworthy pitches up, or, care that there's at least one murderer on the loose.

'I mean, it's only Dr Jane that you haven't interviewed so far,' says Lamorna, looking up while Jago studies the board. 'And I'm sure you'll catch up with her at some point – especially if someone else croaks it, because you'll need a doctor to identify the body. Have you noticed what a useful guest a doctor at a house party is, Donna? I reckon whenever we have dinner parties at Penberth we need to make it a rule that we always invite a doctor along, just in case. Do we know any doctors?'

'No, we don't. And in case what?' asks Donna.

Lamorna doesn't have the chance to answer because Jago makes a show of toppling his own king. He shakes Lamorna's hand then turns around. 'And how have you two been getting along?' he asks.

'He means in terms of the murder inquiry,' says Lamorna. 'Rather than asking for an update on how you're getting along after spending the night together, although I'm more interested in the latter, to be honest.'

Joe considers protesting his innocence on that front, but Lamorna doesn't grant him the time because she adds, 'Oh, and I think I know how Miles was murdered, by the way; although Auntie Donna possibly guessed first. I meant to tell you earlier, but I got so involved with keeping the prisoners amused I forgot. It's on a YouTube clip.'

'Miles's murder is on YouTube?!' exclaims Uncle Jago. 'My God! Whatever will they think of next.'

'What YouTube clip is this?' asks Joe, who is becoming so familiar with the Nightshades that he's adopted Donna's habit of stepping straight over most of Jago's comments.

'The one I found of a person being blown up in the bath – when I say person, it's a crash-test dummy. I found it on a kid's TV show.'

'How, when you haven't got a phone or an iPad?' asks Donna.

'I borrowed Auntie Donna's while she was in the study with you two – I think she must have borrowed it from a prison officer by the looks of the photos. I was thinking about how Miles could have been bumped off, so it seemed pretty obvious to just type, 'How to blow up someone in a bath' in the YouTube search, although I could have asked an AI site, too, of course, or Google. Auntie Donna has been using YouTube for cooking tutorials. She says there's absolutely nothing you can't find on there, so like I said, I typed in, 'How to blow someone up in a bath' and there it was – easy. If you're wondering where Auntie Donna is, by the way, she's either in the kitchen finishing preparing lunch or back at the cottage – she refuses to be pinned down as she gets enough of that in prison.'

Joe takes a very deep breath. Why does he always feel like he's on the back foot whenever the Nightshades are around?

Probably because he usually is.

Chapter Thirty-Two

DONNA

It turns out that there's an element called rubidium that explodes when it becomes wet. Who knew? Jago probably. And by 3pm, having discussed it from the thread to the needle – and watched a couple of YouTube videos on the subject on my phone – we reckon that the easiest way to blow someone up using rubidium is to create a bath bomb – like the scented ones that are the size of tennis balls that you buy in Lush. Lamorna was right – so easy. But how to get the thing into Miles's room was the question we kept coming back to. As a method for murder, it seems the opposite of fool proof.

'But that's it exactly – Miles *was* a fool, apparently,' says Lamorna. 'At least, Dr Jane thinks so. And the murderer probably just slipped it into Miles's gift bag – you know, the goodie bag of free gifts they all got on arrival. They were labelled so it would have been easy enough to target him.'

My sister really is a treasure.

We dispatch Lamorna and Jago (always travel in twos) to the dining room to interrupt lunch to ask the guests to nip to their rooms one by one and return with their goodie bags to the foyer. As the oldest and therefore most dispensable member of the family, Jago is tasked to go with them and inspect the bags to see if there were bath bombs in there, or if anyone had used one already.

On her return to the dining room Lamorna goes through the last half an hour of her life in great detail, before saying, 'Anyhow, Dr Jane said that it wasn't surprising that whoever it was that slotted Miles used something as … well, girly, as a bath bomb, because he was a man who respected his appearance. That's why his teeth were so white. His nose was a completely different shape compared to when they last saw him, too.'

'Well, it's certainly a different shape now!' scoffs Jago, who has just arrived. 'And to answer your question…' he turns to Joe, who is sitting in the chair Jago vacated at the chess table and looking a little vacant, but then he is under a lot of pressure from Penworthy, 'I can confirm – having placed myself in a great deal of danger – that although there is a different variety of Cornish consumables in all of the bags, the one thing that they all have in common is the same bath bomb, which has been placed in *all* of the goodie bags, and I'm feeling really rather uncomfortable with the fact that they're in the foyer; because if they're all laced with the stuff, that amount of rubidium could take the roof off, and Lady Helen won't be impressed because she's just had the ceiling repainted.'

'It's unlikely that someone was trying to kill the whole lot of them,' says Joe. 'I reckon the others are safe.'

'Except if some of the bath bombs are the glittery type,' I

say. 'Because that stuff is a nightmare to get off.' I laugh at my own joke.

'Ooh, but how thrilling would that be!?' says Lamorna, rushing to the window and throwing it open to let the storm in. 'A proper blood bath over the course of the weekend where absolutely everyone gets blown up!'

We all penetrate Lamorna with the stare of judgement.

'Well, it would,' she protests. 'It's not like they're lovely people. Auntie Donna says they're all complete idiots!'

My angelic sister is becoming far too influenced by Auntie Donna these days for my liking.

'There is one obvious way to find out,' I offer, having lassoed my sister with a double glance and dragged her back to the point. 'I mean … we could throw the remaining bath bombs in water and just, you know, see if they blow up?'

'Too dangerous,' says Joe.

'Lady Helen wouldn't like it,' says Jago.

'I'm on it!' shouts Lamorna, jumping up.

Half an hour later, while Jago takes Patch and Ruby back to the cottage, Joe – having insisted that if anyone was going to risk life and limb as an amateur explosives expert then it had better be him – returns from the battlements soaking wet with all limbs intact and confirms that his earlier theory that all the others were exactly what it said on the tin – 'fragranced salts for dissolving in warm bath water for the purpose of rest and relaxation' – was correct. He now smells just like a field of roses – and is that a bit of glitter on his nose?

There is one final thing that we need to do to confirm Lamorna's bath-bomb theory, however. We need to return to Miles's room to see if the bath bomb in the goodie bag has been used. If it has, then it's a firm possibility that bizarrely, Lamorna is right: Miles Johnson was blown up by a rubidium-infused relaxing bath bomb.

'Lamorna,' I say, interrupting a new game of chess she's playing by herself, 'do me a favour and find Auntie Donna to make sure that she's behaving herself. And after that, I want you to wait at the harbour cottage with Jago for further instructions.'

'And under no circumstances are you to go wandering around the castle by yourself,' adds Joe, using his firm voice. 'Because if the bath bomb in Miles's goodie bag has been used, then it points the finger towards someone here at the castle having done it.'

'But of course, they did, Joe,' says Lamorna. 'I think that that's rather a given, don't you?'

Chapter Thirty-Three

DONNA

'There's no bath bomb in here,' says Joe, tipping the contents of Miles's goodie bag onto his bed. It's a high-quality bag – hessian with a bamboo handle. Neither of us relished heading back up the stairs and stepping through the broken door into the anti-chamber of hell, but it had to be done.

I take a look at the contents of the bag: Cornish biscuits, Cornish fudge, Cornish cider, Cornish tea (grown in India, packaged in Falmouth), Cornish honey, Cornish soap and Cornish jam. Which leads us to the almost indisputable conclusion that Lamorna was right about the rubidium bath bomb.

'You've got to admit, it's pretty cool,' I say, picking up the Cornish fudge, opening the packet and popping a nice, tasty morsel into my mouth.

'What are you doing?' says Joe, who's walked to my side of the bed and is looking at me like I'm certifiably insane. I quickly swallow the fudge.

'It's not like he can enjoy it, is it?' I nod towards hell. 'All of his teeth are stuck on the bathroom ceiling!'

Joe's mouth opens and closes several times before he says, 'Firstly, that packet probably has traces of rubidium on it, which won't be healthy. And secondly…' he gesticulates towards the detritus of Cornish-ness lying on the bed, 'it's all evidence, Donna. And your prints will be all over the stuff now. Why did you think I tucked my hands into my jumper when I tipped it all onto the bed?'

While Joe waffles on and on about the best way to conduct a search, I notice a name tag with a raffia tie poking out from under the tin of biscuits (ginger stem). If I'm not mistaken the name written on the card is none other than 'Nadine Pinkerton-Smyth'. I hook the sleeve of my chunky knitted jumper over my hand and fish out the tag.

'Blimey!' I say. 'This should have been Pinky's bag. The bags must have been swapped somehow.'

Joe offers me a smile that tells me that my previous misdemeanour is forgiven and that I've done good.

'Which means presumably that Miles's goodie bag is in Pinky's room,' says Joe. He has a moment of head scratching until I see the copper's internal light bulb switch on. 'Yes! I remember now. Perkin handed the bag to her in the foyer when we arrived yesterday. She was completely dismissive about it; didn't say thank you and didn't even look at the tag.'

'You're not saying that Perkin...?'

'No … no. At least, I hope not.' Joe thinks for a moment. 'Pinky was the last to arrive and the bag Perkin gave to her was the only one left on the table. Perkin would have just presumed it was hers, perhaps.'

'Where is he, by the way?' I ask.

'Perkin? He's probably doing what any sensible person would do and keeping safely out of the way, except for going around keeping the fires going, unless there's a house elf, which wouldn't surprise me with this place, frankly.'

I tuck the remaining fudge into my pocket.

Joe glares at me.

'What? It can't be evidence if I've eaten it, can it?' I offer a friendly shoulder nudge his way.

Joe frowns, then smiles, then laughs. Then he grabs me gently on each arm, leans forward and kisses me on the cheek. 'You're an absolute tonic, Donna Nightshade,' he says, 'and I bloody well—'

His phone rings. 'My Heart Will Go On'.

'Demelza,' he says, answering his phone.

'And this contact … he's sure about this?' Joe looks me in the eye while listening for the answer, but I can't read his expression, which is annoying – and unusual. I used to be able to read Joe Enys like a book. I conclude that it must be some kind of Demelza effect.

'OK, well, keep working on it, Dem.' He throws me another half-arsed smile. 'And see what you can find out about the others on the list.'

'I suppose the sergeant of the year has cracked the case?' I say as we head down the corridor. (Demelza actually was Sergeant of the Year last year.)

'Not yet. But guess what? Sienna Blackville *is not* the journalist who wrote the book about Pinky's past … Miles was. He'd already sent it to a publisher, too, faking being a journalist. The blackmail was just bullshit to get extra cash. And you'll never guess what the juiciest bit of it all is…'

'That Pinky was a drag queen called Simon and was about to go on a tour of the North?'

'No. Better than that,' says Joe.

'Go on.'

'The mother – Pinky's mother – didn't commit suicide, at all. She was murdered. And guess what?'

'What?' (He's dragging this out a bit, but let's go with it.)

'It was the sibling who did it!'

'Crikey. And the sibling is?'

Joe frowns.

'That's the bit Demelza's mate couldn't find out, because Miles couldn't either. It's apparently buried so deeply within Home Office records that it's simply untraceable.'

We begin to walk down the corridor at a rush.

'We need to interview Sienna again,' says Joe.

'And Dr Jane,' I add as we run down a long corridor lined with yet more weapons and portraits of the St Clement family of days gone by. 'Because the sooner we get this wrapped up and get off this blood-soaked island and away from the bathroom of the living dead, the better.'

Chapter Thirty-Four

To Joe's surprise – and relief – the remaining guests have conveniently assembled themselves in the library for after-lunch coffee provided by Auntie Donna, who slunk out of the dining room when Joe arrived and seems to have taken on the sinister gait of Mrs Danvers in *Rebecca*. Joe ignores the melodrama of the senior Nightshade and has the distinct feeling, looking around at the ashen faces of the group, that they've decided to adopt the strategy of safety in numbers, either that or they really are in it together and are plotting their next move with the help of Auntie Donna. Joe doesn't want to even consider that option. Matt and Rupert are sitting opposite each other at the card table and Sienna is perched on the window seat, looking out at the forever-raging storm.

'Well?' begins Atticus, who is standing by the fire like an advert for *SAGA* magazine. 'Are we about to explode in our baths or are we all safe to go to Body Shop again?'

'None of your bath bombs blew up,' says Joe. 'Which

means that only Miles's bath bomb was … to coin a phrase, loaded.'

'Bloody ridiculous notion,' concludes Atticus.

'I don't think Miles would have thought there was anything ridiculous about the notion when he found himself splattered across the room,' spits out Jane, reading Joe's mind. 'So if you could stop the bluff and bullying act of the outraged brigadier, Atticus, we'd all be very grateful.'

Atticus skulks to a chair in the corner like a scolded dog.

'Now, what we'd like to know,' begins Donna, who is standing by the door, notepad in hand. 'Is whose idea it was to provide goodie bags for the weekend?'

Everyone offers a puzzled expression except for Rupert, who says, 'I can answer that. One of the shops in Marazion put them together. Lady Helen wanted to promote Cornish products, what with the Home Secretary coming to stay…' He trails off. Many pairs of shoes are looked at.

'I suppose the point you're getting at,' says Matt. 'Is that whoever swapped Miles's bath bomb for the rubidium-laced one, knew that there would be bath bombs in the bags in the first place. Which rules all of us out, clearly.'

'Not at all,' says Donna. 'The invitation said there would be a complementary goodie bag on arrival, so all the person had to do was bring several bath bombs with them and remember to lace only one.'

'Wait a minute…' says Rupert. 'I saw Miles looking inside all the goodie bags when we arrived. He put one back and took another one and winked at me when he did it. Which must mean that…'

'Miles got Pinky's bag, and Pinky ended up with Miles's

bag,' says Joe, remembering the label on the bag in Miles's room. He concludes with, 'Which means that Miles wasn't the target at all – Pinky was.'

'Except that I did that, too,' says Sienna quietly.

Joe has a sinking feeling that he knows exactly where this is going and that his nice little theory that Miles got caught in the crossfire and that he's only looking for one murderer who intended to kill just one person is an ever-fading mirage of false hope.

'I'm embarrassed to admit it now,' she says, 'but I did the same as Miles – I looked in the bags and chose the one with the goodies that I liked the most. I don't like rum-and-raisin fudge, you see, I like it plain, so I swapped my tag for Pinky's, left it on the table with the other bags, and picked it up after we'd all said hello.'

'Which means that the bomb would have possibly started off in Sienna's bag,' says Matt, stealing Joe's 'ta da' moment. 'And that inadvertently became Pinky's bag once the tag was changed, and then Miles stole Pinky's bag, so the bomb ended up with him. It's like that trick with the ball under the cups. Unlucky bugger!'

'It also means that the bomb was possibly meant for you, old thing,' says Rupert, looking at Sienna. He crosses to the window and places an arm around her shoulders. If she was ashen-faced before then she is nothing but a translucent shimmer now.

'Can you think of any reason why someone would want to kill you, Sienna?' asks Donna.

Sienna shrugs. 'None whatsoever.'

Donna glances up from her notebook to look at Joe.

'And you're certain about that, Ms Blackville?' asks Joe, who notices that most pairs of eyes in the room avert his gaze.

'Of course,' says Sienna, edging further into Rupert's embrace.

'It all seems rather too convenient,' says Atticus, finding his voice again.

'What does?' asks Jane, whose tone, Joe notices, suggests that she is finding Atticus to be a bit of a pompous arse. Either that or she's annoyed because lover boy Rupert has his arm around yet another woman.

'That the invitation mentioned the goodie bags,' offers Atticus. 'That kind of detail isn't usually put on the invitations.'

Everyone looks at Rupert.

'Now hold it right there!' says Rupert, reclaiming his arm and jumping up. 'Don't start putting this at my door. That wasn't my idea. I didn't even write out the invitations!'

'Then who did?' asks Donna.

Rupert glances around the room. 'Nadine. She said she'd get her assistant to send them out to save me a job.'

There's a pause because Joe's thought processes need to catch up. Donna doesn't miss a beat and quickly says, 'Miss Blackville. Would you mind stepping into the study please, only there are a few details that we'd like to clear up.' Donna nods towards the door in a kind of no-nonsense way that only an ex-con could get away with. With shoulders hunched, Sienna heads towards the door.

'I'll ask you again,' says Donna, who has parked herself very firmly in the interviewer's chair leaving Joe to perch on the window seat. 'Who on this island might want to see you dead?'

'The only person who might have any inclination of killing me,' says Sienna, 'is dead. Unless this is bigger than that.'

'You mean Nadine.'

'I do.'

'Why?'

'Because I know things about her that would not be a great look for the Home Secretary.'

'That her sibling killed her mother, you mean?' says Donna.

Joe can't help but think that Sienna's expression of utter shock is understandable. Personally, he would have gone in slower with the build-up himself. But this is Donna, and there's no pissing around with Donna Nightshade when her dander's up.

'How do you know all this?' asks Sienna, who looks like she's building up to take Donna on, toe-to-toe. Joe feels that he really ought to tell Sienna that the last person who did that found herself on the losing end of death, but he's happy to watch it play out for now.

Donna leans forwards. 'I might be Cornish, sweetheart, but my family is older than Agincourt and suitably well connected. We know people who know people who know people who know stuff – *comprenez-vous*?'

A trickle of a smile floats its way across Joe's lips, although he doubts that Demelza would be at all happy to be classed as 'people who know people'.

'Come on then,' presses Donna. 'How did you uncover Pinky's secrets?'

'It's nothing clandestine, if that's what you think. She told me. We all told far too many secrets to each other during our time on the roof in Basra. One night, when it was just me and Pinky, she told me everything, or almost everything. Miles came into the conversation halfway through. When I got wind of him also writing his Iraq memoirs, I suspected that he'd been hiding in the shadows and had heard everything. Without looking at his manuscript I have no clue what's in there. I'd have given anything to know, though, I'll tell you that.'

'Why?'

'Quite simple. I'm writing my own memoirs and I don't want Miles – even a dead Miles – to steal my thunder.'

'About the Home Secretary's matricidal sibling?'

'No! I'd never write about that.'

'I suppose that's why you were in his room,' says Joe. 'Why you lost the tip of your heel. You were looking for his manuscript.'

Sienna turns to Joe. 'Guilty as charged, M'lud. Listen, I want to get off this island ASAP. I thought Miles had murdered Pinky, then killed himself. Or perhaps they had somehow killed each other – that he'd killed her, but she had already put the bomb in his goodie bag, and then he'd jumped in the bath to wash her blood off.'

Joe considers this last statement thinking how plausible it is and wondering why on earth he hadn't thought of it himself – probably because he hasn't had time to scratch his arse since the bomb went off.

Sienna has more. 'When we talked about it amongst the group earlier, the only person who thought the rubidium theory was ridiculous was Atticus – make of that what you will.'

'Wait. Go back a bit,' says Donna. 'What do you mean, lithium thing?' She puts her sharpie behind her ear and flicks through the notes in her book – Joe knew she'd latch onto that. Donna glances up. 'When we asked you earlier what you knew about the lithium project, you said, and I quote, "I know nothing about Cornish lithium. I *do* know, however, that there is a global scarcity of lithium." And I wrote all of that down because I'm a landowner and my land is bound to be laced with the stuff.'

'Look, it wasn't a lie. I don't know anything about it per se,' says Sienna, entirely unfazed. 'Although I am aware that we've been considering investing heavily in that area. Atticus gave us a file to read. I haven't read mine yet, what with what's happened today.' She offers a sigh of superiority and boredom, which Joe knows will grip Donna's shit.

'And why would you think that Nadine and Miles would be at such loggerheads about it that they would kill each other?' asks Donna.

'Because Miles wasn't interested in future investments. He wanted a quicker and bigger return on his money. Investing in the lithium deal meant leaving all the money in the consortium for at least three years without a dividend – longer, I should imagine.'

'Why not just boot Miles out?' asks Joe.

'We wanted to, especially after last night's antics.'

Donna and Joe wait.

'I exposed Miles's plan for his book to the group ... and let's just say that they were less than pleased.'

'You exposed Miles while keeping your own book a secret?' says Donna.

Sienna shrugs. 'Think of me what you will,' she says. 'My own book only targets the legality of the Iraq War, and I don't mention the consortium, for obvious reasons. Nadine's life has been ... interesting, colourful ... deceptive. I brush on it, but it's nothing that would completely ruin her, not that she wouldn't – hasn't – quashed me in the past.'

'So we gather,' says Donna.

'And why would the consortium be angry at Miles for writing a book about their dealings?' asks Joe, who, while applauding Donna's arrow-sharp interviewing skills, needs to return to the earlier point before it's lost.

'Because initially we used information we shouldn't have to make deals we shouldn't have made with people in the middle east we shouldn't have been influencing.'

'And are you all complicit?' asks Joe. 'You *all* have something to lose if the book is published?'

'We do. The consortium was created in such a way that requires one hundred per cent agreement – we were all much closer and idealistic back in the day, when the contract was drawn up. There's a non-disclosure agreement too, which is why none of us will want to tell you anything about it, and why Miles shouldn't have been writing his book.'

'Except that you *are* telling us...' says Joe.

'Only to save my life.'

She takes a packet of cigarettes out of one side pocket on her designer combats and a lighter out of another. After lighting up and taking a very long, slow drag, she says, 'Take my advice, the two of you…' The cigarette hangs expertly from her fingertips, her head turns from Donna to Joe and back again. 'Do your level best to keep us alive for the next few hours until the causeway opens, but other than that, leave everything well alone. When the causeway is open and the storm's passed through, call in a clean-up team and get the hell out of Dodge. No offence, but this thing is much bigger than an ex-con, two-bit, flower farmer – yes, I've looked you up – and the local copper.'

'What do you mean, bigger?' asks Joe, who's taking over because Donna is still processing how to react to being called an ex-con, two-bit, flower farmer.

'Grow up, Joe. What do you think I mean? I'm talking espionage; I'm talking hitmen; I'm talking possible government plots here – do I have to spell it out? Pinky was the Home Secretary for Christ's sake, and someone clearly wanted her dead – and I'm not talking about the so-called deported South American she extradited. What if someone in the government wanted rid of her? The woman was a hand grenade who was winding a lot of people up. Have you seen her Twitter feed? It's dynamite.'

'Then why are you concerned about your own safety?' asks Donna, quite reasonably, thinks Joe.

'Because, with all the talk of the swapped labels, I can't be sure that the bath bomb was meant for me. I've made quite a few enemies over the years, reporting things that many people did not want reporting. Quite a few people – and I'm not talking about the syndicate – should be very concerned about what's written in my book, and if it's somehow been leaked from the publishers…'

The door opens.

'*Lord of the Flies,*' says Lamorna, who wanders in looking more windswept than ever.

'My thoughts exactly,' says Donna.

'I suppose it is a little,' says Sienna, who is looking decidedly less polished around the edges than a few hours ago.

Joe has never read *Lord of the Flies* because he was in a different class to Donna in English Literature and was forced to study *Dr Faustus* instead, but he can imagine the general gist.

'I guess we're coming to the conclusion,' says Donna, turning to Joe, 'that the bath bomb was meant for Sienna for reasons unconfirmed but might have something to do with her book and that Pinky may have been killed by Miles, who is now also accidentally dead because he nicked her goodie bag. Which means that one of the murderers that we're looking for – just in case there are two – is potentially not Miles's killer at all…'

'But someone that was trying to kill me…' says Sienna, following up with an appropriate gulp.

'So let me get this straight,' says Donna. 'The bomb began its journey by being put into your bag, either before you arrived or after.'

'Correct.'

'You swapped name tags shortly after you arrived with Pinky, who hadn't arrived yet, because you wanted her fudge.'

'Correct again.'

'Why not just swap the fudge?'

'Because she basically had a better lot of goodies all round – I don't like stem ginger biscuits.'

'OK. So now the bomb is in Pinky's bag, and Miles comes along while all the bags are still on the table and has a sneaky peak. He then fancies the goodies in Pinky's bag.'

'He would have been after the cider, I should think,' says Sienna.

'And then he runs a bath and gets blown up,' says Donna. 'The question being, did Miles kill Pinky not knowing that he was about to be blown up? It would have been tight, but possible.' Donna starts chewing on her sharpie having worn her way through the top of Joe's pencil already. 'If only we had more clues,' she says.

Joe makes a mental note to remind Donna to refer to clues as 'evidence' in order to sound more professional in front of the punters, but yes, he has to agree, they are distinctly lacking an amount of heft in the clue department.

'I might have something for you,' says Lamorna, brightly. 'The light is starting to fade so I took Patch out for a bit of a tinkle – Jago is knackered with all the walking up and down the castle steps so he's having a nap. Anyhow, Patch ran off towards the north rocks, so I called him back, and he came running back with this in his mouth.' Lamorna takes a medical syringe out of her coat pocket. 'It looks fairly new,' she says. 'Maybe it's a clue?'

'Hmm,' murmurs Sienna.

'Odd,' says Donna.

'The litter of a local drug addict,' surmises Joe.

'I suppose I'd better return to the fold,' says Sienna, standing. 'They will want a full rundown on what you've asked me. I suppose there is no way off the island until later?'

Joe looks at his watch. 'Not for three hours,' he says.

Sienna walks to the window and looks over Joe's shoulder towards the darkening skies.

'It'll be dark by then,' she says quietly, and not without a little lip wobble in Joe's direction, which he notices. He rests a reassuring hand on her arm.

'It'll be dark within the hour in fact,' says Donna sharply, throwing Joe a little side-eye. He removes his hand. 'If you don't mind...' Donna nods towards the door curtly, thereby reversing the process of how Sienna found herself in the study in the first place.

'I was hoping you would offer me protection,' says Sienna, her eyes fixed on Joe. 'You have your own accommodation at the harbour, don't you? Couldn't I stay there until the tide goes out?'

Joe doesn't need to look to sense Donna's jaw tightening.

'I can't guarantee you'd be any safer there,' says Joe. 'I honestly believe that if you all stick together then you have safety in numbers.'

'We could ask Perkin?' offers Lamorna. 'If we can find him. I could ask him to let you stay in his quarters with him. Or you could hang around with Jago at our cottage. You could trot down there with me now.'

Sienna looks at Donna for her say so.

'If you would just wait in the library, Miss Blackville,' says Donna. 'We'll discuss what's best and let you know.'

'Just one last thing...' says Joe as Sienna goes to open the door. 'You're the first of the group to not advise me to go easy on Dr MacAvoy. All of the others seem to believe that she's much more vulnerable than we realise, and that Nadine's death will be harder for her than she lets on. Why is that do you think?'

Sienna does not rush to reply. Glances are exchanged while she has a think.

'Old sins cast long shadows,' she says. 'But other than that, I'm sorry, and I can't say any more.'

The door opens. The door closes. Donna groans.

'Some people get a thrill out of being melodramatic,' she says. 'I bet she knows bugger all about Dr Jane and she's just trying to be mysterious.' Donna turns to Lamorna. 'And you're not going anywhere with that one on your own.'

'You aren't going to let her stay at our cottage, then?' asks Lamorna.

'She can if she wants to,' says Donna, surprising Joe. 'Because I've got the best guard dog in Britain watching over the place.'

'Patch?' exclaim Joe and Lamorna in harmony.

'Don't be daft. I mean our wonderful auntie. Sienna won't have a clue what's hit her if she steps even one little toe out of line with Auntie Donna, not to mention what could happen if she annoys Ruby when her dander's up.'

'But that's like sending her out of the frying pan and into the fire,' says Joe.

Donna smiles. 'She shouldn't have called me an "ex-con, two-bit, flower farmer" then, should she!'

Chapter Thirty-Five

While Donna heads off into the wild outdoors towards the harbour with Lamorna and Sienna in tow, Joe decides to interview Dr MacAvoy. Donna is going to be mad as all hell that he's done it without her, but as the saying goes, time and tide waits for no man, and never was there a truer word than on this occasion, thinks Joe.

'Sorry it's taken a while to speak to you privately,' he says, gesturing that she take a seat opposite him at the now very familiar desk. 'It's been…

He was going to say, 'One of those days,' and throw in an eye roll, but bearing in mind this woman has seen the dead bodies of two of her friends and the other guests have all said that Joe should go gently on her, he goes for, 'a difficult day,' remembering to follow up with, 'How are you?'

Jane allows herself a half smile. 'I'm fine,' she says, before returning her face to a blankness Joe hasn't seen since he interviewed Auntie Donna the first time he arrested her for the attempted murder of her husband.

'How are the others bearing up?' he asks.

'Honestly?'

'Of course.'

'Well, Sienna believes we're all out to murder her since the bath-bomb revelation. Atticus is in a mood – I think he was a little bit in love with Pinky, so he's bound to be feeling grim. Matt has some odd stuff going down and keeps disappearing off, so he's either got a stomach bug or something to hide, I would assume the latter because he would have asked me for Imodium. And, Rupert … is being Rupert.'

'Which is?'

'Changeable. Although he seems more relaxed now that Miles is dead.'

'With you or with everyone?'

'Why just with me?'

'Because he might be nervous about the affair getting out.'

'What affair?' she says, leading Joe to wonder why people can't just sit in front of a policeman and be honest.

'The love affair he's having with you. We know that Miles had tried to blackmail him with a photo he took yesterday – the two of you were in an embrace. Didn't Rupert tell you?'

Jane glances away, processing this. 'So that's why he's been off,' she murmurs. 'Where was the photo taken?'

'On the beach at Marazion.'

'We weren't exactly discreet,' she says.

'You don't seem cross about having been seen.'

'I'm not. I have nothing to lose.'

'But Rupert has,' says Joe.

'That's not what he said when he propositioned me.'

Joe notices the trace of a smile cross her lips and a very slight eyebrow raise. So much for her so-called fragility.

'It's over, anyhow.' Jane straightens herself in her seat and sighs. 'Time to move on.'

The conversation has been too quick and has left Joe a little dislodged from his train of thought. He expected Jane to be furious at being found out – at having her private life questioned, but she hasn't given a stuff. And where has that line of questioning got him? Nowhere. Unless she's bluffing about not knowing that Miles had tried to blackmail Rupert and so took her revenge on Miles for Rupert's sake … but hasn't he come to the conclusion that Miles wasn't the intended victim and that Sienna was the real target?

Maybe Sienna was right. Maybe this should be left to Scotland Yard and a clean-up team, and he should get himself and the Nightshades off the Mount as soon as possible. But then … what *about* the Nightshades? Where do they stand in all this? Can he really, hand on heart, say that he can trust anyone that he's holed up with at the Mount?

Yes, he can: Donna. He can trust Donna. And he's ninety-nine-point-nine per cent sure of that.

'Will there be anything else?' asks Jane.

Will there? Joe's brain is addled. He remembers something Donna said.

'My colleague said that Pinky dropped to the floor clutching her chest, this was followed by oozing blood, which would imply that she'd been shot. But at such a short range, most guns would have caused – forgive me for being blunt – a mess to come out of her back when the bullet travelled through her. What are your thoughts on that?'

'Why do you think she was shot from close range?'

'Because it's likely that the murderer was hidden in a dark section of the room. The Garrison Room is an unilluminable room – it's a conjuring trick. And if not from there, with Donna standing at the door, then how could she have been shot?'

'From the window, clearly,' says Jane, as if she's talking to a particularly dim school child who has spent half of the year bunking off. 'It was open. The unilluminable room thing seems utterly farfetched.'

'Farfetched,' repeats Joe. 'Surely you want to know more detail before you pass it off as unlikely?'

'Not really,' says Jane. 'The older chap – the one who wouldn't stop singing sea shanties – spent a whole twenty minutes or so boring us to death about it.'

'So you think it much more likely that someone abseiled to the window, shot her, remained hanging off the rope (in a storm), waited for Donna to dash upstairs – to get you – wait for the two of you to leave, remove the body, and then – if it was one of your group – get back into the house, leave no wet footsteps, and manage to be as calm as a cucumber when you were all rounded up.'

'You'd be amazed at what humans are physically and mentally capable of,' she says. 'Trust me. I've seen soldiers carry out seemingly impossible tasks and then rip open their ration pack like they're back in their hometown and tucking into a MacDonald's without a care in the world. And anyway, what makes you think that he or she was working alone?'

'How heavy was Nadine?' asks Joe.

'Not heavy at all. Nine stone, roughly?'

'Which means that anyone could have pulled her through the corridors and thrown her into the sea … even a woman?'

'I suppose so,' confirms Jane. 'Although they would only have had to manoeuvre her onto the trolley. Anyone could have pulled her through those corridors after that.'

'Trolley?' says Joe. 'What trolley?'

'There was a trolley – one of those low metal ones. It was parked in the hallway outside the Garrison Room when I went down to see Nadine. Didn't your colleague tell you?'

'She can't have noticed it,' says Joe, defensively.

'Not much of a detective, is she?'

No, she probably isn't. But Joe's not going to admit that to this cold fish. 'A woman had just been shot in front of her,' he says. 'Can you imagine how that felt?'

'I don't have to imagine, officer.'

Touché.

'Do you want to know what I think?' says Jane.

'Go on.'

'I think that one of two things happened: One – Miles killed Pinky in the Garrison Room and Pinky killed Miles with the prearranged bath bomb.'

'Sienna said that too,' says Joe.

'Or, two, your pal, Donna, did it. Also, I think you've all got yourselves caught up in a mess with the Sienna bath-bomb thing – who's to say she's telling the truth and hasn't got her own agenda going down. I mean, Pinky *did* get Sienna's BBC Iraq documentary cancelled, and she was a sure bet to get a BAFTA for it too. Sienna has *always* wanted a BAFTA.'

It's all coming out now, thinks Joe.

'But her documentary was benign – compared to what could have been in Miles's book.'

'Benign?' repeats Joe. 'By your own admission it was impactful enough to have been a BAFTA contender, which means that it was most likely incendiary, don't you think?'

Jane shrugs and this little action is finally the little detail that makes Joe flip – not a big somersault flip, more of a flick flack.

'Dr MacAvoy, for once will someone – you, preferably – just tell me what the hell was in that documentary that caused Nadine to close it down?'

'No,' is her basic answer. But then, as a gift from the heavens above, Joe's phone pings and it's a text from Demelza.

Demelza to Joe: *Guess what. Miles wrote in the book that Atticus stole secrets from the Iraqi oilmen during the Hearts and Minds operation in 2003. That's why they set up the consortium. More to follow.*

'That was my sergeant who's been in touch with the BBC,' says Joe. It's a lie but needs must. 'We know that Atticus used Iraqi contracts to steal secret information, and I'm about to find out a whole lot more. So do you think, perhaps, that it's time to just start talking?'

Jane chews on this for a moment before saying, 'OK, but there's not as much to tell as you think. We made a few quid, so what? The mistake was allowing Miles in, of course. But he was always hanging around us, smoking his Marlboro Lights on the roof into the early hours of the morning. I never trusted him.'

'Atticus in particular would be worried about any word getting out about the consortium in its early days wouldn't he?' asks Joe.

'I would say that's pretty much a certainty. Sienna can take the moral high ground with the consortium because she pulled out of any dealings we had with the oil industry. She's only invested in certain other investments these days.'

'Why?'

'Because it wouldn't do for a woman who is always preaching to the rest of the world about the morality of Western society to be found out to be bent herself – it's her thing, preaching on TV, so she has to be seen to be whiter than white, even if it is a sham. Fair enough. We're all arseholes deep down anyhow – like your pal Donna, who would be suspect number one if you weren't taken in by her.'

'That's not the case,' says Joe.

'Really, then tell me why you're looking for clandestine explanations of hidden corners in a room or abseiling psychopaths when you have an ex-con with a reputation for knife crime who was standing in the room at the very moment Nadine was shot.'

Joe wants to say, 'That simply didn't happen,' because he's as sure as he's ever been in his life that Donna is innocent, but he needs to look like a neutral copper who's not blinkered in any way by a gorgeous brunette and is, therefore, investigating all lines of inquiry. So he says, 'Hmm,' and leaves it there.

'Look,' continues Jane, 'in my experience, and probably in yours if you take a moment to think about it clearly – which you haven't done all day, by the way – the obvious answer to all this is the one to go with i.e. – that the Nightshade woman did it. You won't though.'

This interview has been turned on its head to such an extent that Joe might as well hand in his warrant card.

'Why?' he asks.

'Because love is blind and you're clearly smitten with her – the pirate-looking, dark-haired one. So do yourself – and all of us – a favour and present the idea to your boss – who will surely want this wrapping up immediately – that they killed each other and then we can all walk away.' She sits back in her chair and sighs. 'Are we done here?'

Joe tries to think. 'Not quite,' he says. 'If someone wanted to get hold of rubidium, how would they do that?'

'I'm a doctor, not a chemist. I have absolutely no idea.'

'In that case,' says Joe. 'We're done.'

Jane pauses at the door. 'Listen. Do yourself a favour and ask Donna what she did with the gun.'

Joe's had enough of this. 'You saw her with a gun?' he says, fatigue melting off every word.

'No. But there was just something about her when she came to find me after Nadine had been shot. It was like she was play-acting… I can't put my finger on it, but I know Nadine brought a gun with her and I've looked in her room and it isn't there. If I'm right, Donna will react accordingly. If I'm wrong, you'll know. Consider it a basic tip from a medic who's seen a lot of utter crap go down over the years – and I won't even charge you for the consultation.'

With that, she leaves.

Balls to you thinks Joe.

But she might have a point about that gun…

Chapter Thirty-Six

DONNA

On our way down the hill, Sienna, Lamorna and I cross paths with Auntie Donna who's battling her way up the hill towards the castle wearing Kerensa's lollipop-lady sou'wester hat.

'Off to prep for an early dinner for the guests,' she shouts, rain dripping off the hat, the ends of her long, strawberry-blonde curls soaked through with rain. 'Thought I'd get them fed before the hoards arrive! Oh, and Jago has gone to find Perkin – for an early snifter, he said.'

'Right-oh!' I shout back, but she's ten steps further up the Mount by the time my voice reaches her through the wind. 'And don't forget to feed Joe, too!'

She turns to face me, forcing herself to remain upright by leaning into the wind and makes the gesture of cupping an ear.

'I said … don't forget to take Joe Enys some food. He's in the study. And save some food for Jago and Perkin and feed them too!'

It's no good. Auntie Donna hasn't a clue what I'm saying

and has thrown up her hands and carried on along her way – either that or she heard perfectly well and has no intention of feeding the resident policeman.

Sienna and Lamorna, with the wind behind them, are several paces ahead of me by the time I carry on down the hill alone. I'm not sure how I feel about Sienna Blackville – uncertain, I suppose. But then I feel uncertain about all of them – the Pimpernel Club. It's like they're almost complete strangers to each other, but that's the thing with reunions, which I find to be odd affairs at the best of times and tend to steer away from them; they're well-intended and generally good in principle, but awkward in execution and usually organised by a woman who's lost a lot of weight and wants to wear a revenge dress in front of the guy who dumped her. Fair enough. Not that we have too many reunions in this part of Cornwall; we're born here, we stay here, we love each other, we fall out, we make up, we know each other well, and occasionally, but more in days of old, we wreck and pillage the shit out of each other, but only when absolutely necessary. But this lot … there's no heart to them, no soul to the club, and that's a shame. Maybe when you've seen the things that these people have seen – the real stuff that happens in wartime that the rest of us only catch glimpses of on the telly – then perhaps it leads to one being a little more guarded. Truth is, I don't think we've got a real glimpse of genuine military camaraderie here, not one bit. I think that perhaps what unified them in Iraq was the fact that as individuals they didn't fit in there – their respective roles and personalities separated them from the rest, and that's why they formed the bond. I hurry my footsteps because there is a seed of a theory festering deep within my subconscious, except, for my theory to be correct, there are a couple of key links that simply don't add up.

Enough of my windswept perusals because having arrived at the bottom of the steps and fought my way across an open lawned area, I'm now making a direct line to the harbour cottages through a snicket that cuts through a group of stone outbuildings. During the tourist season these buildings house a café, a shop and an ice-cream kiosk. Today all the buildings are battened up, and the island seems to have cloaked itself in a sense of its own impending doom in a way that leads me to feel as though I'm surrounded by the ghosts of the island's colourful past, a thought which makes me feel better, actually. Because if there is such a thing as ghosts – which there isn't, but just in case – I'm pretty sure that this lot will be rooting for me, if only because I'm one of their own and not a blow-in.

Looking down towards the familiar row of harbourside cottages I see that to my right, in a courtyard beyond a low wall, there is something I never knew existed at the Mount – a tramway track. After vaulting over the wall to take a closer look, I see that the track leads under a low tunnel towards the castle. On the track, resting against the stoppers, there is a tram that looks like a coal cart of olden times, something used in a gold mine in the American west. This one is covered and takes on the look of a large, treasure chest, eight-feet long by four-foot high. There is a sign attached to the side of the cart that says, 'Dreckly Express'. Looking around the yard further I come to the conclusion that this whole set up must be an electrically powered subterranean delivery service. I also see a Tesco carrier bag hanging off the cart and, on looking inside, find an empty sandwich box and a half bottle of champagne that's been polished off – Moët, no less. Those St Clements certainly know how to have a picnic!

Does Joe know that this exists? Does Jago? Surely Jago knows. He knows everything.

One of those missing links may have just slotted into place.

I clamber out of the yard, look across at the backs of the harbour cottages and see a light come on in the kitchen of my own cottage. Sienna is taking a seat at the table. Lamorna appears with Ruby on her shoulder and is filling the kettle at the sink. There's another light on, too, in the back bedroom in Joe's cottage which is the bedroom I slept in last night. The curtains are drawn but I remember opening them this morning, and I definitely didn't leave the light on. A shadow crosses the window…

Lamorna and Sienna are in the cottage next door; Joe is interviewing Dr Jane in the study – and the other guests were all in the dining room when I left. Auntie Donna has just gone up to the castle, and Jago is apparently with Perkin in Perkin's quarters.

So, I ask the question… Who is in Joe's cottage?

No idea.

Now, there are times in life when a woman has to make a decision – to be or not to be dicked about by a hidden murderer / samurai ghost?

Not to be.

As I put a hand on the handle of Joe's back door, which leads straight into the kitchen, I glance skyward through the raging wind and rain and send up a prayer to all the past Belladonna Nightshades; and in a whisper, because I don't want the ghost to hear me, I say, 'Auntie Donnas of days gone by, please, please can you watch over me for the next ten minutes or so, because I'm about to do something really, *really* stupid…'

A reply echoes back to me down the ages and is whispered in the wind, 'Crack on, me hearty!' it says. 'And put the swine in your book! PS A cutlass would be handy right now…'

They're right, but that's Lamorna's domain. I'm more of a bare-knuckle kind of a gal.

The handle turns and I step inside.

A low, stormy twilight gives the kitchen a sinister glow and filters through to the hallway sufficiently to light my way to the bottom of the stairs.

'There is no such thing as ghosts,' I murmur, working my way up the staircase. 'There is no such thing as ghosts…'

I place my hand on Joe's bedroom-door handle while a cartoon heart beats out of my chest at a thousand beats a minute. The door swings open and I take in the room from the safety of the landing. It's economically furnished, with whitewashed walls and storm-grey woodwork; the double bed is opposite the door and the eiderdown cover is ruffled. The bed was made this morning, so either Goldilocks has been here or someone else, someone with a physical rather than spiritual form. A 1930s-style wardrobe and a set of drawers complete the furnishings. If there is someone hiding in this room, they are either behind the door, under the bed, or in the wardrobe.

I push the door open further until it hits the wall. No one there. I consider the fact that no one knows where I am and that, if there is someone hiding here, it's quite possibly the murderer. Taking a very deep breath I also consider that the would-be murderer is hiding from me, and so I, therefore, am the predator. We often find fear where none exists. All one has to do is to take on the bloody-mindedness of the Nightshades and have belief in the absolute invincibility of the self and everything will generally be OK; at least, that's what I'm telling myself as I drop down and peer under the bed.

Nothing doing.

The wardrobe it is then.

I open the door a crack and a whiff of something familiar wafts towards me; namely Marc Jacobs, *Eau So Fresh,* which I can't afford to buy but it's my favourite perfume and Lamorna and I always have a cheeky spray of it on the rare occasion we venture up country to Truro.

Another deep breath.

The door opens wider, and a voice cries out from the hallway behind me – 'Don't open that door!' it cries.

I turn around. It's Sienna.

Right. I'm opening the door.

Chapter Thirty-Seven

The interview with Jane has left Joe feeling odd. Odd and sad. Sad for the woman herself, so washed through with the sight of bloodshed over the years that she seems to have become devoid of any true emotion, and sad for the rest of the group. They all seem so … robotic and the opposite of the Nightshades, except for Pinky and Miles, who at least had wild personalities. He's done a quick google of the premise of *Lord of the Flies* and Lamorna is quite right: this lot would definitely start eating each other if the chips were down.

Joe takes a deep breath and crosses to the study window. He kneels on the seat and presses his forehead against the cold frame. Looking out from his position of height through the sea spray and murk he can just about make out the small village of Perranuthnoe in the low light across the bay. The Cabin Café above the beach will be closed today, what with the storm, although it always surprises Joe just how much craptastic weather tourists are prepared to battle through in order to make the most of their Cornish experience. He looks at his watch. Two hours until the causeway opens, at which point he will have no choice but to call this in. Penworthy will want answers, but the question is, does he have any?

He takes out his notebook and flicks through the interviews, documented in bullet points and his own brand of hieroglyphics – mainly emoji faces, in this case. Flicking through the pages of each member of the group is like flicking through an animated flicker book, except the picture doesn't change; it's one sad face after another.

His phone pings not once, but twice. The first is from Penworthy, the second from Demelza.

Penworthy: *What news from the bloodbath?*

Joe: *No new deaths yet. Lines of enquiry are leading to certain conclusions. More anon.*

Penworthy: *Yet? If one more person dies on the island, then you'll be the next and by my own bare hands. My Botox bill is going through the roof btw.*

Joe scratches his head and thinks of Penworthy's furrowed brow creasing itself into oblivion when she sees him later. No amount of filler is going to sort that kind of deep crease out if Joe can't come to some kind of conclusion and quickly. He moves on to Demelza's text:

Demelza: *My pal at Scotland Yard has a pal in MI6 who has a pal at Somerset House… Pinky's sibling was registered as Samantha at birth. The same mates are trying to find out what she's called now. Don't worry; they know it's hush-hush. I had a good look through her engagements over the past few months and guess what? Nadine went on a trip to Bodmin Prison six months ago. I phoned the prison to see how the visit went and it turns out not well. There was an altercation between Nadine and … can you guess? One very irate Belladonna Nightshade (senior). Also, (another guess what?) Perkin was a butler at Number 10 (as in Downing Street) for several years until he came to the Mount three years ago. He MUST have met Nadine Pinkerton before… Interesting, eh?*

Joe looks up to the heavens and lets out a silent scream.

Chapter Thirty-Eight

DONNA

It turns out that the samurai warrior is a woman called Claire. She's nineteen and is the love child of Matt and Pinky, who had a quickie on Pinky's last day in Iraq (broom-cupboard antics by the sounds of things). As is usually the way with quickies, Pinky fell pregnant. Having decided to leave Matt in the dark regarding the matter, she took a post-war sabbatical from the Civil Service and carried the pregnancy to term, taking cover at a friend's manor in the Cotswolds (in days of old it would have been called 'entering into confinement'). Nine months later Nadine offered the child up for adoption and after a quick wash down and some intensive Pilates workouts, Pinky went back to work and presumably forgot about the whole thing.

Until last year, when Claire sent her DNA away to be analysed by an ancestry website only to find that a man called Matt Lewis had done the same thing, wanting to prove that he had Irish ancestry in order to secure an Irish passport, which could come in very handy post-Brexit. The website informed

Claire and Matt that they were father and daughter, which was a shock to both of them. Claire subsequently met up with Matt and asked to be told who her mother was. Matt, having worked out the dates and feeling more than a little aggrieved with Pinky (he had always wanted children, but his ex-wife was steadfastly against it) didn't hesitate in informing Claire that her mother was none other than the present Home Secretary. Pinky confirmed that she wanted nothing to do with the child and no, she wouldn't meet up for brunch. Claire quoted Pinky as saying, 'Today's news is simply tomorrow's fish-and-chip papers. I've ridden out worse shit storms than this hiccup,' which was understandably upsetting for Claire. As an aside, albeit a judgemental one, the fact that Claire exists at all leaves me wondering if I've judged Pinky harshly, because I can't help but see her as having been someone who would terminate a pregnancy for the sake of her career. It's presumptuous and judgemental of me, but there you are. More questions need to be asked on the matter I fear, if subtly.

Desperate to persuade Pinky to engage with her daughter, Matt decided to take advantage of the reunion weekend where Pinky would, for part of the time, be trapped on a tidal island. It seemed to be the ideal opportunity to force Pinky to enter into talks with her daughter. There was to be a big reveal at dinner this evening. Claire was initially holed up in the castle with Sienna, who was in on it, but when she got cold feet on the issue of stowing Claire in her room, Matt paid off 'that butler bloke' to let Claire stay in the family's quarters (had he, now?). Having gone walkabout last night, Claire frightened herself to death because of the basic fact that the castle is spooky as all hell, put on the samurai cloak to keep warm, and this morning had run down to the harbour looking for shelter. With all the Nightshades holed up at the castle, just like our very own Goldilocks, Claire had tried the handle on each of the cottage doors until she found one that was unlocked and it was Joe's (that would be my cock-up). She had then messaged Matt to say where she was, and he had said that there was possibly a change of plan, but he'd let her know.

On asking Claire why on earth Sienna was in on the caper, too, Claire said something about Sienna being keen to help formulate a positive outcome because, being someone who desperately wanted to keep hold of her own daughter, she didn't want Pinky to throw away her own, which I can understand.

Matt had subsequently told Sienna that Claire had decamped to the 'copper's cottage' as it was referred to, which was partly the reason she had asked to come to the harbour so that she could tell her to get herself off the island sharpish rather than become embroiled in a murder case.

'But why didn't Matt come down and tell me himself?' asks Claire, tears edging to almost overflow levels on her lower lashes.

'I should imagine it's because we're keeping the guests under surveillance in the castle for their own protection,' I explain.

Sienna laughs out loud. 'No, it isn't. It's because all men are basically shits who only think of themselves!'

(Sienna's response is somewhat telling.)

'I just can't believe it,' says Claire, her voice a broken whisper. 'Nadine Pinkerton – my mother – is dead!'

Sienna reaches across the table to take her hand while Ruby, not helping, starts squawking, 'Dead, dead,' from her viewing platform on Lamorna's dungaree strap. Lamorna is surprisingly quiet, but then she is staring at Claire like Claire is a goddess descended down from heaven above, so that explains that.

'Where did it happen?' asks Claire, quickly adding, '*How* did it happen?'

Lamorna jumps straight into an explanation, and I hope to God she tones it down a bit.

Explanation complete, Claire says, 'In the Garrison Room? The room with all the weapons and that samurai guy that I stole the coat from?'

'That's the one,' says Lamorna.

'How awful. Is Matt upset?' Claire glances around for an answer. When we all don't respond she says, 'About Pinky, I mean?'

'Ah, very,' I say. 'But possibly only because he can't do his big reveal tonight.'

Those lashes are looking awfully full.

'And … er, do you know if Nadine had any other family?' asks Claire.

Without thinking I say, 'Well, we know that she was put into care when her own mother died, and we also know that she had a sibling.'

'Do you know who the sibling is?' asks Claire, edging her chair away a little from Lamorna.

(The kind side of my heart says that she's hoping for a family; the cynical side wonders if she's considering any possible inheritance that she might be entitled to.)

'I'm afraid not,' says Sienna, reaching down to stroke Patch.

'In that case,' says Claire, visibly pulling herself together 'When the causeway opens, and the storm settles down, I'll get out of here. I'm already in touch with Matt and there's nothing else for me to hang around here for—'

My phone pings. It's a message from Joe. Something about Pinky visiting Bodmin Prison six months ago and having an altercation with Auntie Donna. I hit reply:

Me: *I know about that already. They argued about Pinky's voting record. TBF Auntie has had altercations with every MP that's ever visited the prison. Means nothing.*

Joe: *OK.*

Me: *I'll be up in a minute. I've found our ghost.*

Joe: *I've interviewed Jane – interesting.*

Me: *You interviewed Jane … without me?!*

Joe: *You found a ghost … without me? I needed to crack on. Tick-tock. By the way, Jane said there was a trolley in the corridor outside the Garrison Room when Pinky was shot but it's gone now. Did you see it?*

Me: *No. But my mind was elsewhere.*

I put my phone away and turn to Claire.

'I'm afraid that as there is a murder inquiry going on, like it or not, you'll have to stay because you were on the Mount when it happened.'

Her mouth opens. She looks at Sienna. Sienna looks at me pleadingly but nothing doing.

I grab my coat. 'Come on, ghost girl,' I say. 'There's someone I want you to meet.'

Claire grabs my hand. 'But … please, I'm begging you! Don't make me go up to that castle again…'

'Why?' we all ask, even Ruby.

Claire makes a song and dance about answering before eventually saying, 'Because I bumped into this barking mad woman this morning – in the family's quarters, near to the Garrison Room. I've never seen anyone with such wild eyes! She told me that if I told anyone that I'd seen her there – anyone at all – that she'd feed me to the dolphins … limb by limb.'

I look at Lamorna.

Lamorna looks at me.

Ruby says, 'Uh-oh.'

'What did she look like, this woman?' asks Lamorna.

Claire takes a moment to think before saying, 'A bit crazy, you know? Long, curly red hair. Good body.' She scratches her head. 'Mid-fifties, maybe? She was dressed like a hippy and carrying a lollipop-lady type coat…'

That, as Joe would say, is all I need. Time to search Auntie Donna's room.

Chapter Thirty-Nine

Not for the first time in his career Joe Enys finds himself sitting alone and wondering if he's got himself tangled in yet another web within a web that the Nightshades have spun. Do they have their own private reason for popping off the Home Secretary, he wonders? Have they been paid to do it? Donna would sell a kidney to keep Penberth in the family, so she might not say no to a few easy quid for carrying out the perfect murder. He knows Donna's politics, too; not that she's politically active, but her very ethos is the exact opposite of Pinky's.

And then there was Penworthy's initial summation... Penworthy, after all, has a knack of getting straight to the heart of the murderer from the off and she had thought it obvious that Donna Nightshade had done it. But then, she always thought that Donna Nightshade had done whatever it was that was occurring in Penzance at the time. And yet ... Donna *was* alone in the Garrison Room with Pinky one minute and then the next ... Pinky was dead. And was it a coincidence that Jago just happened to know about the part of the room that was unilluminable or was it always planned that way?

Joe shakes his head.

'I will not suspect, Donna Nightshade,' he says aloud. And again: 'I will not suspect Donna Nightshade.'

Having said that, he might have to interview her ... but he'd make it look like she wasn't being interviewed somehow, more like a friendly discussion between colleagues.

His phone rings. It's Demelza and she's very excited.

The gist of the conversation is that an elderly lady who was on the National Express bus with Miles Johnson yesterday sent her grandson into the police station with a memory stick. 'In this weather!' exclaims Demelza. He left it on the seat when he got up but when she shouted after him, he didn't turn around.

'It has some kind of manuscript for a book on it,' she says. 'Thought it might be the so-called, tell-all book.'

Joe nearly falls off his chair. He tells Demelza to skim-read any chapters about Iraq and to get straight back to him if she reads anything juicy or odd concerning the Home Secretary.

'But how will I know what's juicy or odd?'

'Trust me. You'll know,' says Joe, hanging up.

With the distinct feeling that he might be getting somewhere, although he's not exactly sure where that somewhere is, Joe takes himself to the kitchen to put the kettle on. Auntie Donna is standing over the Aga and stirring the contents of a steaming pot like she's a Shakespearean witch brewing up a storm. (A Shakespearean witch who wore a chef's hat and a pinny with the body of Superwoman on the front).

Jago is sitting at the table. He has a pen in his hand and a book of crosswords in front of him. His chin is resting on his hand. So much for finishing his book, thinks Joe.

'I'm supposed to be with Perkin so I'm not really here,' says Jago, without looking up.

Never a truer word, thinks Joe.

'Solved it yet?' asks Auntie Donna. Is that a smile, Joe wonders? And for him?

'Getting there,' says Joe, returning the smile.

'Of course you are,' she titters and turns back to the stew. 'You know where the kettle is, if that's what you're after.'

Joe is, but he doesn't have time to fill it because the kitchen door opens with a bang, announcing the arrival of a very wet Donna (the younger) who seems to have brought a friend to the party: an equally wet young woman wearing a samurai coat, who, if Joe isn't mistaken, recoils when she claps eyes on Auntie Donna.

'Hi, Joe,' says Donna, brightly. 'Let me introduce you to Claire. Our ghost.' She grabs a tea towel and wipes the rain from her face.

Auntie Donna, having let out an expletive that causes even Joe to blush, lifts the pot from the Aga and places it on a marble worktop. 'That's lunch made,' she says. 'And there's bread in the oven. So, if you don't mind, the causeway will be open soon and it's time that I headed off back to the old homestead…'

Donna closes the door and stands against it, shaking slightly. Joe wonders if she's caught a chill until she says, her voice quivering slightly, 'I'm sorry, Auntie, but you're going nowhere until you've answered some questions.'

She gestures to the table. Auntie Donna bristles but

nevertheless takes a seat next to Jago, who mouths, 'What have you done now?'

Donna says that the young woman – Claire – should also take a seat at the table.

'Don't worry, she won't hurt you,' she says to Claire.

Joe has no idea where this is going, but there is not one scenario he can think of where this can possibly turn out well.

'Right then, Auntie,' says Donna, also sitting down. 'Perhaps you could explain a couple of things to me. One, why were you in the St Clement family quarters this morning just before eleven? And two, why, when you bumped into Claire here in the aforementioned family quarters, did you say that if she ever told anyone that she'd seen you, you would hunt her down and feed her organs to the sharks?'

'Dolphins,' corrects Auntie Donna. 'I said I'd feed her to the dolphins. We don't tend to get sharks bobbing around Cornish waters these days.'

'We do,' says Jago. 'Not often, but we do. Don't we, Joe?'

Joe, for his part, is far too confused (and worried) to say anything other than, 'Well, yes.'

'Auntie?'

'Firstly, it is none of your or anyone else's business why I was in the family's quarters this morning. All I will say is that I was on government business and you, Donna Nightshade, are my own kith and kin: and whether I have murdered someone or not, we Nightshades stick together, and this interrogation,' she waves her hand back and forth ,'is unacceptable. I will forgive you this once because you are under the influence of this ... this...' She looks at Joe.

'Policeman?' offers Jago.

'Amoeba,' says Auntie Donna, following on with, 'And as for this little shrimp here,' (she means Claire) 'my telling her that I would feed her to the dolphins was better than the alternative.'

'Which was?' asks Donna.

'*Actually* feeding her to the dolphins. Now, if you don't mind, I'm heading back to the cottage where my favourite niece will no doubt be waiting for me. Other than that, my lips are, and have to be forever more, sealed.'

Donna unzips her coat and takes a plastic sandwich bag out of her bra.

'Not before you've explained this to me,' she says, sliding it across the table.

Auntie Donna sighs the sigh of extreme boredom and slips the contents out of the bag. From what Joe can gather, within the sandwich bag is another see-through plastic bag and it has an ampoule inside it.

Auntie Donna takes her glasses from the top of her head and reads the label.

'I found it in your room fifteen minutes ago,' says Donna. 'In the side pocket of your bag, hidden inside a box of Tampax.'

'Tampax?' says Auntie, looking up. 'Why would I have Tampax when I haven't menstruated in years?'

She reads the label on the envelope and suddenly, just like a hen trying to escape a fox in a hen house, Auntie Donna goes mental. Joe reaches across the table to take a look at the ampoule for himself and understands why.

It's rubidium. But Joe hasn't the time to process this because Auntie Donna has grabbed a meat cleaver and is heading for the door.

'Back in a tick,' she says. 'I've just got someone's liver to cut out and feed to the damn dolphins.'

'Sharks,' says Jago, not looking up from his crossword.

Chapter Forty

DONNA

By the time we catch up with her in the library, Auntie Donna has Jane pinned against a bookshelf, a hand around her neck. Atticus and Matt are here, too, playing chess. Matt offers a double take when he notices that Claire is now in tow – as well he might.

'Back off!' shouts Auntie in the direction of Atticus, who is trying to grab Auntie's arm – not the one holding Jane by the neck, but the one with a knife at the end of it. 'This little tiff is between me and her.' A nod in Jane's direction.

Auntie Donna releases her grip slightly allowing Jane just enough breath to speak.

'How the hell could I plant rubidium in your bag when I haven't left the castle since I arrived – ask anyone.' She glances around. 'For God's sake, find a taser, someone!'

'Taser my arse,' says Auntie Donna. 'I had a deal with Nadine. And by the terms of that deal, if I helped you with your little scheme this weekend, she would secure me an early release – and then rubidium pitches up in my bag. Double-crossing bitches! And don't think that I don't know exactly who you are and your part in it all, you so-called doctor… I've been watching out for a double-cross considering your pedigree, but this? I'll bloody kill the lot of you!'

Joe manages to grab Auntie's arm and do a little manoeuvre that not only knocks the knife out of her hand, which lands with a satisfactory clank, but also enables him to grapple her to the floor.

'Let her go,' says Jane, rubbing her neck while looking down at Auntie Donna. Atticus picks up the knife. 'We'll go into the study. Better to talk in there.' She turns to Donna. 'Perhaps you could bring some strong drinks through. Your auntie and I need to talk.' She looks at Joe. 'Privately, this time.'

It's taken me a while (at least two minutes) to persuade Joe to allow the two of them to speak in private, but the truth is, we don't need to hear what they say to each other because I already know exactly what's happened here this weekend – well, kind of. There may be a couple of bits that I can't account for, but if I'm right, the people who need to squeal will be squealing soon enough.

I urgently need to get back to the cottage to check on my sister, but first, I've got a date with an aspidistra. Joe is following on behind asking what the hell I'm playing at, but I don't have time to answer, because if my theory is correct then the first thing I need to do is to retrieve the only tangible piece of evidence I've gathered. I reach into the aspidistra pot and take out…

'A gun,' says Joe. His voice is flat. His expression is unreadable. His eyes are cold.

I would have preferred a reaction. I know where I stand with a reaction.

'It's Pinky's,' I say. 'She took it with her to the Garrison Room. It was in her hand when I ran in… So, I took it.'

'You took it.'

Still deadpan.

'Of course. I needed to run back through the castle to find you and for all I knew there was a murderer on the loose. And it wasn't any use to Pinky anymore, so…'

Still deadpan.

'But then I realised what it must look like … an ex-con running around a castle with a loaded gun – at least, I guessed it was loaded. Which is why I hid it.'

'In the aspidistra?'

'Yes.'

'And you didn't think to tell me?'

'Old habits?'

Joe takes a deep breath. I feel a lecture coming on, which needs nipping in the bud because we simply don't have the time.

'Look,' I begin, while applying the safety catch and releasing the gun's magazine. 'If you're going to have a go at me, can it wait because there's something way more important we have to do now.' I show him the end of the magazine. Look. Only one bullet has gone.'

I slip the magazine back into the holder and head to the door.

'Where are we going now?' Joe chases after me as I retrace

my steps while running through the library and the study with a loaded gun in my hand. The guests look at me aghast, whereas Auntie Donna, who I'm relieved to see is having a cheeky fag by the window in the study with Jane, says, 'That's my girl…'

'To the Garrison Room!' I shout, legging it down picture-lined corridors until we hit the staircase that leads to the bowels of the house. If I can just find what I'm looking for, then we might be able to get Joe off the hook with Penworthy and prevent a media shitstorm descending on Penzance (oh, and get me back into Joe's good books, which is the most important thing). I turn the handle to the Garrison Room, and we go inside. The poor samurai is still missing his coat. I must speak to Claire about putting that back before Lady Helen comes home. I turn to Joe.

'Answer me this,' I say, heading towards the spot where Pinky was shot. 'Why did Pinky take a gun along to a meeting with a person she regarded as a pussy cat?'

Joe's face is a catalogue of unanswered questions.

'And why did she ask me to set up watch in the corridor? Why was it so important to her to make sure no one else ventured in?'

'Just stop a minute, Nancy Drew,' says Joe, 'and tell me what you're looking for.'

I pat my hands around the walls. No joy. Then step inside the unilluminable cubby hole, take out my phone and turn on the torch.

'A bullet hole,' I say, examining the walls once again.

We step into the lit part of the room. I glance down at the floor where Pinky's body had been lying just a few hours before; the smear of blood tracing a telltale line to the door. And there it is, exactly what I'm looking for – a cracked tile. It lifts easily, and beneath it, in the concrete underneath, is not at all what I was looking for, which is a hole with a bullet in it, but there is a scorch mark, and the concrete has been messed up.

'When a gun fires a blank bullet, can it leave scorch marks and a bit of a mess?' I ask.

Joe shrugs. 'It depends, but yes, I should imagine it would.'

I don't try to hide the smugness that's edging ear-wards from my twitching mouth.

I jump up. 'Come on,' I say. 'We're nearly there.'

'Nearly where?' shouts Joe, after me.

'*There*!' I shout back, being purposefully vague while skidding out into the subterranean, brick-lined corridor, coming moments later to a halt at the glass-panelled door to the family's quarters, which is locked.

Where is Perkin when you need him? Stoking a fire, most likely.

I look through the keyhole and deduce that the key is in the lock on the other side. 'I don't suppose you have your truncheon on you?' I ask.

Joe's simple reply of, 'No' is laced with sarcasm.

'In that case…' I hand him the gun. 'You'll have to use this to break the glass, and before you ask why, just give me the pleasure of my delayed "ta da" moment by getting me to the other side of this door.'

To my surprise, Joe makes sure that the gun isn't cocked, takes off his jacket, wraps it around his hand, smashes the glass, reaches in and turns the key.

A little way down the corridor is…

'A trolley,' says Joe. 'It must be the one that Jane saw parked outside the Garrison Room. *Unbelievably* good of the murderer to bring it back after dumping the body,' he adds. 'We'll get forensics to check it for blood when they…'

'No need for that,' I shout from halfway down the corridor, because as far as the investigation goes, I've moved on.

I open door after door. We're still in the bowels of the house so this is pretty much the utility area – boiler room, laundry room, storage room…

A hand, a firm one, grasps my shoulder, pausing me.

'Enough,' says Joe. 'The causeway opens in under an hour and I've got your psychotic aunt upstairs who's not only threatening to kill people but clearly embroiled in the thing – the chief suspect, you might say. And I'm sorry, I know she's your aunt, but there's no way I can let this particular sleeping dog lie. Tell me, finally, what are we looking for?'

We step through a door that opens into a cell-like room that has a rail track running into it. The mouth of the tunnel mirrors Joe's mouth perfectly – a gaping void.

I send out my hand with a flourish. 'Ta da! I give you, the Dreckly Express.'

'Blimey!' says Joe. (He's such a pleasant man. It'll be "crikey" next). 'A tunnel! Which must lead to…'

'The harbour. To the back of the cottages if you want exact details. My guess is that it's for transporting heavy goods … coal, furniture, dead bodies…'

'Crikey!' says Joe, the light bulb flickering into life.

I hit a very large button on the wall that is conveniently

labelled 'Start' and various bits of machinery begin to click into place, leaving me the time, finally, to turn to face Joe and explain my thoughts, which are almost coherent enough to understand.

'Ask yourself this,' I begin. 'Why was Auntie Donna in the family's quarters at around eleven o'clock this morning?'

'Oh, believe me,' says Joe. 'That is exactly the question that I do want to ask, and I'd be posing it to the very person who can answer it if we weren't playing Cagney and Lacey.'

I let it slide.

'And remind me: who was it that made a point of telling you about the trolley being in the corridor?'

'Jane.'

'Exactly. And she did that – clearly – so that you wouldn't rule out the ease with which Pinky's body could have been removed from the castle. But they didn't need the trolley, did they?

'Who didn't?'

'Pinky and my auntie, who are clearly in cahoots in the whole thing. You said yourself that they met at the prison. I bet the whole "didn't get along" thing is nothing but smoke and mirrors because they strike me as exactly the type of women who would get along swimmingly. No, this whole debacle has Auntie Donna's stamp all over it – which is the Nightshade stamp of high drama with just a little bit of madness thrown in. And I would know, I inherited the gene.'

'I know,' says Joe, his eyes rolling so far back that they almost forget to roll forward again. 'I've been in the audience for it all my life.'

I'll let that slide, too.

'Although somehow it's gone a bit wrong, and Miles got blown up.'

Joe cocks his head to allow the final cog to click into place. 'You don't think ... surely not?

'That Pinky is in cahoots with my auntie to organise her own murder…?' I say. 'Yes, I do. Well, sort of. Joe – don't you see? The reason there was nobody to find in the Garrison Room this morning was because there was no *body* to find, because Pinky is not actually—'

'Dead?' says Joe.

'Exactly. My guess is that Auntie Donna has helped her to fake her own death – either because of the death threats from one of the many people that she's annoyed since she's been in government – and before, probably – or because of the scandalous details that were due to come out in Miles's and Sienna's books. Maybe she's in cahoots with Auntie so that she can disappear with all the consortium's money and has set up a whole other identity without fear of being killed and start again. Maybe she's having a wild affair with Auntie Donna? Who knows. A few minutes ago, Auntie Donna said that she agreed to "help" in order to get an early release, remember?'

Joe looks at me like he's still not certain, but as the mechanism continues to whine and whir, bringing the little carriage towards us under the Mount from the harbour, if he wants more proof, I'll soon have it – hopefully.

'Remember how I said that the blood I saw on Pinky's blouse was a very dark red,' I say. 'Think about it ... it shouldn't have been. It should have been brighter, recently oxygenated blood. I think the smear on the floor was intentional…'

'A kind of dye, you mean?'

'No, they're far too savvy for that.' I nod sagely because I'm on a roll. 'It will be Pinky's blood all right, forensics will confirm it. And I reckon that it was blood taken by Jane last night – you said she went to her room after the party with her medical bag.'

'And the gun?'

'Hello!? She needed a gun to make the noise of gunshot. The mistake she made was telling me that the person she was meeting was a pussycat, but who takes a gun to meet a harmless pussycat? Auntie Donna will be sooo mad that Pinky made that rooky mistake. I panicked last minute you see … said we should get you to come along with us rather than go to the Garrison Room alone. I suppose that you – a policeman – wouldn't have been factored into their original plan, so she had to think on the hoof. Think about it, Joe. Who was it that sent out the invitations? Nadine! Jago worked it out straight away. He tried to tell us, remember? He said something along the lines of, "presuming she was shot".'

Joe's face is beginning to brighten as he puts the pieces together. 'But what about the first murder attempt last night – the nut thing?'

'A set-up, clearly. To show that there was a murderer on the loose, no doubt to add gravitas to the murder ruse they were intending to pull off the next day. I bet Pinky doesn't even have a nut allergy, and I bet that the syringe Patch found was the one Jane used to draw the blood. She must have thrown it away and it's obviously washed back onto the rocks. Remember the note Pinky said she received: telling her to go to the Garrison Room? Where is it now? Nowhere, because there is no note like there is no body – it's all a mirage. No wonder she was setting her accounts straight with Atticus. Pinky had every intention of killing herself off and leaving Blighty for good.'

'But that means Jane must be in on it, too,' he says. 'But why would she do that?'

'Who knows with these things? Loyalty? Camaraderie? Auntie Donna must have been waiting in the family's quarters to unlock the adjoining door when Pinky walked into the Garrison Room and faked being shot. As for the blood – my guess is that she released an ampoule of her own blood – blood that Jane had taken – across her blouse. Who better than a doctor to pronounce someone as dead? Lamorna said so herself. Then, when we retreated to the main part of the house, as she knew we would, Auntie Donna unlocked the door to the family's quarters from the other side so that Pinky, who had smeared her own blood along the floor, could escape to the locked part of the house, after pulling the trolley behind the door to show that it had been moved – she must have put it there earlier.'

'But ... wait a minute,' says Joe. 'Auntie Donna wasn't even supposed to be on the island for the weekend. She wouldn't have been here at all if Jago hadn't phoned her to moan about being sacked.'

He has a point, but the answer just makes me smile. 'Ah, but that was the clever bit. Oh, Joe. Don't you know us at all? Auntie Donna knew that if Pinky criticised Jago's cooking – if she insisted that he was fired – he would take the huff and call his sister because that's *exactly* what Jago always does. Calls his sister when he's upset!'

Joe doesn't look so sure. 'Or maybe he's just in on it, too?' he says.

'My wonderful, gentle uncle? In on it? No way. He's as pure as the driven snow.'

'Hmm,' says Joe, adding, 'But how did Auntie Donna get into the family quarters in the first place if they're all locked up?'

This, I admit, requires a little poetic licence.

'It must have been Perkin,' I say. 'He was bought off by Matt, after all.'

Joe thinks about this before nodding his agreement, which is a surprise. I thought he'd just laugh.

'I suppose he *was* the butler at Number 10 for a few years,' says Joe. 'That's before he came here. Maybe he met Pinky then?'

I *would* question him about not keeping me in the loop about that little titbit, but I've hardly been squeaky clean on the divulging information front, so I go with a simple, 'There you go, then. Although Auntie Donna could easily have paid Perkin off or bribed him. All of which means – thank God – that Auntie Donna is in the clear on the murdering of Pinky front.'

'Except for the rubidium found in her bedroom,' says Joe. 'And the other murder of Miles…'

He would bring that up.

'And given Auntie's reaction,' I'm quick to say, 'I think we can conclude that that was a set-up.'

Joe looks at me.

I look at Joe.

We both smile and there's a 'moment' suddenly. And even

though we're caught up in the high point – the most frenetic part – of this murder enquiry. Joe steps towards me and I say (seductively), 'About last night…'

And then the carriage arrives and crashes into the bumper stop.

'If Pinky is alive,' says Joe, stepping back and pulling himself together. 'Where is she?'

I nod towards the carriage.

'No!' shouts Joe.

'Yes!' I shout back. 'My theory is that Auntie Donna put Pinky in the carriage, sent her to the harbour and left her there with the idea that Pinky could simply jump out of the cart and walk over the causeway when the tide went out – in plain sight – while the police were coming the other way, or perhaps she would be in disguise.'

Joe doesn't respond so I add. 'OK, it's all pure conjecture and based on nothing more than the fact that it's exactly the kind of bonkers plan that Auntie Donna (and, OK, I) would come up with. But the fact that there was a Tesco carrier bag – with half a prawn sandwich and an empty bottle of champagne inside it – by the carriage at the harbour, boosts my confidence in the theory. I reckon Auntie Donna left it there earlier for Pinky's lunch. She just hasn't picked up the rubbish yet!'

Joe puts his hand on the carriage lid handle and is just about to raise the lid when a voice cries out, 'Don't open that lid!'

Joe, being a good copper, ignores the instruction and lifts the lid, anyway, without looking around or flinching; while I, being a rookie detective, turn around to see Jane and Auntie

Donna standing at the door. Auntie Donna throws me a wink, but Jane looks mad as all hell and runs to the carriage, throwing her weight on the lid to hold it down while Joe tries, and succeeds, in lifting it.

He looks in the carriage and then looks up at me. There is no 'ta da' expression on his face – it's quite the opposite. His eyes are out on stalks. Dr Jane steps backwards and slides down the damp wall, defeated.

Auntie Donna and I run to the carriage and look in.

'Well, that wasn't part of the plan,' says Auntie Donna, who scratches her head and looks in bemusement inside the carriage. 'And before you ask,' she says, looking up at Joe, 'this is one particular murder that has absolutely nothing to do with me.'

Joe's phone pings. He reads the message and hands the phone to me.

Demelza: *I've gone through Miles's manuscript. Jane MacAvoy is Nadine Pinkerton's biological sister. Be careful Jo, she sounds like a complete nutter.*

Joe looks inside the carriage again while murmuring something about orphans sticking together.

That explains that then.

Chapter Forty-One

Jane is sitting with her back to the wall with her knees up and her head in her hands while Joe looks down on the crumpled – semi-naked – form of Rupert, which takes up most of the miner's cart known as the Dreckly Express.

That's all Joe needs, another dead body on his patch.

Donna places a supportive hand on his arm, but Auntie Donna is the first to speak, directing her conversation towards Jane.

'Isn't this the fella that you've been shagging, Jane?' she says, before looking back at the body and prodding it.

Jane takes her head out of her hands, looks at Auntie Donna and with a shrug says, 'What can I say, he behaved like an absolute twat this weekend…'

Auntie Donna adopts her 'fair enough' face and says, 'It's not a problem. We'll put him on our boat and dump him. We've got loads of mine shafts on our land. No one will ever know. Job done.'

Joe looks at Donna.

Donna mouths, 'I'm *so* so sorry.'

Jane stands, brushes herself down, looks in the cart herself and says, 'He's not dead, more's the pity. He's just … sleeping. I thought I'd teach him a lesson about not messing with women who can fight back.' She looks at Auntie Donna. 'You know the kind of thing…'

'Oh, I certainly do, Sister,' says Auntie Donna, nodding sagely. 'I could have written a book on the subject. In fact, I still might.' She laughs her villainous laugh. 'I think I'll call it, *Disappointing Men And What To Do With Them*. It'll be better than Jago's book, anyhow.'

Both older women tip their heads to one side while looking in at Rupert. Jane says, 'Aww' and Donna senior says, 'Not too late to quickly slit his throat if you've changed your mind? Perkin could have it cleaned up in a jiffy.'

Joe, as ever, needs to grip this.

'Dr Jane MacAvoy,' says Joe, 'I'm arresting you on suspicion of the murders of Nadine Pinkerton-Smyth and Miles Johnson. You don't have to…'

And Auntie Donna says. 'Arresting her? Don't be ridiculous, man!'

Joe doesn't think he's being ridiculous. In fact, he's going to arrest Auntie Donna, too, in a moment – if only he had some cuffs! He says as much to the assembled triumvirate, leading Auntie Donna to laugh out loud, and after looking at Jane with an offer of consolation because she's about to give the game away, says, 'Firstly, as we speak Nadine is having sushi with Perkin and Jago in Perkin's quarters, so…'

'Jago is?!' exclaims Donna. 'Uncle Jago is in on this?!'

Auntie Donna eye rolls in Joe's direction. 'Oh, darling,

don't worry. You can keep those rose-coloured spectacles on a little longer. Jago guessed what we'd done early doors, and with him spending so much time with Perkin this weekend we kind of had to tell him.'

Joe could scream, although he's chuffed to bits that the Home Secretary isn't dead because that was going to create a mountain of paperwork. 'The arrest still stands for Jane regarding the American, though,' he says, with a trace of the haha! about him. He turns to Jane. 'Not to mention the heinous crime, whatever it is, that you've committed against Rupert here.' A nod in the direction of the cart.

'Jane? Kill the American? Whatever would the motive be?' asks Auntie Donna, who seems surprisingly pally with Jane considering she had her hands around her neck not twenty minutes ago.

Joe turns to Jane. 'Look. We know all about your mother – that you killed her. And we know that Miles was going to include details of it in his book.'

Auntie Donna flashes Jane a 'you're on your own with this one' shrug.

Then Jane lets out a very long and very tired-sounding sigh. 'I had every reason to kill Miles,' she says, 'but I'm into saving lives, these days, not taking them.'

Four pairs of eyes look towards the cart. Low moans have started to emanate from the comatose Rupert.

'He's coming to, that's all,' says Dr Jane.

'But if not you,' says Donna, referring to the contents of the eighth circle of hell, 'then who?'

'Who knows?' says Jane. 'And frankly, who cares? The man was a complete pain in the arse.'

Auntie Donna lets out a snort. 'Whoever did it did a fantastic job, though, because in my experience those kinds of men are usually an absolute pig to kill.' She glances around and adds, 'But I can categorically say that I did not make a rubidium bath bomb. The rubidium you found in my room was a plant, on Nightshade honour. I thought that Jane here had done it, but we've had a bit of a chat and I believe her when she says that she hasn't left the castle all day. I suppose what you have to ask yourself, Joseph Enys, is who out of the other guests that aren't dead or pretending to be dead, had the motive but also the means to kill him ... and when you find out, tell me, because I'll take that spare rubidium vile and stuff it up their a—'

'Auntie Donna! Enough!' says young Donna, shaking her head but also, just a little bit, Joe notices, smiling.

Joe rests himself against the cart and takes out his notebook. Despite everything he's been through with Auntie Donna over the years, incredibly, he believes her. He's also just remembered that he left the gun on the floor by the door to the family's quarters.

Shoddy, Joe. Shoddy.

If only he'd got some sleep last night, he might just be able to think clearly: think, and not leave loaded weapons lying around the place.

'Come on, Joe,' he murmurs to himself. 'Think!'

He runs through the past twenty-four hours in his mind; the interviews, the double glances, the little comments. He's looking for something, some particular glaring reason for one of the Pimpernel Club to dispose of Miles. He takes out his notebook – it's mainly doodles – but he runs through each guest in turn while instructing Dr Jane and Auntie Donna not to move a muscle.

'But we're not looking for a murderer for Miles, are we?' says Donna, looking over his shoulder, reading his mind (she could always read his mind) and breaking his flow. 'We're looking for someone who wanted rid of Sienna – remember? That whole bag-swap thing? That's why she's down at the harbour, hiding out with Lamorna.'

'She's what?!' shouts Auntie Donna. 'Are you telling me, Belladonna Nightshade the Thirteenth, that you've left my precious, angel of a niece with one of *that* lot!? They're a bunch of complete nutters!'

If that's not the pot calling the kettle black Joe doesn't know what is, and he can't help but notice that Auntie Donna really does have the look of an eighteenth century pirate about her these days, that's if eighteenth-century pirates had an incredibly healthy, vibrant and 'bordering on the edge of sanity' look about them – wild hair, ruddy sea-swept complexion, buckled boots, big trousers with a thick belt pulling in a shirt around a trim waist (not as trim as Kerensa's Joe notices now, but trim), a Superwoman pinny, a pistol tucked into the pinny's pocket…

Ah.

'It's all right, Auntie,' says Donna. 'Lamorna is fine. She's got Ruby with her, and anyway it turns out that Sienna was the intended victim of the bath bomb, so…'

'Yeah, right,' scoffs Jane, throwing Auntie Donna a 'how naïve is this kid?' eye roll, and before Joe knows what's happened, Auntie Donna has pointed the gun, loaded and cocked, firmly and directly at Jane's head.

That's new.

'Right!' spits Auntie Donna. 'I've been dick-dancing around on behalf of you and your sister for long enough. If you know something about this bath-bomb business, stop with the eye rolls and the 'whoever it was, I don't blame them' bullshit, and 'fess up, or you'll find yourself – quite literally – forever holding your peace.' She nods towards the cart. 'And you won't find me to be as lenient as you've been with *your* enemies, I'll tell you that for nothing! I told your sister that at the start that I don't piss around, so squeal, bitch!'

Not for the first time Jane takes a deep breath, sighs, and says, 'All I'm saying is that Sienna has always been the most ambitious of all of us, really. Even more so than Pinky. And it's just like Mr Nightshade said... Who's to say Sienna is telling the truth about the goodie bag swap, anyhow?'

Joe looks at his notes ... did Jago say that? Not that Joe can remember, but then he's never really interviewed him.

Shoddy, Joe. Shoddy.

'When did Mr Nightshade say that?' asks Joe.

'Oh, sometime when he popped in while you two were concentrating on solving Nadine's murder rather than concentrating on the really important thing – who killed Miles? You got caught up in the fact that she was the Home Secretary and wanted to cover your own arses...' She looks at Auntie Donna. 'Credit to you; you predicted that they would.'

Auntie Donna offers a little bow but does not lower the gun.

'Wait,' says young Donna. 'You're saying Sienna might have killed Miles just to stop him from publishing a book?

They weren't even going to publish the same guff! It all seems a bit extreme just to get the scoop on a war memoir.'

'I'm not saying that she would,' says Jane. 'I'm not really saying anything at all, I just found it odd that you all seemed so quick to believe her about the bag swap thing. Honestly, I doubt you'll ever unpick this whole thing. I'm only saying this now because I've got a gun to my head, clearly.'

'No, you're not,' says Joe, who's not really been listening as he's been preoccupied with his notebook. 'You, Jane MacAvoy, know exactly who killed Miles Johnson and why, because you've been in on it from the start. And I wouldn't be the least bit surprised if it wasn't you who lit the touchpaper to kick the whole thing off with Pinky and Sienna.'

There's a click. Auntie Donna has cocked the gun but Jane just shrugs.

'You haven't got the balls,' says Jane to Auntie Donna, which Joe thinks is a very silly move.

He'd better do some talking and quickly, especially as Donna the younger is looking at him pleadingly, like the world has gone mad.

'Look,' begins Joe. 'We know that Sienna Blackville has a daughter – a very sick daughter – and as the lead scientist at an Oxford institute, the very person who can cure her is you, Dr Jane MacAvoy, which means that…'

'If Miles had published his book ousting the Home Secretary's sister as a murderer, then the sister – you – would have lost your job at the institute,' concludes Donna, her voice reflecting the fact that she's really quite surprised to have reached such a satisfactory conclusion.

'They wouldn't have dismissed me necessarily,' says Jane.

'Employment law is tight on that, but I would have been drummed out one way or another, that's for sure.' She looks at Auntie Donna kindly, despite the gun in her face. 'Be warned. People can be a bit funny about working with convicted murderers. And Sylvie – well, she's always been so protective of me.'

'Sylvie?' says Donna.

'That was Nadine's name at birth,' says Joe.

'Oh, of course,' says Donna. 'Go on…'

'There isn't much to go on about,' says Jane, 'except that she – Sylvie, Nadine, whoever – couldn't bare for me to be maligned in the press. Mother was a nightmare to me. There was a great deal of abuse – mental abuse mainly. Sylvie always felt responsible somehow, but she wasn't. I knew what I was doing when I took a knife to Mother, and honestly, I don't regret it. Ms Nightshade here' – a nod in Auntie Donna's direction – 'cooked up the idea to fake Nadine's death, thereby putting her real predators – the South American cartel – off the scent and Nadine agreed to allow it to be leaked that she – not I – killed our mother, thereby releasing me to carry on with my research with the hope of saving Sienna's daughter's life. My sister is a very nice person, really. All that bravado on Twitter is just a smoke screen. And she's bored of the whole political scene these days and wants out.'

Donna turns to her auntie.

'And you were involved, Auntie, because…?'

Donna senior shrugs. 'It was actually Kerensa who hit it off with Nadine initially, and they asked if I could think of something, because sisters with odd sisters need to stick together, or something like that…'

'There's also the carrot of her arranging an early release for you,' says Joe.

'Well, yes. That too.'

'Out? Early?' says Donna, looking – and Joe can't blame her – disappointed.

'Fingers crossed!' says Auntie Donna.

'But how would Nadine manage to arrange this for you if she was dead?'

Auntie Donna shrugs. 'She left notes?'

'But how did Miles know about your childhood in the first place?' asks Joe of Jane. 'That kind of detail is buried in the vaults of the Home Office, surely?'

'Nadine was far too loose with sharing her life story during our time in Iraq,' says Jane. 'She and Sienna were very close. They got talking on the roof one evening and they always suspected that Miles had overheard them – and clearly, he had. This was always going to happen if he found himself short of money. It was just a matter of time, really.'

There's one thing that Joe doesn't understand, however. 'Why were you *both* there?' he asks. 'In Iraq, I mean?'

Jane smiles the smile of absolute love for her sister. 'We were separated after Mother died, but Sylvie didn't rest until she found me when we were in our early twenties. When she discovered that I'd joined the army as a doctor and was off to Iraq, she volunteered to come too – as political advisor. She's very protective of me, you see.'

'She was probably just scared that you might kick off on another murder spree once you were given a gun!' says Auntie Donna, stating it as a fact and without a trace of irony, before adding, 'And that's what *I* believed the fake murder to be really all about. Pinky said that she was going to let it be "leaked" after her death that she, not Jane, killed their mother, thereby putting an end to any claim in Miles's book about Jane. But we were never supposed to kill him! No way. I'd have charged more for that!'

Joe squeezes his eyebrows together. The beginnings of a headache is creeping up his temples and heading for his frontal lobe.

'And where was Nadine going to live afterwards, and how?' asks Donna, intrigued. 'The Caymans? Cannes?'

Jane and Auntie Donna laugh and fist bump.

'Nowhere so exotic,' says Jane. 'No, she was going to go up to the Pennines – somewhere on the moors to the west of Barnsley. Hidden in plain sight is always the best way – that's what you said, isn't it?' A nod in Auntie Donna's direction. 'And do lower that gun, because honestly, it's full of blanks.'

Joe can't help but smile. Auntie Donna really has met her match with this one.

Even so, he needs to get back on track, because Jane was quite correct earlier when she said that when it came down to it, he needed to find out who the hell it was that made a bath bomb out of rubidium and blew Miles Johnson to kingdom come.

'But back to Sienna,' says Joe, just as Auntie Donna steps into the corridor and fires a shot leading to another eye roll from Jane. 'If you're right, then why would Sienna kill Miles if Nadine was going to take the rap for your mother's murder?'

'Maybe because there were too many things that could go wrong with the plan,' says young Donna.

'She's right. Blanks,' says Auntie Donna, stepping back into the room. She throws the gun into the cart with Rupert, who's still groaning.

'I suppose it was you who sowed the seed with Sienna,' continues young Donna. 'Perhaps you just happened to mention that even with Nadine taking the hit, he could still publish, and you could lose your job anyhow and not find a cure for her daughter. Nadine might not have been prepared to kill for you to keep your job, but Sienna might have been, if only for the sake of her daughter.'

'I can neither confirm nor deny that summation,' says Jane, which is when Auntie Donna grabs her by the throat once again and slips a knife out of her knickers. The knife finds its way to Jane's throat. Blood is spilt, but only a little bit.

'Tell me now. Is my niece holed up with a murderer or not?' she snarls.

And Jane, her voice catching, what with having her airway suppressed, says, 'Considering the fact that she insisted on getting here early so that she could walk over and not catch the boat, and that rubidium does not mix well with water … I would say that that is the most likely possibility, yes.'

Chapter Forty-Two

DONNA

The first thing we discover on stepping out into the blustery Cornish outdoors is that the rain has stopped. It's still incredibly windy – blow you off your feet stuff – but the worst of the storm has passed. It's completely dark now, with the streetlights across the water in Marazion offering a glimpse of unaccustomed normality. Joe offers me his hand in the dark as we attempt to rush down the hill, admittedly tentatively on account of the slippery rocks, etc. I wonder if he would have taken my hand if he knew that I'd purloined the American's lottery ticket. Speaking of which, I must check the numbers.

'To think that we spent all that time looking for Pinky's murderer when she wasn't actually dead!' I say, raising my voice to be heard above the wind. 'I'd call that wasting police time. You could charge her for that!'

No response.

'And can you believe that it was Auntie Donna who came up with the whole "fake death" thing in the first place? – don't answer that. But honestly, fancy the Home Secretary becoming friendly with Auntie Donna – an inmate!'

No response. Oh, well. In for a penny…

'Clever move on my part, though, stumbling across the Dreckly Express like that and putting two and two together and realising what was really going on. I'd say Lady Helen owes me a few extra quid for this.'

No response, except, he's stopped walking.

'I thought we were partners,' he says. 'In this weekend's investigation, I mean.'

'We are.'

'Right. So how come you found a gun and didn't tell me about it?'

He continues down the hill.

I grab his arm. 'Come on, Joe. Would you have believed me that I didn't shoot Pinky?'

He stops.

'Can you honestly put your hand on your heart and tell me that you wouldn't have suspected me, even just a little bit?'

He looks at me like I'm from Mars and he's from Venus.

'Yes,' he says. 'I can, and I wouldn't have.'

'OK, I got that wrong. Sorry.'

There's a pause. 'Apology accepted,' he says.

(Men are such an easy breed of human to deal with, really.)

I turn to carry on down the hill, but it's his turn to grab my arm.

'When things get hectic later,' he says, 'because I'll probably get caught up with Penworthy when the squad arrives, I want you to know that despite the fact that the past twenty-four hours has been a complete and unprecedented disaster, and despite having had an American blow up in a bath and a missing (presumed dead) Home Secretary on my patch, and despite being told by Penworthy that I'd be back on the beat next week for letting Pinky get slotted…'

He pauses. I'm nervous. Where's he going with this?

'I've loved this,' he says, smiling and putting his hands in his pockets.

That's where he's going. Crikey!

'Especially last night. I loved the *Scooby-Doo* search, I loved having a laugh on the sofa, I loved interviewing the psychopaths together… It was all great. And … what I'm trying to say is that I don't want this to be the last time we're together like this.' He wafts his hand between us. 'And most especially, I don't want to spend my life thinking … what if?'

He's waiting for me to say something. All I can think about is the ringtone whenever Demelza phones him – 'My Heart Will Go On' – and I can't work out if he's saying that he wants our friendship to blossom or if he wants more than that.

Sod it. I'm no shrinking violet. I'll ask.

'So, let me get this right. Are you saying you want us to be—'

'Argh!!!'

We hear a scream – a woman's scream, carried by the wind from the direction of the cottages.

'My sister!' I shout. 'That's my sister screaming!'

Despite Joe's protestations as we run down the hill, protestations that we shouldn't run straight into the cottage –

the lion's den, he calls it – without staking the place out first, I throw open the door and run through to the kitchen before Joe can say, 'I think we may need backup.'

The scene on arriving in the kitchen is surprising to both of us, although given that members of my family are involved in the debacle, it shouldn't be.

Sienna is in the kitchen and is as quiet as a mouse, mainly because she's tied to the chair and has been gagged using a Givenchy scarf belonging to Auntie Kerensa (bought before she went fair trade). Auntie Donna must have borrowed it. Lamorna, Jago and Ruby are also sitting at the table and they're playing cards. Ruby likes to be dealt a hand, although she has difficulty understanding the rules and tends to throw cards into the pile randomly, but very occasionally she wins, because if you say 'snap' randomly over and over again, you can nail it. Patch is sitting on Jago's knee and after a cursory, 'Oh, hi, Mum' tail-wag thrown my way, he forgets all about me and throws himself in Joe's arms and sets about washing his face with his tongue.

'We heard a scream,' says Joe as an explanation as to why I'm hugging my sister like she just survived an earthquake.

'That was Lamorna,' explains Jago who, after shuffling the cards like a Vegas pro, starts to deal. 'She popped upstairs to the loo and thought she saw the samurai ghost, but it was just the costume hanging on a bedroom door. I thought that I had better retrieve it from next door – you may remember that the Home Secretary's love child had left it there. Your turn for first pick up, Ruby,' he says.

Sienna is emitting high-pitched noises and alternating her pleading gaze between myself and Joe, not that she has much of a gaze going on, what with one eye being partially shut and well, bleeding. Joe, saying something about the laws of arrest, goes to release the gag. I rest a hand on his hand (there may have been a little static) and say, 'Just, give me a minute.'

I turn to Lamorna while gesturing towards Sienna and say, 'What happened?'

'Sienna killed Miles,' says Lamorna. 'Uncle Jago told me, but I'd kind of guessed, anyway.'

I turn to Jago and I'm feeling … well, to be completely honest, put out. *I'm* supposed to be the detective here, not Jago, and he's stolen my thunder, rather.

'Sorry to piss on your parade, Donna,' he says. 'But when I saw on the old CCTV that you'd left our little Lamorna here alone with a woman that Perkin had reliably informed me had had no qualms about blowing up a man in a bath—'

'Wait! What?!' This from Joe. (I thought he'd flash at that.) 'What do you mean, CCTV?'

'Snap!' shouts Ruby.

Jago collects the cards from the pile for Ruby. He looks up from the cards, pushes his glasses further up his nose and says, 'Yes, I meant to tell you both about that. Perkin had to knock it off because of the whole Fake Death of the Home Secretary fiasco – Nadine paid him enough to buy a new boat, you see, so he couldn't mess that up. I'm afraid the excuse about turning it off because of the cost-of-living crisis while the tide was in was … well … a lie. Which is why we knew Sienna had tried to take Lamorna as hostage … on account of the CCTV.' He nods towards a tiny camera perched on top of the bread bin.

'I thought she would, by the way,' says Lamorna. 'That's

why I engineered it that I'd be alone with her. And once I told her the game was up over a cup of tea' – Lamorna looks at Sienna – 'which was a wild guess on my part by the way so you could have just laughed at me and got away with it – she did what I thought she'd do, and she attacked me.'

'Except that she hadn't reckoned on Ruby,' says Jago. 'Who attacked *her* – hence the dicky eye.' He turns to Sienna. 'And yes, I heard everything you said about the American chap being a scoundrel who deserved his comeuppance, but a bath bomb is a step too far, young lady.' He turns to address Joe. 'Feel free to release her if you've got cuffs on you. I don't think she's necessarily dangerous, but unlike you, Donna Nightshade, I wasn't prepared to risk her going full psycho with my own niece!'

Joe unfastens the gag.

'These people are insane!' spits out Sienna. 'And the bird? It's a menace. Someone ought to wring its damn neck!'

'Good luck with that,' murmurs Lamorna. 'Snap!'

Sienna looks at Joe who has taken a seat next to Lamorna. 'Aren't you going to untie me?' she asks.

Joe considers this. 'No,' he says.

'You can't really think that I…?'

'Murdered Miles?' he says. 'Yep. That's pretty much my – our – main theory.' He looks at his watch. 'The causeway is about to open, and my boss will be here soon, so I'd save your breath for her if I were you.'

Jago puts down his cards and says, 'Well, I for one think we could all do with a nice cup of tea. I'll make it milky, and your woman here can have a straw.'

Sienna continues to persist her innocence but Lamorna, of all people, finds the words to throw water on Sienna's flames.

'I'm afraid that I clocked you once we knew about the rubidium because you were the only one not to catch the boat – probably because you didn't want the Rubidium to get wet. When you asked to go to the loo – when my sister was sorting out Claire the Samurai ghost woman – I popped outside and stood on the wheelie bin to look through the bathroom window, just to check that you were having a pee and not doing anything dodgy, and you didn't even go into the bathroom. You went into Auntie Donna's bedroom, presumably to put the rubidium in her bag – that was a big mistake, Sister,' says Lamorna, adopting the accent of a lady from the American Midwest. 'Big mistake. I've learned a lot from looking in windows this weekend.' Lamorna turns to me. 'Maybe I should clean windows for a living?'

Sienna drops her head and starts to sob.

'What have I done?' she says. 'Oh, dear God. What have I done. I can't go to prison. I just can't.'

'They all say that,' says Jago, who's standing by the worktop waiting for the kettle to boil. 'You'll get used to it.'

'Do you have a twin by any chance?' asks Lamorna. 'Because they can come in very handy…'

Sienna, after double glancing at Jago and Lamorna, looks pleadingly at Joe. 'You don't understand,' she cries. 'My daughter needs me.' Tears are now flowing as snot-inducing sobs. 'And honestly, he wasn't supposed to die, just get a shock – a shot across the bow, that's what I…'

'Carry on,' presses Joe.

Sienna shakes her head. 'It doesn't matter. But honestly, he wasn't supposed to get anything except a scorched penis and maybe lose an eyebrow or two.'

'Well, accident or not, that must have been some pretty high-grade stuff you used,' says Jago. 'Where on earth did you get it?'

Sienna, whose eye is looking particularly nasty now that the blood has infused with the tears, drops her head and says, 'I'm sorry but I just can't tell you.'

'It was Jane, wasn't it?' says Joe. 'She works in a lab, and it wouldn't be too hard to find out if they keep rubidium there, or even better, if she took some…'

Sienna shakes her head. Time to go in for the kill.

'Your loyalty is touching,' I say, 'but you should know that loyalty between the group has not been a two-way street. Jane grassed you up without a moment's thought.'

'Yes, OK. I got it from Jane,' she says. 'She told me how much rubidium to use and how to make the bomb.'

Well, that was easy!

'But the bomb wasn't my idea, I don't think it was even Jane's.'

'Likely story,' says Jago.

'No, honestly. Nadine took up with some kind of convict who told her how to make bath bombs after watching something similar on YouTube…'

'Moving on,' says Jago. 'Get the cuffs out, Joe. She might not have had the original idea, or bought the rubidium, or designed the bomb, but pound to a pinch of salt this little madam was the one who made the bomb, put it in the American's goodie bag and then sat back and waited for the big boom!'

Sienna looks up, her tears now subsiding.

'Yes, you're right, and I may well have been a mug – a foil – for other people's machinations, but I couldn't risk Jane losing her job. She's so close to finding a cure for my daughter's disease. Nadine and Atticus have piled incredible amounts of money into Jane's research projects, you wouldn't believe it. Oh, I know that you'll all look at the Pimpernel Club and see a bunch of money-laundering criminals, but eighty per cent of every penny from all of us – except for Miles's share – has gone into Jane's research projects. We felt we needed to do something good, after all the bad we had seen in Iraq.'

'Of course ... LWF,' I murmur, remembering the file of financial accounts. 'Lest we forget.'

'Well, yes. That's what the Pimpernel Club is really all about – a society to set things right. When my own daughter became ill, I couldn't believe that Jane's work might ultimately save her life. But Miles ... he always wanted a cut for his own personal greed, not for charity. Tell me, wouldn't you have done the same to save your daughter?'

'Cold-blooded murder to save my daughter?' I look at Lamorna, who in many ways *is* my daughter. 'Yes,' I say. 'I would. Definitely.'

'Honestly, though,' Sienna pleads. 'Jane told me that he'd just have his feathers singed, not that he'd ... well...'

'Have his teeth blown into the roof?' says Lamorna.

'I'm so, so sorry,' says Sienna, looking down.

For the first time in twenty-four hours, I believe that everything the person sitting opposite me is saying is true, and I feel sorry for her. Life really does deal you a crap hand sometimes. As for the Pimpernel Club turning out to be a philanthropic enterprise knowingly breaking money-trading laws for the greater good, like some kind of a modern-day gang of Robin Hoods? Crack on, that's what I say. I make a mental note to be less judgemental about people until I've known them for a while, or at least longer than twenty-four hours. Maybe Nadine Pinkerton isn't so bad after all?

But what to do about Sienna?

Joe must be thinking the same thing because he's looking … troubled.

'Let sleeping dogs lie?' I mumble, stroking Patch who has fallen asleep on my knee.

We hear the front door open and heavy steps march through to the kitchen. I'm expecting Auntie Donna, but when the door opens, it's DCI Penworthy who blows in. She peels off her waterproofs revealing a power suit that badly needs an iron. Her shoulder-length mousey hair is stuck to her head and her mascara is forming long streaks down her face. Oh, what I'd give to take this woman in hand. The causeway must be open. And where Penworthy treads, other coppers will follow.

Penworthy says, 'Why is this woman tied to a chair?'

No one answers.

'And is that a gag that's loose around her neck … and who pecked her eye out?'

Eventually, Joe says, 'This is Sienna Blackville. She's a famous journalist and she murdered the American.'

And Lamorna says, 'But we want to let her off.'

And Jago says, 'I think we need more tea.'

And Ruby says, 'Snap!'

Chapter Forty-Three

It's 9pm and DS Joe Enys is sitting at what he now regards as *his* desk in the study. He's looking around and smiling, mainly because he's reliving the twenty-four hours he's just spent with Donna. He's also waiting for Penworthy to appear because, after having gone to Perkin's quarters to find Pinky, she immediately instructed Joe, who went with her, to 'give them a moment'. Pinky, on being uncovered in Perkin's quarters, did not give the impression of being in any way contrite at having tried to fake her own murder, rather, she made it perfectly clear that she was excessively annoyed at Joe for figuring the whole thing out. When he explained that Donna Nightshade had been the one who had done most of the work, Penworthy said, 'She's still not going to let you into her knickers, Joe. Even if you do let her have all the glory.'

Joe glances out of the window towards Marazion and wonders why there are no flashing blue lights rushing across the causeway, no ambulances to take away the dead. Penworthy had been told that Pinky was dead, after all, so why on earth did she cross the causeway on foot in the dark and alone?

'I need to speak to the Home Secretary first,' was all Penworthy had offered by way of explanation, and so here Joe is, alone in the study and smiling to himself that they actually did it … that somehow, he and Donna solved the case. Even so, he can't help but feel sorry for Sienna who not only has a very sick daughter but has been led astray by Dr Jane, who might be a genius in a science lab, but is almost certainly one ruthless woman – a psycho maybe? A mother killer! Joe shrugs. Maybe even Jane isn't so bad, not really. No one but Pinky knew what depths of despair her mother had driven her to, and Rupert had behaved like an arse, after all – shit, he'd forgotten all about Rupert stuck in the Dreckly Express! And as for Miles … didn't he kind of deserve his comeuppance, too? Joe visualises the eighth circle of hell and decides that no, Miles probably didn't quite deserve to have his limbs ripped apart.

At half past nine, with the fire having gone out hours ago, Joe finds himself sitting opposite Penworthy, waiting to be debriefed. Suddenly, the whole Mount seems deadly, deadly quiet.

Penworthy takes a deep breath.

'The thing is, Joe,' she begins. 'The Home Secretary and I have come to the conclusion that what you reported to me this morning didn't actually happen. In fact, you probably dreamt the whole thing.' This is said as a matter-of-fact statement and Penworthy doesn't flinch. 'There was a reunion, yes, which was a success, but that's all. The Pimpernel Club have also been brought up to date with the present situation regarding the Home Secretary and everyone is in agreement that you must have had a few beers too many – maybe a bit of LSD – and you've been tripping out. The Home Secretary murdered on the Mount? As if!'

'I see,' says Joe, following on with, 'Actually, I don't see. What's that again?'

Penworthy doesn't answer but says, 'The issue regarding the American's manuscript has gone away – or it will have when all the evidence has been deleted, when operatives break into the houses of Demelza's stream of contacts, which means that there is no longer any need for the Home Secretary to take the rap for her sister and disappear to some kind of Cayman Island underworld…'

'She was going to Barnsley,' says Joe.

'That's just the LSD speaking,' says Penworthy. 'Which means that the Home Secretary's mad sister can carry on curing her incurable conditions and the greater good has been served and no one needs to do any paperwork.'

'Right, absolutely,' says Joe, because really, what else can he say? Except…

'What about the South American cartel that put a price on Pinky's head? Wouldn't it be safer for her to disappear anyway?'

Penworthy takes a hairbrush out of her handbag and attempts to smooth down her wayward hair, which has dried in a frizzy tangle. 'Oh, she doesn't really care about that. Made of stern stuff is Nadine Pinkerton. But, get this… It was an inmate she met on a prison visit that gave her the idea for the murder that never happened, if you know what I mean. They became penfriends and that's how it all started. How absolutely barking is that?'

'Totally barking,' says Joe. 'But what about Miles Johnson?' he adds, his smile fading. 'You know that bits of his body have created a new paint colour in one of the guest bathrooms? I don't think Lady Helen is going to think I imagined that particular nightmare when she gets home.'

Penworthy doesn't miss a beat. 'That's all sorted. Perkin is going to do a clean-up job for me, if you know what I mean...'

'Perkin? Is that fair?'

'Best man for the job,' says Penworthy. 'You know he used to be MI6?'

Joe didn't, but nothing surprises him anymore.

'The only rub in the whole thing is the Nightshades,' says Penworthy. 'Do you think they will talk? Could be a good earner selling this to the press?'

'They won't talk,' says Joe, remembering the deal that Nadine made with Auntie Donna. But how to word this to Penworthy without giving the game away? 'Perhaps the Home Secretary could find a way to secure the early release of Donna's aunt as a softener?' he offers.

Penworthy shrugs. 'You mean release the mad old fish that tried to kill Jack Crowlas all those years ago?'

'That's the one,' says Joe.

'Consider it done.'

She stands.

Joe stands.

It's over.

'Good work, by the way,' says Penworthy, heading to the door. 'Shame I won't be able to write you up for it, but we'll make a DCI of you yet, Enys. And the Home Secretary was impressed with you, too – annoyed as all hell, but impressed.

There was talk of you going to London on promotion… Fancy that? She even said you could work for her. I think she fancies you so watch out!'

Joe is flattered, clearly. But as they step out of the castle into the biting night air, the storm having worn itself out on the rugged Cornish cliffs and moors, which have seen off greater storms than this one, Joe looks westward towards the lights of his hometown, Penzance, and sees the 21:45 Great Western train slowing to a stop at the end of the line on a track that parallels the sea front. He thinks of his new house on Chapel Street and all the great fish he's yet to catch…

'Nah. I'm happy here,' he says. 'Thanks anyway, though.'

As they walk slowly down the rocks towards the harbour and the clouds part and a full moon appears, Penworthy says, 'Did you get your leg over with the Nightshade woman, or what?'

And Joe, too tired to play games, takes a woolly hat out of his coat pocket, puts it on, sighs and says, 'No, but maybe one day she'll have me. There's just something – someone – I need to sort out first.'

'Ah, the present squeeze,' says Penworthy.

Joe shrugs. 'We shouldn't take hold of the hand of a new love, until we've let go of the hand of the old one,' he says. 'That's what my mum taught me, and she was right.'

'Demelza?' says Penworthy.

'Demelza,' says Joe.

'Would it help if I told you that she's about to be promoted and transferred? Her star, as they say, is rising. Knowing Demelza, I wouldn't be surprised if she's *my* boss before too long.'

Joe's heart leaps, and then he feels terribly guilty for even committing to a leap in the first place because, God, he's such an arsehole, and Demelza is *such* a great sergeant. But still…

'I'd miss her,' he admits. 'She's a wonderful woman and an incredible operator, but yes, it would help. Where would she be sent to?'

Penworthy pats his arm. 'You've got the Home Secretary in your pocket now, kiddo. I'd say that the answer to that is … wherever you'd like her to go. But I was thinking … Bristol?'

Joe allows himself the luxury of a nod and a smile, and for the first time since he made the error of taking Demelza for a drink five months ago, he allows himself to breathe out.

Chapter Forty-Four

DONNA

What a day that was!

Penworthy has given strict instructions that it's best if Lady Helen never knows about the bathroom incident, as we now refer to it – there are certain things that one does not wish to know about one's own house. Jago has agreed to stay on and return to his duties as chef until the guests leave tomorrow morning – Pinky has apologised to him for the whole nut accusation thing and offered to show him around the House of Commons the next time he is in London, to which Jago replied, 'Madam, I will *never* be in London.'

It was odd how easily Pinky returned to the fold of the Pimpernel Club. They were all delighted to see her – well, the ones who weren't in on it were delighted, which was basically just the men; read into that what you will. Matt was especially pleased because it meant that he finally had his big reveal moment with Pinky and Claire, which turned out to be a bit of a damp squib. Pinky walked up to her (Claire) in the library, held out her hand and said, 'Hello, I'm your biological mother, and I'm sorry – for everything.' And Claire nodded and said, 'I know.' They retreated to the study, not arm in arm, but not having a blazing row, either, which is a start; and that's where they are now, making up for lost time, if that's possible, which it isn't.

As for the rest of the Nightshades? Auntie Donna, Lamorna, Ruby, Patch and I are tucked up in the kitchen at our harbour cottage. Auntie and I are playing whist (we moved on from snap as Ruby started getting arsy about not winning every time) and Lamorna is playing the guitar softly in the background. We're all enjoying Auntie Donna's last night of freedom before she returns to the old homestead tomorrow.

I try to look at my phone surreptitiously because I'm meeting Joe in a minute…

'Going somewhere, Darling?' asks Auntie Donna who, like a sharp-eyed owl spotting a scampering mouse, notices my time check, even though she has just started dealing a fresh hand like a one-handed card sharp.

'No, no, just checking the time,' I say. 'Patch likes being taken out for his last pee around now.'

'Right.' She glances up, still dealing. 'You wouldn't be thinking about nipping next door to see that policeman chap, would you?'

'His name is Joe,' says Lamorna, who returns immediately to singing the Adele classic,'When We Were Young'.

'I've seen the way you look at him,' says Auntie Donna. 'And I'll tell you this for nothing… You're giving far too much away with your eyes. I've told you before: always be the one to *be* kissed rather than the one who initiates the kissing. A man needs to be kept wondering if you're staying around, even if your heart does break for him every time he leaves the room. Trust me, it will save you a great deal of heartache in the end.' She glances up from the cards and smiles at me. 'Read Nancy Mitford, *The Pursuit of Love,* that will set you straight; or Elizabeth Von Arnim, the one about her German Garden, there's something in there about love and advice to her children.' She sighs. 'I wish I'd been more sensible when I was younger – I wouldn't have ended up being banged up at the old Homestead for one thing! No offence to the Enys boy, but I'm not sure that you can be a true Nightshade if you hang around with a policeman, but I suppose … he's not too bad a stick for all that. After all, he hasn't grassed me up to the feds, has he? Although, it did mess things up having a detective here this weekend. I do wish you'd have run that by me first, Donna. Everything would have gone off very nicely if it hadn't been for you meddling kids.'

'But *I'm* a detective, Auntie!' I protest. 'Surely you should have realised that *I* would work it out. And I did, mainly.'

'Oh, Darling,' she says, patting my hand. 'Of course you are and of *course* you did.' She sniffs. 'Now then, isn't it time you took Patch out for that little stroll? You might bump into that nice policeman while you're at it … and you might invite him to Penberth for lunch sometime, you know, when I'm not incarcerated.'

I throw my cards down and lurch forward to give her a hug.

'Oh, Auntie,' I say, 'I do love you.'

She bats me off while saying something about, 'that's enough of that,' and I grab my coat and scarf and head for the door, beckoning Patch to run after me. Lamorna offers me her bobble hat, which isn't exactly the look I'm going for, but it's blooming nippy outside so needs must.

'He's the great love of her life, you know,' says Lamorna to Auntie Donna. And as the door closes behind me, I hear Auntie Donna reply, sadly, 'Oh, Darling. One always thinks that. Every, every time.'

I'm standing with Patch at my feet by the harbour wall as Joe walks towards me. He's lit by the light of an olde worlde streetlamp. Thanks to Perkin, who has forgotten all about Lady Helen's cost-of-living-crisis economy drive, the island is lit by beautiful uplights that drench the Mount in a soft lilac colour. It's a perfect end to a less than perfect day (if you're Miles Johnson, that is). Joe is wearing his waterproof jacket, jeans and walking boots; he's wearing a woolly hat and he's carrying his rucksack jauntily over one shoulder. Most importantly, he's smiling at me, for once.

Now that Penworthy has 'tidied everything up', as she put it, Joe has been told to hotfoot it back to Penzance so that there can be no gossip about why DS Enys was holed up on the Mount for the whole weekend. Rather than call for a car, he's decided to take a late-night walk home along the beach from Marazion to Penzance. It's not too far, a mile or so. Patch and I have offered to walk him across the causeway with the excuse of Patch needing his bedtime pee.

Patch jumps up to greet his favourite person and, without words, we turn to walk down the cobbles that lead away from the Mount and merge with the causeway proper. Our footsteps are lit beautifully by a silvery moon.

It feels like a first date.

Which seems ludicrous given the chaos of the past twenty-four hours, but there you are.

Thirty seconds in and I've decided that Joe wants to walk in silence – to take in the ambience of the night and have some peace after the antics of the day. OK. Good idea. I can do that. Only…

'Was that a crazy ride or what?' I turn to look up at him as we walk. 'You should have seen your face when we thought we'd seen the samurai ghost! God, I wish the CCTV had been turned on – I'd have had your face freeze-framed and sent it to Bill Smiley to put front page on the Penzance Packet!'

Joe smiles and carries on walking.

'To be perfectly honest,' I say – because it doesn't matter now, 'I did start to wonder if it was all too much of a coincidence that people started to die once my Auntie Donna arrived…'

'Mmm,' says Joe, still walking.

'But this time … I just knew – *knew* – that she hadn't done it.'

He smiles again.

'I am worried about Pinky, though…'

This gets a response. 'Why?'

'Because Auntie Donna said she cursed her – wrote her name in the Nightshade book of curses and everything, for sacking Jago. But let's hope she made that bit up, and let's face it she probably did, because Pinky would be shark food by now if she had.'

'Dolphin food,' corrects Joe, leading us both to laugh.

More silence.

More walking.

We reach the end of the causeway and turn to look back at the Mount. The village of Marazion, the beach, the earth … all is perfectly still and quiet. It's time for us to say goodbye.

'Why didn't you stay tonight?' I ask. 'You could have come over to us. Auntie Donna is warming to you, by the way. She even called you "that nice policeman" earlier.'

Joe swallows. 'Maybe because we didn't finish our conversation,' he says.

'No, we didn't. But before we do – *if* we do – there's something I need to tell you first – to confess to.'

His expression darkens. 'Go on.'

'You know how when we searched Miles's room I went through his wallet…'

'Yes…'

'Well, there was a lottery ticket in there…'

'Donna…'

'Which I stole.'

'Jesus.'

'And I've checked the numbers, and well, I've won.'

'What?'

'Oh, not the full thing. Just *part* of it.'

'How much?'

'Two hundred and fifty-eight thousand pounds and forty-nine pence. And the thing is, I'm going to keep it – the money. To have the roof fixed. And to buy Lamorna some clothes. And Jago fancies a trip to Bora Bora.'

'But, that's wonderful news!' he says.

'You're not mad?'

He shakes his head. 'Not a bit.'

'But anyway, now that that's out – phew – in the conversation we were having before Lamorna screamed, you were saying how much you'd enjoyed last night.' I step ever so slightly closer. 'How you loved our *Scooby-Doo* moment with the ghost and everything. Great, wasn't it, by the way?' I make an eek face. 'Except for the Miles thing, obviously. I'll remember the sight of those teeth in the ceiling for ever I think... Nice teeth, though.'

Joe takes my gloved hand in his bare one.

'What I was actually saying,' he says, 'is that I don't want it to be the last time that we're together like this...'

That's my cue to say, 'Like what?' and then he could kiss me, but I'm still not quite one-hundred per cent sure that this is the direction of travel, so I smile and say, 'Oh, it won't be, Joe! We're friends now, remember? I'm sure we'll have lots of fresh cases in the future...'

He shakes his head and takes my other hand.

Right.

That direction.

Blimey.

'Are you still seeing that Interpol knob, or...?'

Should I lie?

Yep, I should definitely lie.

'No. No. Well, not really. Not often. He's in Mongolia infiltrating a Chinese sect. He might not be back for years.'

Thinking about it, that isn't a lie. Not any of it.

'Let's just hope he stays there,' says Joe, before adding.

'Look, I've got things that I need to sort out, but when they're sorted, could I call by at Penberth some time?'

'In a panda car?' I joke.

'No.'

'Will you book the love seat at the Newlyn cinema this time?' I ask, edging ever closer.

But Joe can't answer because a car has pulled onto the slipway, causing Joe and I to break hands to shield our eyes from the glare of the headlights.

Jase Clarkson – the Interpol knob, as Joe called him – gets out of the car and walks towards me. He's lost the head brace, but his arm is in a sling and he's limping severely. When he reaches me he says, 'Demelza told me I'd find you here.' He takes something out of his jacket pocket and tries to drop down to one knee but fails on account of the leg injury.

Patch, who has never warmed to Jase, takes a running jump and clamps his jaws around his coat sleeve, growling and ragging at the coat like he's trying to shake Jase to death.

'In the words of the Simply Red song "Something Got Me Started",' begins Jase, *'I'd give it all up for you.'* (I'm only half listening because of the need to tease open the dog's jaw.) I tuck the snapping dog under my arm and tell him to shush.

'Sorry, Jase, you were saying?'

Jase, who has lost his thread, looks at Joe for a nudge.

'You'd got to the "I'd give it all up for you" bit,' says Joe, battery acid dripping off every word.

'Right, yes,' says Jase. 'Which is my daft way of saying that during the past three months, I've realised that my life – even with all the excitement and money that comes with being a secret agent, which is *amazing* – even then, it's not worth living if I'm living it without you…'

Jase opens a small box and the moonlight illuminates what looks to be a *massive* diamond.

'Donna Nightshade,' he says. 'Will you tame this wandering fool and marry me?'

I look at Joe.

Joe looks at me, and within two seconds, maybe three, Joe's fist has connected with Jase's face causing Jase to drop to the floor.

Joe picks up his rucksack, gives Patch a quick and very loving pat, and with a final look towards the Mount, says, 'Until next time, Donna Nightshade,' and walks quietly away.

Author's Note

Although I have visited St Michael's Mount many times, I afraid that I have no idea what the bedrooms look like (or where they are situated in the castle). I have never met the family who live there, either; although I have it on good account that they are not in any way bonkers like my imaginary St Clement family are, which is, perhaps, a shame. Should Lord and Lady St Leven ever read this book (I doubt it, but you never know) I beg forgiveness for turning their castle into an odd mash-up of reality and my imagination.

Additionally, as I served on the general's staff in Iraq in 2003, I can categorically say that none of the characters in the book reflect any of the soldiers or civilians that I served with during my time with the army.

Acknowledgments

My heartfelt thanks to Charlotte Ledger and the whole team at One More Chapter, and to my agent, Hannah Todd. A further note of thanks go to my good friends, Emily and Ade Clark. Emily is a consultant in paediatric and palliative care at Helen & Douglas House Hospice, and yet despite this she always finds the time to read my latest novel, usually confirming that although I'm almost certainly bonkers, I can just about get away with the way I set about killing people (in my books, to be very clear).

The author and One More Chapter would like to thank everyone who contributed to the publication of this story...

Analytics
Emma Harvey
Maria Osa

Audio
Fionnuala Barrett
Ciara Briggs

Contracts
Georgina Hoffman
Florence Shepherd

Design
Lucy Bennett
Fiona Greenway
Holly Macdonald
Liane Payne
Dean Russell

Digital Sales
Laura Daley
Michael Davies
Georgina Ugen

Editorial
Arsalan Isa
Charlotte Ledger
Lydia Mason
Jennie Rothwell
Tony Russell
Kimberley Young

Harper360
Emily Gerbner
Jean Marie Kelly
Juliette Pasquini
emma sullivan
Sophia Walker

International Sales
Bethan Moore

Marketing & Publicity
Chloe Cummings
Emma Petfield

Operations
Melissa Okusanya
Hannah Stamp

Production
Emily Chan
Denis Manson
Francesca Tuzzeo

Rights
Lana Beckwith
Rachel McCarron
Agnes Rigou
Hany Sheikh
Mohamed
Zoe Shine
Aisling Smyth

The HarperCollins Distribution Team

The HarperCollins Finance & Royalties Team

The HarperCollins Legal Team

The HarperCollins Technology Team

Trade Marketing
Ben Hurd

UK Sales
Yazmeen Akhtar
Laura Carpenter
Isabel Coburn
Jay Cochrane
Alice Gomer
Gemma Rayner
Erin White
Harriet Williams
Leah Woods

And every other essential link in the chain from delivery drivers to booksellers to librarians and beyond!